The Accidental Native

D0744874

a novel by

J.L. Torres

Arte Público Press
Houston, Texas

The Accidental Native is made possible through grants from the City of Houston through the Houston Arts Alliance and the National Endowment for the Arts.

Recovering the past, creating the future

Arte Público Press
University of Houston
4902 Gulf Fwy, Bldg 19, Rm 100
Houston, Texas 77204-2004

Cover design and art by William David Powell

Torres-Padilla, José L.
  The accidental native / By J.L. Torres.—First Edition.
     p. cm.
  ISBN 978-1-55885-777-3 (alk. paper)
     1. Parents—Death—Fiction. 2. Traffic accidents—Fiction.
  3. Birthmothers—Fiction. 4. Puerto Ricans—United States—
  Fiction. I. Title.
  PS3620.O62A64 2013
  813'.6--dc23
                                                   2013022187
                                                         CIP

♾ The paper used in this publication meets the requirements of the American National Standard for Information Sciences—Permanence of Paper for Printed Library Materials, ANSI Z39.48-1984.

13 14 15 16 17 18 19 20   10 9 8 7 6 5 4 3 2 1

Acknowledgments

Many thanks to the Fulbright Program for granting me an opportunity to teach at the Universidad de Barcelona and Universidad Autónoma de Barcelona. While on the Fulbright, I was also able to work on this novel. Special thanks to the Departments of English and German Philology in each institution. My Barcelona colleagues and friends, Cristina Alsina, Rodrigo Andrés and Raquel Serrano, I owe you so much for your hospitality, companionship and encouragement.

Thanks to my stateside friends and colleagues, Michael Carrino and Elizabeth Cohen for your insightful, thorough reading of early drafts of this novel. Your feedback helped tremendously; your encouragement and advice lifted me in moments of doubt. Thelma Carrino thanks for being such a great supportive friend. My colleagues at SUNY Plattsburgh, thanks for providing me with a wonderful, relatively sane place to work and grow.

I had the opportunity to receive encouragement and advice from Diana López and Selena Mclemore at the National Latino Writers Conference early in the process of writing this novel. Thanks to both of you and to the conference. David Powell, thank you so much for your artistic vision, designing gifts and patience. Lisa Sánchez González, Joanna B. Marshall, José Santos, thanks for your cover art feedback. My most appreciative thanks to Judith Ortiz Cofer, Ernesto Quiñonez, Ilan Stavans and Esmeralda Santiago for graciously offering their thoughts and comments on the novel.

This novel is set in Puerto Rico, not only geographically but emotionally. To my homeland and compatriots: I anguish with you until the decision that frees us. To those friends and colleagues who befriended me while living there, my warmest appreciation.

To those agents who passed on this novel but took time to offer constructive criticism, my sincerest thanks for your genuine comments that I incorporated into my revision.

My most profound gratitude to Arte Público Press for supporting Latina/o writers so they do not have to write to Peoria to be heard. To Nicolás Kanellos, your comments and edits made this novel better, and for that I am forever grateful. Un millón de gracias for having faith in my work. Gabriela Baeza Ventura, thanks for your meticulous reading of this novel and your spot on recommendations. Adelaida Mendoza, thank you for putting up with all my questions and anxieties. To the marketing and publicity crew at APP—Marina, Ashley and Carmen: you are the greatest; thanks for helping me to get out the word.

To the growing Latina/o reading population, thank you for supporting the literary voices of our communities.

As always, mucho amor y cariño to my wife Lee and sons, Alex and Julian, for your unconditional love and support, and for keeping my uprooted spirit grounded.

My deepest love to my mother, Marcelina Padilla, for always guiding me with her strength of character and moral fortitude; and my sister, Gladys and niece, Yari, por ese apoyo, siempre seguro. Thanks to my second familia: Celia López Vera, Ev, Big E, Lil and Mikey for the laughs, the big hugs and all that good food and love that goes with it.

Dedication

For every returning Puerto Rican;
and to those who remain unhomed.

Home is where one starts from.

T.S. Eliot

One

Sometimes your life runs like a film with a damn good script and you're the lead. You're hitting all your marks, and you're not even finished with act one. That's how it felt for me until she entered the scene like an extra gone rogue. After her, everything was upended, and I realized my entire life up to that moment had really been more like a movie about deception which had hit its major twist.

It all started with the violent, freakish deaths of my parents. They both swore they'd be buried in Puerto Rico. They belonged to that generation of Boricuas who grew up on equal helpings of rice and beans and nostalgia for Puerto Rico. They believed in the Puerto Rican Dream, which meant work in the U.S. to live your golden years in the island. So, they slaved to buy a house there but never returned, and they never did get around to buying a plot. Why would they? They were years from retiring, and too preoccupied with living. But I knew, because half-jokingly they made me promise, that if anything happened to them I had to step up and grant them that wish.

The funeral home in Jersey held them in their private morgue until I could buy a plot in Baná, their hometown. Erin drove me to the airport, where I made the classic request for "the next plane out"—in this case, San Juan. I had only opaque memories of Puerto Rico from a childhood visit, knew only the little my parents spoon fed me about it. How appropriate my journey into this new life of deception should start there. The Enchanted Island.

Picture a tropical paradise. Warm sunshine on happy faces focused on making you comfortable, accommodating your every whim. By the beach the ocean laps the sand as you drink the cool rum-spiked milk from a coconut dropped down to the ground by a sultry breeze. Everywhere you see bronzed, curvaceous women and Latin Lovers strutting half-naked along the inviting, turquoise water. Life is wonderful, swinging in your hammock, listening to the steady afro-Caribbean sensual rhythms stirring your loins.

Okay. Now, let's take ourselves out of the tourism commercial and talk reality, or as the natives say, "vamos a hablar inglés," let's talk English. If you look at all the important national statistics— from unemployment to mortality rates—Puerto Rico persistently ranks low. And then you have the power outages, water shortages, work stoppages, the corrupt governments, the high crime rate, the lousy service you get most places you go, the horrific traffic and drivers, the increasing water and air pollution. Yet, every year Puerto Rico comes out in the list of the top five happiest nations. Puerto Ricans consistently say they are happy. The Puerto Rican avoidance strategy is to create a fantasy world and call it enchant-ed. But I didn't know any of this. I was just going down to this tropical Disneyland to bury my parents.

The only place I could find to stay in the area at the last minute was a "fuck motel." A place where you drive into a garage, out of nowhere someone closes the garage door, and you walk through a side door into a room without windows. The bed vibrates with a few quarters and if you want a "night pack" with toothbrush, toothpaste, condoms, you call and a few minutes later there's a rap at the sliding window. It was half an hour from Baná.

At Baná Memorial Cemetery, the director told me that he had a few plots in the cemetery's new extension, Monte Paraíso, and threw in a discount because he knew about my parents. He hand-ed me a business card with the name of a local tombstone compa-ny. After I signed the paperwork and paid for the plots, he grabbed the phone to call the nearest funeral home. "I'll take care of every-thing," he said, patting me on the back.

My parents came from small families, and death seemed fond of both sides. Most of my few aunts and uncles had already passed

on. Both sets of grandparents: gone (or so I thought). The one
remaining uncle I knew, from all accounts was ill and feeble, suffering from Alzheimer's. Cousins, I didn't keep track of, couldn't
care less about the extended family thing, anyway. There wasn't
anyone to contact on the island other than my sickly uncle, Mario.
No wake; they had waited long enough. So, I stood alone, dressed
in ritual black, sweating like a pig over a roast pit, without as
much as an umbrella for shade. My head was throbbing, my shoes
sinking into mud.

Four cemetery workers lowered the caskets with canvas rope,
one at a time, on top of each other, into a hole dug by the towable
excavator parked a few feet away. Behind me, the director's assistant held a corona, a complimentary crown of plastic flowers,
which would be used again for another hurried ceremony later in
the day.

Past them, under a large tree about a hundred yards back, a
woman dressed in a smart pantsuit, appeared to be watching me,
the entire scene, although I couldn't tell for sure because she wore
sunglasses. Even from that distance, she was the type of woman
who stole your attention. But I didn't make much of it. I just
thought she was waiting for another funeral.

My mother often referred to Puerto Rico as "this little piece of
patria." I thought of that as I tossed a handful of dirt over their
remains. The "house priest" had his concerned face on when he
told me, "They're in a better place." I didn't know about "better,"
but they now slept in eternal peace in the muddy, undeveloped
and barren extension of the municipal cemetery of this raggedy-
ass town in central Puerto Rico. Right next to their neighbor for
life, "María Lazos, 1920-2009."

"Welcome home," I whispered, shaking my head.

I shook the priest's hand, thanked the assistant. Wiped the
sweat trickling down my face, took one last look at the gravesite.
The church bells rang three times. *Game over, I thought.*

Not knowing what else to do or where to go, I wandered into
town.

I passed a couple of teens kissing on a corner, an older couple
having a heated discussion, the wife waving a hand backwards in

dismissal, a man scraping at a big block of ice to make snow cones, school kids fidgeting around him. At one point, I had the sensation someone was following me. Thinking back, did I see her slink into a small grocery store, hear her stiletto heels clicking on the sidewalk? I soon blended into the flow of faces looking like mine, but everything was foreign, distant.

I hit the plaza, drained and exhausted, and sat on a dirty, wooden bench. Mami claimed that as a young girl she had seen my father as a young boy in this very plaza and knew she would see him again. My father, the historian, called that improbable because his family had been established in San Juan for decades and only returned to their home in Baná during summers. Perhaps they never were here together at the same time, but for sure at some time both had individually stood here to watch pigeons waddling about, to people watch, to admire the majestic ceiba trees or to daydream about the future. As a group of children in school uniforms marched by, I started to cry, the back of a hand on my mouth, attempting to silence the sobs. The kids turned around, stunned at first, then started to laugh, pointing at me as if I were a freak.

The dark-haired woman, dressed in a navy blue pantsuit, scolded the children. They ran off, screaming and laughing. She walked over to me and slid by my side and offered tissues. As I grabbed them, she took off her sunglasses and I looked up to her eyes, red and teary, nervously scanning, almost devouring my face.

"I must look like shit," I joked.

"You're okay," she said, rubbing my back.

I stared at her, my head askance. Her English was near native with only the thinnest trace of an accent. She panned my face with eyes entrenched in hardness; everything from the eyebrows to the few wrinkles framing the sockets signified a life of fighting, of burdening pain and hardships. Yet, at that moment, they softened just slightly so.

"I was at the cemetery." She offered this as an explanation, but it only confused me more.

"I thought I was alone."

"No, you were not," she responded, defiantly. "I was there, right behind you."

"I saw you," I told her. "Did you know my mother and father?" She lowered her head. "Yes," she said, nodding. "Yes, I did."

A longer pause. I returned some of the unused tissues and she wiped her nose.

"Long ago," she told me, widening her fleshy lips into a smile. "Your father and I were together . . . "

I looked at her like she was speaking in tongues.

"It seems like another time and place." Another smile, this one sad and lost. She dabbed at her eyes.

"No fuckin' way," I said, more to myself in a near whisper as I squinted at her like an apparition, trying to make sure she was real. But she heard me.

Her brows knitted; her eyes regained their hardness and pinned mine. Her reddened cheeks inflated, the fist brandishing soiled tissues in front of my face uncoiled a pointer finger.

"A little more respect," she demanded.

I looked down into embarrassed silence.

And then she blurted it out.

I thought she was nuts. A fifty-something whack job with maternal yearnings who stalked vulnerable grieving orphans. And I was about to say "Okay, bitch, this is no time to be fucking with my head," or something along those lines. But she pushed that piece of paper in front of me before I could say anything: the birth certificate. There they were: my name, her name, my father's—all interconnected forever on that piece of paper. I kept looking at it, at her, shaking my head. Re-reading it until it got blurry. It hit me that every time I had needed a birth certificate for some official purpose, my parents took care of sending it to the right place. Too lazy and indifferent, I never asked why. Now, my head spun with anger, confusion, my throat and chest tightened by grief.

The woman took me by the arm and walked me over to a hole-in-the-wall diner by the plaza for coffee and a sandwich, the birth certificate dangling from my hand.

"In due time, in due time," she repeated, "I will explain."

I threw the certificate back at her. Stared at the sandwich, hungry but thinking I would retch if I took a bite.

"I know it's a horrible time for you," she said, folding the certificate back into her purse, "but fate has given me a little happiness by returning you to me."

I shook my head, put up my hand for her to stop.

"Please, just give me a chance to know you, that's all," she said, giving me her business card with her home address and cell number scribbled on the back.

She took both my hands in hers, and brushed back my hair. I couldn't look at her as she walked away, her heels clicking against the plaza's stonework. I crumpled the card.

Two

The first time she called, I hung up. The following calls, I didn't answer. I just couldn't. Her persistence and the sad-ass but optimistic messages she left made me finally cave in. Those early conversations were limited, guarded on my side, forced. Part of me grew to enjoy her calls, and then our Skyping, more than I wanted to admit, because my parents' death, only a couple of months earlier, had left me a walking shell. But that connection with her would diminish minutes later as I wondered why a woman would abandon her baby son. What could possibly make her do that? Was she one of those career women who put ambition before her child? How selfish. How convenient to play the comforting mom after someone does all the work to raise your kid. And why didn't my parents tell me? What were they hiding? What other secrets were they keeping from me? I started thinking this and would end up angry at their lie and betrayal. But then she would call again and our conversations flowed and all angry thoughts about not wanting to ever see this woman again would disappear. She would always end by assuring me that her home was mine, even suggesting the move to the island after obtaining my degree.

I didn't want to attend graduation. It would remind me of my parents' absence, of how alone I was. Once there, not even Erin's loud presence cheered me up (she made enough noise by herself when my name was called to compete with any larger family contingent). In fact, her being there only made me feel worse—something I would never tell her, but it's true.

Erin was, what, my "girl?" We had an on and off thing centered on sex and this illusion—delusion?—that opposites attract. She was blond, pale, with jade-colored eyes. Part Scottish, Italian—northern, she was fond of reminding me—and some Irish thrown in. She was in marketing, although she always introduced herself as a "designer" in the cosmetics field. Erin believed she had successfully bridged the creative-business divide and urged me to do the same: "put your writing skills to some use, go into advertising."

Something in what she did at work—packaging perfume or soap made from some edible substance in cute, clever ways to baby boomers—must have made her horny. At first, my young adult male brain thought, "wow, great." But after a while, it got scary. There were always bruises, hickies, scratches, teeth marks. I don't think you should have to up your health insurance to cover good sex. Anyway, she didn't think I would break away from the relationship. She believed men were weak that way, that we all thought with our penises. I had never seriously considered our differences before, but they began to irritate me. I left without an explanation other than "this is something I have to do." And I found myself back on a plane headed to Puerto Rico in a flash; this time, the ticket paid by Julia, my biological mother.

My parents had left me a charming chalet tucked away in the idyllic mountains. At least, that's what I got from my parents' description. They considered it a beautiful, airy house—they always emphasized how cool it was up in the mountains, in Baná. The lawyer informed me that it formed part of the "estate." I laughed at the word. My parents had worked so hard as college professors their entire lives, and what they had saved up did not invoke ideas of wealth and legal battles. None of those for me. My parents left me an orphan and the sole heir of their legacy, however minor, and the mourning that follows any loss, which is always huge.

The more I thought about the house, though, the more I actually considered moving down there, especially with Julia's constant pleading. I was adrift. Everything in New York now belonged to a past haunted by phantom memories. Puerto Rico felt like the future, full of the unknown, waiting, calling me, to be discovered.

Getting a teaching job in Puerto Rico pushed me over. After years working as freelance writer, string reporter, wannabe screenwriter and actor, bartender and other odd jobs, I applied and got accepted to an MFA program in creative writing. Now, having earned this fool's degree, I was headed to a tenth-tier college to teach English in a predominately, and later I would find out, resistant to English, Spanish-speaking country. People told me to be thankful I had found a college teaching job, especially in the same town where my parents' had bought their house, on such short notice, right before classes began. It was less about fortune than about contacts and reality. The English department there had a desperate need for teachers, and it didn't hurt that Julia knew one of the deans. I received a tenure-track position without having the hoops others had to jump. But honestly, to the majority of my job-hunting colleagues, Puerto Rico translated to sun, surf and drinks with little umbrellas, not the beginning of a successful academic career.

When I boarded that plane, with only one other suitcase beside a carry-on, I felt new and clean. But I had never taken a noisier, raunchier flight. The Americans on board set the tone. The men with their shorts and T-shirts proclaiming "life was a beach" or some other "I'm on vacation"-type comment. Bikini bottoms jutting out of some of the women's shorts. Lots of flip flops exposing ugly, fungus-ridden toes.

The two young men in front had consumed several rum and Cokes and kept pressing the attendant's button to mess with her. Across the aisle, newlyweds groped and kissed. Pointing to them with her lips, the religious lady with hairy legs sitting next to me whispered, "casi pornográfico." In front of me, a young woman with a freaky haircut talked to a middle-aged bald guy about her philandering husband. Her son, ten or so, slanted his head against the window, his mind drifting with the clouds.

The fat guy in the aisle seat complained about diabetes and blood pressure as he wolfed down a Whopper and big fries. I turned down his offer to share, nauseous at the greasy, prefab chemical smell, and shoved the earphones over my ears to numb the loud laughter, constant chattering and baby crying coming from the crowded plane and to tune out the monotonous preaching of the zealot next to me.

We passed the rawhide-colored beach meeting the opal blue Caribbean water, and soon were flying over dense gray-topped buildings, with only a sliver of green here and there. Inside the plane it was church quiet. The lady next to me had closed her eyes and begun praying. When we touched ground, applause exploded throughout the 757. Seeing my confused face, the diabetic smiled. "Tradition—to celebrate the landing." He had known from the beginning I was not from "here." "Nuyorican?" he asked.

It took close to a half hour to get off that plane, more to retrieve my bags. As I grew agitated, people around me talked and laughed like the delay was no big deal. From the baggage claim area, through large glass panels, I saw relatives and friends picking up passengers. Some pressed against the glass, expectant. Lots of hugging, kissing, crying. Across from me an old woman sat in a wheelchair, probably wearing one of her best dresses. She sat, hands clasped on her lap, eyes scouring, her face full of so much love and hope. Close by, the young woman with freaky hair waited for her bag. She was attractive, although her many tattoos and piercings made her stand out in the middle of conservative Puerto Ricans. Her son sat on their carry-on, chin on fists.

After minutes of waiting for the conveyor belt to start the parade of suitcases, I decided to step into the bathroom. The garbage receptacles were full, and paper towels lay scattered on the floor; puddles of water everywhere, one of the toilets overflowed. I tossed some water on my face. It was getting warmer, and the air conditioning wasn't on very high. In the mirror, the face that stared back at me appeared almost unrecognizable. *Damn, I've lost too much weight.* I tapped the puffy miniature pillows under my eyes, passed a hand through my thick, wavy hair. *Needed a haircut.* I didn't shave in the morning, so from my carry-on I took out the electric shaver my mother had given me.

She usually gave me really crappy gifts—ugly ties, too many briefs, fancy pens I never used, more cologne than I could use. But this last Christmas, I thought with some heartache, she got it right. I started on the wiry stubble. I wasn't a big fan of facial hair.

My father owned a mustache his whole adult life—or maybe it owned him. He once kidded that a real Puerto Rican man always wore one. I finished shaving and splashed more water on my face.

Outside, it felt like I was wearing an invisible, heavy coat. A few steps and I began sweating, rivulets running down my sides, stains spreading on my shirt. I made my way past the crowd, dragging two bags behind me. Illegally parked cars held up traffic even as police officers tried to move people on. The taxi drivers cursed and screamed, waving their hands in frustration.

I spotted Julia, her hands clasped in front of her. She wore a flowery, pleated dress; and I noticed, really noticed, for the first time, her lush hair tumbling down to her shoulders. Noticed a strong proportional, curvy frame. Firm, strong hands with delicately painted fingernails. Her flaming red lips broke into a smile, revealing big, white teeth.

Scanning the airport, I thought how in another time, my parents would have picked me up. They would have made a big deal about my arrival, would have made me feel like a native son. Mami would have been holding balloons.

"Don Marco," Julia said, pointing to my bags. A short skinny guy with lemur eyes and a shaggy mustache covering his lips jumped for my bags. Surprised that I shook his hand, he nodded and grinned, then tossed my bags in the trunk. Julia sat in the back, staring at me for what seemed eternity, grasping my hand. I peeked at the manicured hand at times as if it wasn't touching me but somebody else. She looked away as Don Marco maneuvered his way through frenetic San Juan traffic.

When we left the congested metropolitan area and started passing less denser areas, Julia broke my reverie. She asked, kind of late I thought, how my trip had been. A bit bumpy, I said, and she smiled. She told me that she would have driven to the airport and picked me up alone.

"But this allows me to talk to you easier," she said.

We talked about stupid shit: the weather, sights rolling by. Sometimes she'd respond to a news item on the radio, switching from Spanish and English, almost lecturing, and directed at the driver. To my surprise, he would respond, sometimes heatedly.

The topics would turn to politics, even our conversation about sports, their opinions clashing every time. Halfway through, I wished Julia had not come.

As we drove closer to our destination, the landscape became greener. We had left the last major city heading toward the heart of the island, and although impossible to escape the cement, less urban sprawl confronted us as the elevation rose. The car sped into an expanse of small green mountains and abundant flora, and I breathed freely again. Fifteen minutes later, we passed the last toll booth before exiting the autopista into the town of Baná.

Straight out of the exit, at the light, giant billboards advertised housing units. Not cheap at all, considering the location. To our right, a mall had recently sprung up, the driver informed me. He was a local and beamed with pride at the growth of his hometown. I told him that both my parents claimed this as their hometown, too, and he asked me their names. Julia remained quiet, her gaze set on the horizon. He knew the families. Equally surprising, he did not know what had happened to them. I didn't have the heart or energy to tell him.

Julia asked him to stop at a wooden kiosk near the highway exit and bought me a coffee, which I accepted and sipped as I scanned the surroundings. Around me, middle-aged men huddled at the bar, in this weird wooden shack, drank their midday coffee or beer. The television emitted canned laughter as two on-screen mustached comedians in drag and rollers gossiped.

As towns go, Baná appeared busy and desperate to grow. In the distance, housing developments spotted the green hills. Closer, trucks clogged the feeder road that ran parallel to the autopista; these merged with dozens of cars meandering around orange traffic cones and barrels as they herded traffic toward the new mall. A crane loomed over the scene, swinging to finish the emerging multiplex.

"The air is cooler up here," I told Julia.

"Well, that's at least one good thing about it," she said. "Take a hard look. Sure you don't want to live in San Juan?"

She had tempted me with buying me a car so I could drive to and from the capital to Baná. She insisted a young man needed a livelier place. I declined. I was not going to take anything as luxurious as a car from her.

We rushed back into the car and within minutes were on campus. They deposited me in front of a fading white cement house. "It's the guest house," Don Marco informed me, giving me the keys. I thanked him and extended my hand. He hugged me.

"Bienvenido," he said. Julia hugged me too, and I draped my arms around her.

"I can't believe you're here," she whispered, embracing me harder as if to make sure. She kissed my cheek and looked like she was going to cry, but she wiped the lipstick off with spit and patted my chest. "Call me if you need anything, okay?"

They sped off, Julia waving her arm out of the window. She wanted to stay and help me unpack, invited me to dinner. But the sudden maternal outpouring put me off. Too soon, I thought.

When I entered the house, I noticed the television. Someone else would have looked for the remote. Instead, I turned it around, making the screen face the wall. Then I sat down.

On any trip, I move to other business, start unpacking or just plop on the bed. But I was in Baná, my parents' hometown, where every sense would have elicited a vibrant memory with every morning, each rainfall, any walk into town, had they attained their dream of returning. I threw myself back on the bed and closed my eyes.

"Come with us," my parents had begged. We had not taken a trip together in a while. They handed me the brochure and I contemplated it, knowing I would not go. Milk and Honey Israel Tours, it said. "Experience Israel in a unique way you will never forget." Late in life, my parents had become more serious about religion—the apprehension of approaching retirement, I guess. We were in such different places. I had lost my religion a long time ago and with certainty knew that it would not be rekindled or rediscovered, especially not with some cheesy tour of the Holy Land. I gave back the brochure, which contained an itinerary of various spiritual and sacred landmarks.

One evening when they were still on their trip, the news came on. I watched scenes of screaming people, the disembodied correspondent with hurried stricken voice reporting as officials wearing green vinyl ponchos pushed onlookers away and attempted to drag bodies from smoking, scarred vehicles. A shot repeated over and over of a white rosary atop a pool of blood.

I paced the apartment, nauseous, my heart racing, holding my hand to my forehead, not knowing what to do. I hoped my parents were not involved. But then the news trickled in: The Popular Democratic Jihad taking responsibility for the attack . . . three simultaneous car bombings in the city of Jerusalem . . . detonated in heavy traffic . . . 32 dead . . . 117 wounded . . . a tourist bus partially blown up by one of the suicide car bombers . . . a religious group from the United States on pilgrimage to the Holy Land among the dead and wounded . . . one of the worst terrorist attacks in that troubled part of the world.

Late that night, a young low-level official from the State Department confirmed my fears. I sat dazed, the cell phone clutched in my hand. The silence in the apartment eerie, taunting me toward reflection. My mouth dry, heartburn and anger rising in my chest. Anger and hatred for Israelis and Palestinians alike. With a wrenching wail, I hurled the phone across the room and it smashed against a lithograph of Puerto Rican patriot Albizu Campos waving an angry fist. A gift from them, now shattered, too.

I lay down recalling moments with my parents, trying hard to recall their voices, becoming frustrated I could not faithfully conjure them—having to accept the significance of their loss. *I'm all alone, I thought.* The thought paralyzed me, exhausted me, until I fell into a light sleep on the couch, the ongoing news bulletins streaming from a neighbor's apartment, my machine taking a steady string of messages from family, friends; only to wake to the door opening and Erin's scented body running to me, crying "Oh, baby, sweet baby, I heard."

Three

The doorbell rang. I dried my eyes, blew my nose and ran to open the door. A woman in her mid-thirties tilted her head and grinned. Had dyed reddish, she wore sharp-looking shoes from where glossy red polished toe nails appeared. Her tight dress revealed dazzling wavy shapes. She leaned over and stuck out her hand for me to shake while placing her other hand on her thigh.

"My name is Marisol Santerreguí. Welcome to La Universidad de Baná." We exchanged nods and smiles. "I'm here to pick you up and accompany you to Dr. Roque's office."

I looked around the furnished room for an excuse, but realized this was scheduled, so I'd better go. I thought we were going to walk, but in Puerto Rico people drive their cars everywhere. We drove less than a tenth of a mile in her car, which was so immaculate I asked her if it was new. "No," she replied, laughing. "If it was new, I'd still have the seats covered in factory plastic."

"Puerto Ricans take care of their wheels," she asserted. Then, after a beat: "They love to toss garbage out the window as they speed down the highways in spotless cars." She shrugged, and I nodded.

Marisol drove the long way to show me the campus, small compared to American counterparts. It held three academic buildings, just as many administrative structures. No dormitories. Most students lived in housing provided by town residents, who supplemented their living by gouging rents for no frills, crowded quarters.

On the roof of the student center stood a huge statue of Cano the Coquí, the college mascot, overlooking the well-kept lawns and

17

flowerbeds. The coquí was a tiny tree frog unique to Puerto Rico. Cano stood on two legs and waved an arm in welcome—the other arm held the school flag. The mascot wore a silly cap with the school initials, which I'm sure nobody in Puerto Rico had ever worn.

In the middle of the rotary leading to the college proper stood a replica of Evgeniy Vuchetich's famous United Nations statue, the one with the muscular nude man beating a sword into a plowshare with a hammer. This version had been sculpted to look "native," which meant it wore clothes. Marisol explained the college had once been an American army base. When it closed in the early sixties, the citizens of Baná had petitioned for its transformation into a college campus. With few exceptions, these were the original facilities used by the U.S. Army, including the swimming pool, now closed for repairs.

We drove around the rotary, past an open structure with cement tables and benches. Two stray dogs slept in the shadows of a large ceiba. Along the way, we passed several new BMWs, Mercedes, Volvos, a couple of Lexuses. For a minute, I thought the salaries for professors might compensate for any ill feelings about teaching here.

"Student vehicles," Marisol said, with raised eyebrows. "What their parents were spending on private school tuition they can now spend on new toys."

She parked in the professors' area, with the Hyundais and Toyotas, I knew a teaching gig in Puerto Rico was definitely not the same as in Saudi Arabia or Dubai.

Dr. Roque's office was in The New Academic Building, so named because after six years the college community couldn't agree on someone to name it after. We walked down the English wing, with offices shared by professors. An open area begged for furniture. The architect had that in mind, but the administration didn't want to furnish sofas and armchairs because it promoted student loitering. It remained a big, unused space. As perspiration ran down my face and spotted my clothing, I noticed the building had no air conditioning.

Dr. Pedro Roque's office had the austerity befitting a monk. His working space was sparse and ascetic. Nothing on the walls. A faux wooden bookcase held mostly folders and binders. On top he had three miniature knickknacks, souvenirs really: a porcelain coquí, a *güiro* musical scraper and bookends resembling hands in prayer.

He extended a large, but soft hand with manicured, unpolished nails. A crisp, long green folder, my personnel file, graced his otherwise clean blotter and empty desktop.

"I'm supposed to introduce you to the rector, Dr. Vigo. Pro forma," he said, head slanted, staring at me with deep-set black eyes topped by thick, arching eyebrows.

"I'm sorry about your parents," he said, softly. He meant well, I understood, but it didn't seem right or even his business, and the anger showed on my face.

My mother used to always tell me I wore my emotions on my face. "You really need to learn how to disimular, Rennie," she advised, one day while walking with her at a mall, when lust had captured my adolescent face and I ogled a pretty girl walking by. Learn to feign, dissemble.

"I don't mean to intrude, but it's difficult to know something like that and not feel obligated to say something comforting."

It's not comforting, I thought, when you're trying to forget.

"Personally, and don't take this the wrong way, but I think the unfortunate incident may have helped sway the dean in your favor. In my opinion, there were stronger candidates right here on the island." He smiled as if he had just given me the biggest compliment in the world.

"Well, Dr. Roque, I appreciate the honesty."

"Then we'll get along just fine," he said looking straight into my eyes. I looked at this stooped, lanky man sneering at me, with pasty white skin pockmarked from scarring teenage acne, unflappable gray hair, wearing baggy brown pants, beige guayabera and sandals that made him look like a walking cardboard box. I felt this deep, impending doom.

He sensed the awkwardness and stood up.

"Let's take you to Dr. Vigo."

We walked from the office building without a name in silence, passing the flowerbeds, the fountain in front of Betances Hall, which housed the administrative offices, and across the vast open field where students took naps or read. We walked by the broken pool and the tennis court, where two older professors played a match, until we arrived at a flat, corner building, the Rectoría.

In his office, which in contrast to Dr. Roque's was decorated with many personal artifacts and lithographs done by local artists, Dr. Vigo took my file from Roque and reviewed it.

"Ah, you're Nuyorican," Vigo stated with a smile on his face. Roque rolled his eyes.

"Well, I grew up in Jersey, but yes, I lived in New York City for a while."

"Bien interesante," he commented, looking up from the folder. "This return migration of Puerto Ricans—I'm a sociologist," he offered. "Very under-studied." I stared at him, and he looked like a walrus with glasses. The Beatles' "I am the walrus" ran through my mind. His face turned serious, a studied gravity.

"I heard about your parents." I tensed up. "My heart goes to you, *de verdad, una tragedia.*"

"But, we all have to move on to business. I welcome you to our college and hope you serve with us for many years to come." The little smile on his face disappeared, and he leaned toward me. "You're not involved in any politics, right?"

I turned to Roque, who sat lips pursed.

"No, I'm a writer," I explained.

"I tell all my professors, keep your nose clean, do not get into politics." He gave me his big flipper-like hand, which I shook, and I left numb, almost not remembering Roque had accompanied me out the door. I looked at him, still stunned.

"Can he ask me that?"

"That's how things are here," he said, bothered. I stood on the sidewalk, hands in pockets. Roque directed me toward the guest house.

"You're free now to spend the day as you wish. You should prepare for classes." And he walked back to the building that shall remain nameless.

Classes had to wait.

The taxi took me to *my* house in less than two minutes, and in less time than that my heart sank. In my eyes, it was a shack. Other properties in the area appeared more upscale. But what a hodge-podge neighborhood it was. There were wooden cottages, smaller cement homes, huts with tin roofs and an occasional mansion sprouting like a flower among weeds, built by families with a long history in the area who didn't care about property values.

"This is it," the driver said, breaking my thoughts.

"Are you sure?" I asked.

"Marcos Bortelli 98," he said.

I turned to him and nodded, asked him how close we were to the university, and he laughed. "You can walk from here," he said. I nodded, paid him, and he sped away.

Looking down toward the city center, I could see the top of the church steeple. Cars lined the sloping street that dove into the heart of town. Claustrophobic and third-world urban, I thought. Across from me, a mentally handicapped woman swung back and forth on a rocker, uttering guttural sounds approaching laughter—yah, yah, yah, yah. What was she trying to tell me? Probably, "run, run, run, you stupid fool."

I felt sad that my parents were thinking of retiring to this crowded, fusion house. Fusion, because the house consisted of two parts: a cement portion and an elevated wooden part attached to it. The latter used to be a business—some sort of grocery store. I could not believe my parents were thinking of supplementing their income by running a neighborhood colmado—the thought depressed me. The image of my dad selling bananas actually made me laugh. No, they had good pensions, and I'm sure the proximity to the college had been intentional. Both would probably teach a class or two there to keep them mentally alert and to earn extra income. Most likely, my mother had seen potential in the house. Its quirkiness made her see uniqueness, a bunch of decorating and design challenges, to which, I'm sure, my dad envisioned a retirement full of "projects."

Loud salsa blasted from inside the house. The front door slammed open and a large woman in curlers came out. I had assumed the house was empty. I crossed the narrow sidewalk and stood next to the thick telephone pole in front of the house. I asked the woman if she lived there. Her eyebrows came together in hostile response and she called out for someone—it sounded like "Chu." Chu waddled out, wearing a triple-X Lakers jersey and a menacing glare on his face.

"Excuse me," I began.

"We rent here," he broke in.

It didn't surprise me, because my parents were smart that way. Why lose money on a property if you're not living in it, right? Rent it. And, of course, I didn't know because as usual I never became involved in their affairs, never even became interested in any of their plans. I felt like a crappy son.

"Well, I'm the son of the people you rent from . . . " I said, feeling my voice fade.

"Look, we'll catch up on the rent, okay?" was the reply. "We're a little tight with money right now, okay?" He kept saying "okay" as if he were speaking to an idiot.

"You don't understand. You have to move out. I've decided to move in."

They looked at me, shocked and then angry.

"You can't do that. We live here and pay rent."

"But you just said you owe money."

"Don't matter. We have rights."

"I'm sorry," and I truly was, but I needed a place to live. "You'll have to move. I can give you until the end of the month."

"What? You're crazy, man," this uttered in English. "Crazy."

"That may be true, but you have to move."

"You can't do this. We're poor, but we have rights," said the woman in Spanish.

"Sorry, I need a place to live."

"We don't have to speak with you," said the man. "We do business with Don Juanma and Doña Magda."

I looked toward the mountains rising in the south.

"Well, they won't be able to continue doing business with you. Because they passed away."

They looked at me as if I were lying. But they saw the drop in my mouth and understood that I was not. Apparently, these were the only two people in Puerto Rico who did not know. They said nothing for a while, exchanged glances, lowered their heads.

"I feel sorry for you," said the man. "But we can't move right now, sorry."

They backed themselves into the house, the music blasting away. I stood behind the gate, looking through the rejas, those iron bars that every house in the island installs to protect against the constant threat of crime. Behind the bars, I stretched my neck, trying to peek through the door opening into the place where my parents had chosen to live their golden years.

Four

My parents, Puerto Rican in flesh and spirit, passed on to me their Boricua DNA, but it had failed to manifest itself in any genuine way. They attempted to teach me about the island, about its history and culture. I resisted, and at some level I still do. It is a burden I simply didn't want.

That burden became heavier with Julia's emergence out of thin air. Once on the island, she called me for several lunches and dinners. Fine, she wanted to bond with me. In due time, she kept telling me, she would explain everything about my father and her. I continued going to our get-to-know-each-other meals, but we usually discussed current events, the weather—small talk, really. At the last dinner, she told me how distressed she was that her only son was so ignorant of Puerto Rican history and culture, how distressingly alienated I was from my Puerto Ricaness. In her fashionable pin-striped pants suit, a rose brooch pinned to her lapel, thick dark hair with a few gray strands cut precisely to her neck, her penetrating brown eyes staring at me through Christian Dior frames, she told me how naïve I was about the U.S. involvement in Puerto Rico. I would have rather talked about how difficult it was to hear her call me son, but I listened respectfully as she outlined a plan to "re-integrate" me into Puerto Rican society.

"I have to purge you of the last drop of Yankeeness," she joked, in Spanish.

I googled my biological mother—Julia Matos Canales—and learned she was a founding partner at a law firm in San Juan—Garrutia, Matos and Bustamante—known for taking cases involv-

ing political activists and action lawsuits against the U.S. government. She had a reputation for being a firebrand, an *independentista* who ran for a San Juan senate seat as a Puerto Rican Independence Party candidate, a feminist, an outspoken woman. She
was unmarried and, according to the information I gathered,
childless. Often, she took on high-profile cases defending radical
nationalists whom most Americans would brand as terrorists. She
was born in 1960, which made her five years younger than *papi*—
and in her twenties when she gave birth to me. Started law studies at the University of Puerto Rico but transferred a year later to
the University of Pennsylvania's law school, where she graduated
top of her class. In those details, I knew, was buried the story of
how I came into the world and the aftermath. But Julia was not
ready to share it.

Instead, she dedicated herself to lecturing me on Puerto Rican
history, culture and society. She faxed me a bibliography of "must
read books." The Re-Education of René (she insisted on calling
me by my real name) invigorated her, enlivened her discussions
with me, definitely was shaping our reconnection. These efforts
seemed a way to construct a bridge to narrow our distance, so
awkward and painful between a mother and son. Besides all the
reading, mini lectures, history lessons, she now suggested "cultural field trips" to get a "truer sense of the island and its people."
It was overbearing of her to suggest them, but I signed up anyway,
with the hope of learning about my true past and family history.

So, when she called about the first field trip, to attend the commemoration of the Grito de Lares rebellion, I agreed. Julia had her
secretary send me detailed directions and an address where I was
to stay. She could have put me up in a parador, a small hotel in
Quebradillas, a few miles away, but she wanted me to stay with her
and her "compatriotas."

Excellent directions led me to a former nineteenth-century coffee hacienda, which distant cousins now used as a summer home.
The house overlooked the town of Lares, two kilometers away,
and on a clear day the northwestern coast, known as Costa Brava,
appeared in the distance. Coffee beans still grew but now ended
up drying on the trees, lost amid the fierce foliage surrounding the

house. The owners kept the immediate grounds trimmed and beautiful. Baskets of geraniums, peonies and bougainvillea hung from the bottom of the second floor balcony. Orchids of all colors everywhere; vervain lined the grounds around the many trees.

By a faded wooden sign that read "Hacienda Colibrí" stood the stairs which led up to the second floor, the wrap-around balcony and my room. On a credenza and taped to an incongruous mobile phone, I saw a folded piece of paper with my name scrawled in large letters. A note from Julia, apologizing for not being here to meet me because she had business in town related to the festivities. She was part of the organizing committee and would return to dine with me and show me around. "Enjoy this beautiful house," she wrote, "which is also part of your historical and family heritage."

I circled the house, looking out from the four cardinal points. On the back of the house, a long wooden stairway zigzagged down to a pool. Invigorated by an idea of a swim, I found my room, threw the small carry-on on top of the bed and dug for my swimsuit. A few weeks in Puerto Rico and I had learned to pack a bathing suit, no matter my destination.

At poolside, sitting upright on a padded lounge chair, legs covered by a towel, sat an older woman, someone's abuela, I thought. Next to her sat a burly man, perhaps her son or grandson, dressed in black. He sat at the edge of the chair, alert, hands folded at the space between his knees. He stirred when he saw me, relaxed when he saw my towel and suntan lotion. I nodded a hello. Grandma dropped her copy of *El Día*, looked over her sunglasses and responded "Buenas tardes" in a firm tone. As I kicked my flip-flops off and spread the sun block on, I caught a better glimpse of her. A stern face, with a mouth etched into a smile. She had a large mole under the left side of her lower lip. Beautiful eyebrows fanned out as they approached a fine nose with flaring nostrils. I sensed her watching me behind the sunglasses. What was up with her? This went beyond cougarism—this woman was in her eighties at least.

I dove in and did my usual laps. I had swum varsity in high school and did my standard warm up anytime I hit the water, more out of habit than anything else. After treading water for a few minutes to cool off, I climbed into a floating doughnut, and paddled around a bit. When I reached her side of the pool, she leaned toward me.

"You Julia's son?" she said this in English, heavily accented, but clear.

I wasn't used to hearing myself linked to Julia like that, and I didn't know how this woman knew my mother and her life-long secret.

"You know Julia?" I asked.

She took off her sunglasses, slowly folding them at her waist. "So," she said, smiling, "You are the reluctant prodigal son." Her eyes lit up. An abundant, thick white mane surrounded her elegant face.

Another man dressed in black stood by the stairs, which led back to the house. I jumped off the doughnut, swam up to the side of the pool and pushed myself up and out. I don't know why, but when she said "prodigal son," I saw it as "prodigal sun."

We shook hands and she signaled me to sit by her. She pointed to a pitcher of orange juice filled with ice, her hand trembling a bit, but I declined. She stared at me for a minute longer than I felt comfortable being observed.

"You have Julia's eyes. They burn through you like a laser." She shook a little jokingly. She must have known something, because my lack of response spawned an awkward silence. She patted my thigh.

"Everyone has a burden in life," she said in Spanish, holding her pointer finger up in the air. "And God bears them all."

She asked the nearest guy to her if he was getting hungry.

"Let's get some chicken at the Chinese," she said.

He relayed the message to the other guy, who quickly left to run the errand. She took lipstick out of her purse, applied some and glanced out toward the mountains.

"Me, I have outlived my children," she said. She stared at me, her lively eyes now deflated, and she said to me in a low voice, "Be thankful and happy you still have your mother."

Evening approached; the pool lights came on and mosquitoes buzzed around us. The sky turned a burnt orange.

"You know, this is my hometown," she said as she struggled to get up from the chair.

"Oh, is it?" I said, getting up to help her. The guy next to her was faster and held her arm as she stood up.

"I left many years ago, but the memories they don't leave."

She waved her hand to no one in particular. She walked toward the stairs, holding on to the man's arm. At the base of the stairs, she turned her head.

"Welcome home."

"I'm not from Lares."

"No, welcome home to Puerto Rico."

She ascended the long steps; almost at the top she started singing, "*La vida te da sorpresas, sorpresas te da la vida.*" She slipped into darkness and out of sight.

Home? Mother? Abuela, please. And what was all that stuff about God bearing everyone's pain? I wanted to submerge myself. Instead, I served myself a glass of orange juice, wishing it had some vodka, and stayed at the pool, almost falling asleep, until I couldn't tolerate the mosquitoes, and I remembered my newly found "mom" had invited me to dinner.

Julia had made reservations at the one decent restaurant in the area for seven o'clock, but we left an hour earlier so she could show me the Plaza de la Revolución, where tomorrow hundreds would congregate to commemorate *El Grito*. She parked on a side street and, as we walked on the narrow sidewalk, she seemed like she wanted to grab my arm but hesitated and folded her arms, walking like that for a while. I found the idea of her grabbing on to me unsettling. Did she think that those types of gestures could erase a past of abandonment and neglect? Looking at her I felt sorry, though; ordinarily, Julia possessed a self-confident stride. Now, with folded arms, bumping into people, she appeared awkward, unsure. "Mother" was a role she didn't know how to play.

With the upcoming festivities, the streets of this sleepy town were more crowded than usual. We bumped into people on the slim sidewalks, most of the time forcing us into the streets, joining the human traffic bringing the cars to a dead stop. The town merchants adjacent to the plaza must love this day, I thought.

They added to the congestion by lining the sidewalks with some of their merchandise. For a small town, the noise equaled, at least on this day, that of a city. Cars honked, the merchants hawked their goods, laughter and voices rose from the growing crowds; an electricity flowed through the streets, making the day feel special. In the middle of this, Julia proceeded to give me a historical account of the events in 1868 leading to El Grito, the "ill-fated but heroic" rebellion.

"A Spanish Captain overheard insurgents talking. Typically Puerto Rican: we can't keep our mouths shut when we have to, but when we need to yell to the high heavens, you couldn't pry our mouths open with a crowbar." She said this with a grin, pulling off her glasses and fidgeting with them, a sign I had learned to read as agitation. "Anyway, the Spaniards soon learned of the revolt and the rebels had to move the date from the originally planned 29th of September to the 23rd."

What were my ancestors doing during all this, I thought. What side were they on?

We sat down on a bench by the plaza, similar to so many across the island. She crossed her legs, took a cigarette from a gold case and lit it, breathing in the tobacco deeply and expelling the smoke with vigorous, angry intensity.

"They took this town, Lares, proclaimed the Republic of Puerto Rico, but the Spaniards outnumbered them—it was over almost as soon as it started."

She smoked like she did everything else, with blinded urgency. Mami had been a non-smoker, who had lectured me about the dangers of smoking since an early age; that, and drugs, and STDs. In a way, she had Julia's vitality; she approached everything head-on, never flinching.

Strong women attracted my dad. Strong, attractive women. Because both Mami and Julia were appealing, although in different ways. Julia gravitated toward plumpness, some would say voluptuousness. Mami had always been slender, with wild curly hair; I always envied her beautiful brown skin. Now I knew why I'm pale, looking at Julia and remembering how Mami would kid Papi about being so "jincho." Julia had that hair, though, and

those eyes—also passed on to me, no mistaking it. Anyone who
saw us would assume we were mother and son. Both women had
intriguing faces, with striking features. Julia's eyes, when not
piercing you, when they softened, felt as if, for that moment, you
were the center of the universe. Mami had wonderful light-brown
almond eyes, a slender nose and curvy lips that I thought fortunate enough to have inherited, until I saw Julia's. Julia's high heels,
another difference; Mami would never wear a pair like those. She
was a teacher on her feet for long stretches of time. And she liked
to think she was sensible. Looking at the shoes, I noticed her
shapely legs and that Julia was shorter than Mami.

Our bench faced San José, the Catholic church, and the monument to the Grito: a rectangular stone resembling cinder blocks,
the Lares flag painted on it, no more than six feet tall, with a bust
of Ramón Emeterio Betances on top, all of it standing on a hexagonal base. I had envisioned something larger to equal the significance Julia and her crew gave the bust. Julia read my face. She
pointed to it with the cigarette.

"It's a disgrace, but what can you expect? El Grito isn't even a
national holiday." She looked at me with her piercing eyes, searching for comprehension. "But we do celebrate the United States'
Declaration of Independence, with fireworks and parades." She
shrugged her shoulders and smirked.

Her smirk bothered me. That, and the smoke flowing from her
lips to my face. I didn't give a flying fuck about the shitty monument, about how PR celebrated the Fourth—why not, it's as stupid as anything else Puerto Ricans do—fuck the Grito and Puerto
Rican history. Seeing Julia made me think of my real mother and
that depressed the shit out of me. I had buried her along with
Papi, just a few months ago, and could not grasp the finality of it.
They were gone too soon for me to tell them how much I loved
them. And this woman came along and disturbed the peace I
needed to deal with their deaths. Damn you, Julia, for making me
angry at them for their lies, for turning my life into a lie. For
expecting to replace a love I took for granted. What do you want?
Why am I here with you, in this shithole town commemorating an

event I couldn't care less about? Damn you. I'm alone now, and with all this lecturing you make me feel like an orphan.

She droned on: "Puerto Rican history is a long series of tragedies, René. After so many tragedies, you're left with no other alternative but to laugh." She threw the butt to the ground and crushed it under one red sole of her black Louboutin pumps. Then with a tissue she cleaned the bottom of the shoe and picked up the butt.

"Well, I'm not exactly in a laughing mood," I said.

Her eyebrows knit together, and she nodded. "Bien, let's go eat."

As we were passing a large, shady tree, she stopped. "By the way, this is the famous Tamarindo de Don Pedro."

She looked for some recognition; my shrugging and head shaking evoked an exasperated sigh.

"Gabriela Mistral, the Nobel Prize-winning poet from Chile . . . you know?"

I nodded yes I had heard of her.

"Well, she gave this tree to Pedro Albizu Campos, the leader of the nationalists. It was taken from Bolívar's estate in Venezuela." She slapped her hand against the tree a few times. "It's beautiful, isn't it?"

I nodded. It was indeed a great looking tree.

"It was planted with soil from all the nations of Latin America— a symbol of solidarity with our struggle for freedom and independence." Julia's face turned sad. "The tamarindo is bittersweet, so people say it is a fitting symbol of that struggle."

I wanted to ask, "What's sweet about it?" but held my tongue. Julia's fierce expression demonstrated that she had forgotten everything she had said about laughter and tragedy.

On the way to the car, we passed the famous Lares Ice Cream shop, the one with all the crazy flavors, like garlic and avocado— and I remembered going there as a kid. On a visit to Mami's grandmother. No, I was not from Lares, but my mother—the real one— had family from here. Why didn't I tell that to the old woman?

We drove up route 129 to El Cacique, a dive with ivy crawling up its outside walls. When we entered, I was grateful that Julia had made reservations. The place was packed. I ordered a yucca pie stuffed with shredded beef. Julia ordered a plantain dish filled with seafood, served in a pilón, a wooden mortar used for smashing the fried plantains with garlic. The place was not much for décor, but the food was good. Throughout the meal, I faced two gigantic Puerto Rican flags on the wall, one the more traditional and the other the Lares rebellion flag, replicas of which decorated every corner of this town.

We had settled into our meals, when the old woman from the pool walked in, accompanied by an older gentleman, probably her husband, followed not only by the two guys from the pool, but what seemed like an entourage. The clientele gave her a standing ovation. ¡Ésa es! ¡Ésa es! That's the one! That's the one! Julia stood up, too, so I did the same.

The old woman wore a red dress, her faced done, her lips brilliant with lipstick. Her white hair shone under the restaurant lights. She came over to our table, hugged and kissed Julia and tapped me on the shoulder.

She said to Julia, "I met your son today. Qué guapo es."

This she whispered to Julia, and Julia thanked her, which bothered me. The old woman asked if we wanted to join them in the back, where they had a special room reserved. Julia told her that she wanted to have dinner with me so we could talk.

"I'll see you tomorrow," she said.

They kissed again and the old woman left, talking to others along the way, shaking hands, giving more hugs and kisses, even signing an occasional autograph. Her entourage dressed in black, resembling a funeral procession, followed, apparently accustomed to all the fuss.

"Who the hell is that?" I asked. Julia stared at me as if I had made the worst joke possible, the type that silences a room of people at a party.

"Are you seriously telling me that you don't know who that is?" She asked me this, fork suspended in the air, her blazing eyes a mix of sorrow and incredulity.

"Excuse my ignorance, if I don't know who the old biddy is."

I'm not good at being caught misinformed. Growing up with two college professors who quizzed me on current events, state capitals, you name it, I had acquired a competitive attitude about knowing the correct answer. I pride myself on being well read, being educated at fine schools, so Julia's facial expression stung me. At once, she seemed upset and disgusted with my ignorance.

"No, you are not excused." Down came the fork. She leaned toward me. "You think this is a joke?" she hissed. "That 'old biddy' is Lolita Lebrón, who was willing to die for her country, and you disrespect her?" A quick pat of her lips with the napkin. "What did Juanma teach you? He who always made a big deal about how proud he was of being Puerto Rican."

"Whoa—don't bring Papi into this, okay? And by the way, I have heard of Lebrón. I just didn't know what she looked like. I mean, all the pictures are of her, young and skinny."

Julia rolled her eyes. "For me, she's not buried in some history book. She is alive and still fighting for the cause."

"Well, to others she is nothing but a terrorist."

Silence, an icy stare.

I returned her stare, shocked that she had forgotten my parents had just recently been killed by a suicide bomber in Israel.

She shook her head. "*She . . .* is a patriot, while *you* are a brain-washed pitiyanqui."

I leaned my face right into hers. "Maybe if you hadn't abandoned your son, he'd fucking know who Lolita Lebrón was."

She reached out across the table and slapped me, hard. I was astonished at her strength. By now, people close by stared from their tables, mouths opened in disbelief. The manager made his way toward us. I was thankful we had a corner table, isolated in the back of the restaurant.

"You will respect me," she hissed at me. "And my beliefs. Even if you don't agree." She said this crying, out of breath.

The manager approached us. I walked out.

I stood outside the glass doors, the left side of my face burning. Julia, standing now, laughed, blew her nose. The manager talked to her, his hand on his chest. Still standing, Julia took some bills from her purse and handed them to the man. He kept bowing as he talked to her. I walked over to the car and waited for her.

The car ride was at first quiet. "I'm sorry for hitting you," she said, halfway to the hacienda. "But you don't know what it's like, René," she said almost about to cry, shaking her head in exasperation. "We've been persecuted by the F.B.I.; look how they assassinated Filiberto Ojeda, in his own home, on El Grito, just a few years ago. And what about the carpetas, huh? They should be ashamed that in a so-called democracy they have secret files on people, René. Me, your mother, they had a file on *me*. And why? Because I want freedom and sovereignty for my country, just the same as they did from England. The U.S. government tortured and murdered Don Pedro and they'll do it to anyone who is pro-independence. This is not a joke, René."

Then, glancing at me with a bit of remorse, she added, "And Lolita Lebrón didn't kill anyone." I leaned my head back and closed my eyes.

"Coño," she blurted out a few seconds later, banging her fist against the steering wheel, tears rolling down her cheeks. "You were mean," she said, now sobbing.

I stared out the window at the blurring darkness. "Look, I respect your beliefs, I do." I closed my eyes. "But I didn't come to Puerto Rico for a history lesson."

I turned to her. "Why don't you tell me about how you met my father. About my relatives, their contributions to Puerto Rican history. Just talk to me about you, Julia. About you."

She turned to me, tears streaming down her cheeks, nodded and smiled.

Out of the car, we said nothing and headed to our respective rooms. The next morning, I found a note under my door. It read: "Breakfast on table. Off to the activities. See you later. Your mother." It irked me to no end, how she used "mother" so freely, like she had earned the right. In one of our telephone conversations, I had asked her, out of respect for my real mother, to refer to herself as Julia, until we both could feel comfortable with my calling her "Mom" or "Mami" or whatever.

I remember the silence on the other end, and then she told me she would be forever grateful "her son" had been "blessed" by having a good woman raise him. But, she said, "Magda, may she

rest in peace, did not go through fourteen hours of labor. I did."
The compromise is that she refers to herself as "mother" and calls
me "son," and I call her Julia.

After a breakfast of pan sobao, a soft sweet bread I loved buttered,
strong island coffee, white cheese and fruit, I decided to collect my
stuff and leave. The plan had been to hang out at the Grito ceremony, but I had had enough lectures, and yesterday hadn't been a high
point of our bonding. But I recalled what I had said to her in the
restaurant and felt terrible. She had made an effort to have me experience El Grito; the least I could do was see the activities.

So, I drove into town. I had to park a mile from the plaza; the
area was packed with cars and buses. Along the route to the plaza,
vendors had set up kiosks and tents to sell every imaginable artifact of nationalist pride. A cottage industry of patriotism: T-shirts,
leather key chains, wooden machetes and other handicrafts done
by island artisans, all engraved with some politically charged
motto or saying, like "Viva Puerto Rico Libre." I made my way up
as close to the canopy-covered platform as I could, then heard
marching music and saw the members of the Cadets of the Republic, dressed in their customary black, the standard bearer hoisting
the nationalist flag, a white cross against a black background.
They led the procession, other dignitaries followed, the other
nationalist symbols including the Lares flag in tow, up to the platform, and the entire congregation, hundreds of independentistas,
grew quiet as the band struck up "La Borinqueña," the Puerto
Rican national anthem—the real one, any nationalist will inter-
ject, with the militant lyrics.

In the middle of signs screaming all sorts of political messages,
colorful T-shirts brandishing similar messages or the faces of Ché,
Albizu, Ojeda, Lebrón, the five imprisoned nationalists, I spotted
tired, smiling faces turned solemn by the end of the anthem. Tears
flowed down some cheeks. Then cheers, applause, chanting: Lo-
li-ta, Lo-li-ta. Lo-li-ta.

Today, Lolita Lebrón wore black pants, a white shirt and red tie.
She paraded her outfit to the laughter of the congregation. Then,
she spoke into the microphone: "A tribute to Luisa Capetillo."
Another historical figure absent from my cultural encyclopedia.

The better culturally informed understood and they laughed, cheered and applauded.

In a firm voice, Lebrón began her speech: "Friends and compañeros, today I celebrate and honor Luisa Capetillo because she was a fighter. An independentista to the death. She knew who she was and was proud of it. And was never afraid to fight for her beliefs." Applause and cheers.

Lebrón ranted on against the United States, the crowd eating it up. At one point she quoted Albizu Campos. His comment about how a person not proud of his heritage will never amount to anything because he begins by rejecting himself.

After a few minutes, I turned around and headed back to my car, past Puerto Rican flags patched on butts and hordes of T-shirts claiming pure-bred, deep-rooted Puerto Ricaness.

Five

I was playing with my Hess truck, kneeling on the hard, hospital floor, cool and smooth against my bare knees. My father sat slouched in a chair too small for him, holding my mother's hand as she slept in her cranked up hospital bed, tubes coming and going from her slender body. She looked different, without make-up, beautiful. Her long, wavy hair tied back carelessly with a cheap scrunchie. That moment was perfect, after the crazy week, coming to the hospital every day, hearing my father cry alone in his bedroom after coming home after the surgery. Every day was fine again, peaceful; the only sounds in the room were my parents' breathing, the sounds of the monitor attached to mom's recovering body, the relentless heartbeat filling the room with calm.

The clacking came first, then the strong perfume. I saw the high heels strapped around the slender ankles, looked up and saw her pale, oval face, the cherry red lips breaking into a crooked smile. She was an older woman, but I wouldn't have guessed she was my grandmother, or anybody else's abuela. To my young eyes, she came into that room like an aging movie star. Her green silk dress shone, the fat pearls, rings that swallowed her fingers, the fashionable short haircut, all of it did not spell grandma for me. Because my sense of abuela was my mom's mother, who everyone called Doña Lola and I called Güeli. She was huggingly plump, with heavy arms that held me tight and smelled like coconut flan and coffee. Her hair was always a mess, curly-kinky, a few strands escaping the rubber band that tried holding it all back.

My groggy father arose from his slumber and snapped up to greet his mother, who no one dared called Doña but Isabela, like the queen. My father called her *madre*, not Mami. *Madre*. Mother. They touched each other's cheeks and with pursed lips gave air kisses. Mami always gave me sloppy, wet kisses that landed somewhere on my head, sometimes on my lips. Like Güeli. He called and told me to stand and say "bendición" to Abuela Isabela. I asked for the traditional blessing and she embraced me, the perfume intoxicating me. She rubbed my back with both hands, ran her chiseled, porcelain fingers and long red nails through my hair, and I could see she had tears in her eyes. She collected herself, caressed my father's cheek and asked how Mami was doing. My father nodded and said something in Spanish, which sounded positive.

That was the first time I remember meeting my paternal grandmother. In a hospital room, after my mother's operation. She had seen me before, as a baby, before Mami and she had the falling out. I didn't remember, of course. It comes to me second-hand, and pretty much from my parents' side of things. Not that I need to hear the other side. I believed them when they said Isabela never cut Mami any slack. Like this time in the hospital, she came to help with me, the grandson. Poor woman, Papi would say, she means well, really, she does. But she was set in her ways, old school. And Mami was a new woman, with a career, who grew up in the South Bronx and learned not to take any bullshit from anyone. So she tried to tell my mom what to do, what not to do, offered unwanted advice about how to raise children, how to run a household, what a good wife did for her husband. Pitying her for losing her Puerto Rican ways. Making fun of her Spanish, even though Mami spoke it fluently and taught it.

Mami told me those days were like living in a concentration camp in her own home. Once, she wanted to push the "Nazi witch" out the window. It's horrible to make light of the holocaust. Mami was always conscious of things like that, so imagine how bad my grandmother made her feel. That's when she knew that it wouldn't work. That they would never hit it off and become great friends. And she threw down wife law; and my father had to listen. He accepted her terms, because he loved my mother. He loved his mother and family, but he loved us more. It was simple.

This time around wasn't any better. She had arguments with my father all the time. It's kind of blurry, but I do remember Isabela crying and saying how her own son had turned his back on his mother. I felt bad for her. I felt bad for Dad, too, standing in the kitchen as Isabela tried to cook some terrible dish I wouldn't eat. She kept pointing a spoon at him. He looked trapped, his back against the fridge, ruffling all my artwork that Mami had posted. I could hear them from the living room while I read. It got louder, their yelling, and I knew Mami would be able to hear it across the apartment, from the bedroom, where she was trying to recuperate. Then Isabela started saying stuff I couldn't understand about Mami being hollow, hueca—my father would explain later, although he never told me what it meant. I couldn't understand the rest; it was in Spanish. Sometimes my grandmother would talk in English, which was pretty good. A solid Catholic education, she used to say. Money buys anything in PR, my father would say behind her back.

But they kept it up in Spanish, heated, fast, furious words coming out of their tongues like fuego. They suddenly stopped. My mother stood facing them both in her terrycloth robe, her hand on her stomach. She turned to me and ordered me to my room. I grabbed my book and ran to my bedroom, where I could still see and hear them. Isabela yelled something about "the truth." Mami shuffled closer and stared at my father. "I want her out of here, now!"

Isabela left the next day, on an evening flight to San Juan. I saw her only that one time on the family trip to PR, and not at the funeral, after she died from breast cancer. My father visited her at the hospital in her last days and attended the funeral alone.

Six

The violent dreams continued. They all had the feel of a cheap, hand-held camera movie in an endless horror film festival. In all of them, I kept seeing blood everywhere and heard frantic, disembodied screaming. Every time, I woke up startled, disoriented, and after getting my bearings, would slip into a funk.

I had been living in the Guest House for weeks. I informed the college authorities of my housing situation. Stay as long as you need, they said. Of course, they were charging me, but it wasn't really expensive. But that's not the point. I had my "own" place, my so-called inheritance, and I felt stupid having to pay any kind of rent. Worse, how was I supposed to make the squatters move out? The Riveras owed my parents six months' rent. So on top of everything, I had to file legal proceedings against them. Julia knew nothing about this legal mess. I wasn't even sure she knew about the house. Sad to say, but we weren't at a point where I could confide in her, and I didn't want her involved in something concerning my parents. Miguel "Micco" Montero, a colleague, wished me luck, telling me squatters had ridiculous rights in Puerto Rico.

I was now a perpetual guest, an insomniac and unfocused. I wanted to play some b-ball, run maybe, go lie on the beach, but sometimes I sat on the patio, sipping a cup of strong, sweet, black coffee, and let my thoughts ride the fog drifting over the green central mountains. From where I sat, I could see the neighborhood where my parents' house was located amid houses perched on ground overlooking the college. That would always break the reverie, would upset me, so I had to get up and do something else.

Today, in front of me, the task was reviewing the master syllabi given to me by the department secretary, Nitza. I was supposed to write my own course syllabus for each class and hand them out to students. Uninspiring work, especially with the emphasis on phonetics and grammar—it seemed like the principal objective was to teach the verb "to be."

So, one particular Saturday found me kicking the hacky sack, as I'm bound to do when procrastinating, avoiding a boring task like writing syllabi. I was lost in the rhythmic dance of keeping the sack in the air for minutes, when Micco came to pick me up for a welcome party I didn't even want. Marisol Santerrequi had decided it was the collegial thing to do. Stiegler, a recent hire, told me he never got one. Watch her, Micco had said, referring to Marisol. "She's got it bad for you." I was not pleased by this. Nothing against Marisol. I had scanned her in those tight dresses—the cleavage impossible not to see. Not bad. But the last thing on my mind was having an affair with a colleague. The more I thought about it, the more unsettling it became, because she was persistent, and I didn't need anything else on my plate.

I opened the door and Micco, all five-feet-four and chunky, stood in front of me, dressed in white linen pants and a short sleeve, red silk shirt, his hairless chest held high as if he were displaying a series of medals. He dipped his sunglasses down his nose to look at me, and his from-the-bottle suntanned face turned to shock.

"You're not wearing that." He threw a finger at my outfit, which consisted of army fatigue shorts with a Yankees T-shirt and flip-flops.

"Hell no, let me get ready." I kicked him the hacky sack and he dropped it.

I showered, shaved and dressed, my newly donned clothes—a blue rolled-up sleeved, buttoned-down collared shirt, with khaki pants and boat shoes—did not receive any more of a compliment.

"What's that, Puerto Rican preppie?"

The drive to San Juan from Baná on the autopista is forty minutes, in good traffic, which is rare, but with Micco driving we made it there faster. He drove his little red convertible like a NASCAR wannabe, moving in and out of traffic at a wild speed, turning the wheel in jerky motions, elbows upturned like it was appropriate etiquette. We still had time to chat. I found out he would be my office mate, and I suddenly sensed in him a responsibility to mentor me. All I could think of was that I was having to share such a tiny office with another human being too gabby for me. I liked my privacy, and when it was time to work, I didn't want anyone around me talking stupid crap. In that short drive to San Juan, Montero gave me rundowns on everyone.

"Most of these people," he yelled, over the rushing air and speeding cars around us, "harmless, unless you get in the way of something they want. Like dogs, they'll snap if you try to take the bone they're chewing on."

So much for camaraderie, I thought. Passing us, a pick-up truck carried a huge, plastic cow.

"Pedro, though," he continued, swinging elbows as he steered through dense traffic. "Keep an eye on him. They don't call him The Rock for nothing."

The warm night air slapped at us. We passed congested, residential areas turned commercial, cluttered with signs advertising all types of businesses, and a string of junk food franchises. Montero pointed to one of many residential areas lining the highway, La Sierra Estates. "Freddie Rivas lives there," he said. "A gay man who has yet to accept he's too old to cruise." The university had an unofficial "don't ask, don't tell policy" in place, even before the U.S. Army came up with theirs. No one gay I met there ever admitted it, certainly not in public. Friends knew, but there lingered a tacit hush about how they did their business. It was sad, really. I looked at him as I clenched the dashboard and saw my face reflected off his mirror sunglasses, his tight, black dyed mustache embracing his purplish lips.

"He's into that New Age stuff, with rocks and channeling," he added.

I nodded, though unclear exactly what he meant.

At the exit to Monteverde Mall, traffic thickened. It didn't matter to Micco, who snaked through cars, SUVs and trucks like he was on the last lap at Daytona. At times, he passed vehicles on the shoulder, once almost scraping against the concrete meridian. If he could drive on top of the divider, he would. The other drivers on the road were just as bad or worse. Everyone raced and cut off other drivers.

"Then, we have the resident gringo—the other new guy, Daniel Stiegler."

"What about Foley?"

"Foley," Montero paused. "He's like fog, comes and goes, stealth-like. I think he's CIA." He whispered this and laughed at my surprised expression. Then, added, "Maybe he's here to keep an eye on Stiegler."

Stiegler's wild, bushy-mustached mountain man look came to mind, his unkempt hair, wrinkled clothes and weather-beaten hiking boots recalling his days as a lecturer in Montana.

We exited on Río Piedras, passed the University of Puerto Rico's main campus, an amalgam of huddled, parked automobiles and buildings withered by neglect and weather, and soon entered Marisol's street, which like so many streets in Puerto Rico had no sign. Micco said that to this day he didn't know its name. And like so many other San Juan streets, there wasn't a parking space to be found. Micco drove around for fifteen minutes, past vehicles whose owners had given up and stranded them on sidewalks to await the parking ticket accepted as part of the cost of hanging out in "el área metropolitana." He finally squeezed in between two SUVs, tapping one of the bumpers several times, and we walked to Marisol's high-rise condo, which appeared no better than most "projects" in the Bronx. The same elongated, upturned rectangular, gray-cement structure with a splash of pastels.

Inside, similar long, narrow corridors fronting a series of clone doors. Same hard, waxy, Formica floors. Except here you own the apartment; it was an investment. Once inside the apartment, I saw that it even had the same floor plan. The kitchen area was separated from the living room by a counter and bar stools. A hallway led to two bedrooms and a bathroom. I could find my way blindfolded around this apartment, because I had lived for years in a similar one in the Bronx, before my parents got a deal on a house in New Jersey.

Across the room, a wide, sliding glass door opened onto a slim balcony with a view of San Juan's swarming, concrete cityscape. I was glad for the sake of Marisol's investment that she had more footage than those same floor plans in the South Bronx. The living room was airy and accommodated the dozen individuals already there, sipping mojitos and wine.

"Ah, here's the guest of honor," Marisol chirped, holding a glass of red. "Micco, you brought him late," she scolded. She smiled at me.

"I found the young man shamefully unprepared and utterly unattired," he responded in his awful Brit accent. Montero taught British literature, and on occasion took delight in mimicking a purposefully annoying nasal English accent.

"Ay," clucked Marisol, already tipsy, "at least now we can eat."

It was an inviting room, full of color and practical furniture. White rattan—big in the island—with flowery prints, mostly bright reds against white. She pointed to a Botaño up on a wall. "Its value has gone up," she whispered, "since he died." In a corner swung a Calder mobile replica—the one with red lily pads. On top of a credenza, and other flat surfaces, stood various elongated candles and ceramic knickknacks.

Having announced the go-ahead to eat, everyone approached the buffet spread, a rich combination of seafood paella, several vegetable dishes and a huge spinach salad mixed with tangerines. For appetizers, ham croquettes and miniature alcapurrias. Several colleagues had brought bottles of wine, reds and whites, but I preferred the sangria served in a crystal pitcher.

I was greeted by Cari Rosas, one of several linguists, and her husband, Franco. Much of my conversation with him entailed the many surgical procedures he had undergone. Along with Cari, I met Juan Cedeño and his pretty wife, Anabel; Luis Angel Iglesias, a somber, demure scholarly type, and Rita Gómez, whose English I could barely understand. Stieglitz entrenched himself in a corner with a plate of food.

Juan grabbed a plate with his left hand as he shook my hand with his right. A relatively new hire, he had moved from the United States and complained about the lack of technology on campus. "It's like they're Luddites," he said, grinning, referring to our colleagues as he chewed on a piece of lobster from the paella, and shook his head.

I nodded, drinking the sangria, which was strong.

Marisol served me a plate of food. "Eat something. You could put some meat on those huesitos of yours." She patted my arm, her hand lingering across my forearm.

Opposite from me, Pedro Roque sat talking to Carmela López, whom people called his shadow, and a hooked-nose, hunched woman with short hair, the Chair of the Humanities department, Margo Lasca. She had been chair of that rambunctious group for over fifteen years because no one else could be trusted by the others. Pedro did not look over to me even once. He only talked to me when he approached the food. Holding his hands together and glancing down at everything with caution, he asked if everything was going well, especially with the syllabi. "Yes," I lied.

"Great," he said. "Go by the syllabi—you won't go wrong."

He served himself three croquettes, threw some salad on his plate and walked back to his seat. Today, he wore a frumpy, brown short-sleeved shirt, dark-blue pants and his usual sandals. Not a single strand moved from his newly moussed hair. He resumed the conversation with Lasca and Carmela López. Although Pedro didn't talk much, his deep laughter filled the room whenever one of his colleagues said something humorous.

"People say they're lovers, you know," Micco whispered into my ear. He was buzzed and refilling his glass.

"Which two?" I really didn't care. I just wanted clarification.

"Pedro and Carmela."

It wouldn't have surprised me if Carmela and Pedro were lovers. But people were going on appearances, always dangerous. Carmela hung with Pedro, but they also went back many years. They were two of the most senior faculty in the college. Both were single, although Pedro had gone through a divorce that by all accounts left him bitter and resentful of women. Carmela never married, and no one ever saw her with any other men, and apparently she never shared that part of her life with colleagues. She led a simple life, and by Micco's account, wore slacks all the time in a country where a feminine dress still was considered fashionably desirable. She always kept her hair short and tidy, almost an old fashioned "bob." Her one nod to vanity were earrings—usually tidy hoops or studs—all expensive. "This," she would often say, waving her hand to indicate the college, "is my life—the students, especially." No one could say with certainty if she had ever dated; she could have been a fifty-year-old virgin.

"Here I am," Freddie Rivas announced as he walked through the door, a bottle of champagne in one hand, a bouquet of yellow roses in the other. Behind, a young man hesitated. Freddie turned to the young man. "Ay, come in, nobody's going to bite you." Then, looking at me he said, "Not yet, anyway. Well, nice to see you're still with us," he said, shaking my hand.

Marisol put on a CD by Olga Tañón and gestured to Freddie, hands signaling "come on," her hips moving to the music. Freddie put down the champagne bottle and the flowers, which he was about to put in water. They shook and shuffled to a merengue. Both were good dancers who enjoyed the music. Freddie's friend attended to putting the roses in a vase, smiling at the dancing couple.

Everyone observed the two, spinning like dancing figurines in the center of the floor. Marisol was starting to look good. She wore tight, blue palazzo pants highlighting a formidable behind working overtime to the rhythms of the music. When they stopped, she was perspiring and she dabbed her neck and cleavage with a paper towel.

"Want to dance?" she asked.

I said no, but she took my hand anyway. I was a horrible dancer, a disgrace to Puerto Ricans everywhere, really.

"Shake those hips, nene," Marisol said in a whiny voice.

At one point she placed her hands on my hips, trying to get me in sync with the rhythm. By now, thank God, a few other people were dancing. Montero with Rita Gómez, who was getting into the music and showing off serious dancing skills. Juan with his wife. Cari dancing at bolero speed with Franco. All of us maneuvering around a compact area, until Freddie and Luis Angel moved the sofa and glass coffee table. While spinning once, I glanced at Pedro Roque looking at me grimly, his other two companions equally glum, as Marisol's left hand glided down my back and her hips rubbed against mine.

The dancing didn't last that much longer. Things dwindled down to boleros and soft conversation. In parties like this, people fulfill their sense of obligation and then scoot off to somewhere or something more to their liking. Freddie and his friend took off to a new gay club. Juan and Anabel had children, so they left early. Rita had gone before we realized she was gone. Luis Angel looked like the type who would rather get home to watch a good movie rental. Only Montero, Marisol, Pedro, Carmela and I remained. I found it strange that Roque would stay that long. He didn't seem like a very sociable guy at all, and it didn't look like he had enjoyed himself. Some people just need to see everything until the end; they get a weird power thrill as they witness everyone leave, one by one. I wanted to leave, but Montero was a hardcore partier and my ride.

Midnight found us sitting on the balcony, sipping coffee and looking out to condos and business buildings. The air felt cool, its damp muskiness hinted rain. At a distance, the white and red lights of hundreds of cars undulated through ribbon-like Baldorioty de Castro. I sat, sipping espresso. My mind had been drifting when Montero said something about another referendum over the status issue. Yet again, Puerto Ricans marching to the polls to vote for one of three choices: statehood, independence and the status quo, that is "commonwealth."

"Why can't you guys make up your mind?" I piped in, innocently, reaching the grounds in my coffee.

"You guys?" asked Roque, looking at the others, amused.

"Puerto Ricans."

"You don't consider yourself Puerto Rican?"

"My parents were Puerto Rican, not me."

"How patriotic," Roque said to the others, a smirk on his face as he drank the remains of his coffee.

"Patriotic like the people here?" I responded. "Who kiss every American ass they see?"

Roque's unibrow knitted closer together than usual, his eyes opened wide, his normally pasty face now flushed. He settled the cup and saucer on the plastic patio table and stood up. He tried straightening his rumpled pants, without much success.

"You know, Falto, if you don't like it here, you can always leave." He gasped the last word, almost out of breath, and with that, clutched his car keys and stomped out. Carmela followed.

"Welcome to the department," she said earnestly, waving good-bye as she did.

I blinked at Montero and Marisol.

"Well, the festivities have come to an abrupt and unfortunate turn of events," Montero said in mock-Brit reportage mode.

Marisol sat next to me and patted my arm.

"Don't let Pedro upset you. He's just a bit sensitive about some things."

"Sensitive? He's practically schizoid."

"Let us go then, you and I. . . . " Montero extended an arm to help me out of the chair. At that moment it seemed like I had sunk and needed a hand.

On the way out, Marisol stroked my back. My back tingled and I got goose bumps. She handed me some leftovers, and I thanked her.

We drove back, silent for most of the trip. Montero had the radio on a salsa station with an obnoxious, loud deejay. I asked to change it and turned to soft rock after Micco nodded. He was sedated now, staying in one lane pretty much for the entire trip back to Baná. I was afraid at any moment he would fall asleep. We didn't discuss Roque. Micco only asked me, as we were getting in the car, if I wanted to stay at Marisol's. I laughed and said no.

The thought had crossed my mind. It simply didn't make much sense, though. We were co-workers in a small department, and Marisol was in her mid-thirties—still a young woman—but the idea of having an affair with someone that age was intimidating, even as it turned me on.

Once you drive past the last toll, the autopista turns pitch black and eerie. There is no lighting along the highway, houses too distant to shed light, no public way stations with available gas pumps and bathroom facilities. Sometimes, you spot an individual emerging out of the bushes, walking back toward a sidelined car. The temperature dips as the road climbs up to steeper terrain. I felt my ears pop. As the cool and sweet air whipped against our exposed faces, Micco suddenly veered the convertible toward the next exit. "Need to use the facilities," he said.

In five minutes, we were entering a bar facing the mountain range. "I can never make it home," he said, quickly getting out of the car. Information that told me he frequented this place.

It was a dive like so many others open throughout the island on a Saturday night—una barra de muerte, a death bar, so named because often a macho would get stabbed or shot dead in such a locale, and the story would surface on the front page of *El Vocero*, the island's popular, tacky tabloid. A place that dangerously mixed booze and testosterone.

I expected a more rustic look, but it had a modern decor with a long, elegant wooden bar and comfortable leather swivel chairs. A patio area overlooked the mountains and Baná's city lights.

The emptiness signaled how late it was, approaching two in the morning. Most likely, the pairs who had crowded the dance floor had gone off to the nearby "garage" motels. If there had been a band, they had packed their stuff long ago and were now playing in some metropolitan after hours. A jumbo, CD-playing jukebox played requests while it emitted disco lights that floated across the room. Someone had played a series of boleros that, as the locals say, make you want to slit your wrists. Montero returned and waved for the bartender.

"Haven't you had enough?" I asked.

"Shut up and have a nightcap," he said. I asked for a beer. What the hell, I couldn't sleep anyway.

We sipped quietly, the voices from the jukebox singing about deceit and betrayal.

"Is he always like that, Micco?"

"The Rock?"

I nodded.

He shrugged one shoulder. "Well, he's gone through a lot with his ex."

An investment banker, she had been the love of his life, Montero said. And he recalled how Pedro would look into her eyes, as he'd call her his sweet darling with so much genuine devotion, back when they danced at gatherings like the one today.

"He loved that woman, and she dumped him for a younger, handsome, upscale guy," Montero said. The sweetheart type of love wears thin when one cannot negotiate middle age and realizes wealth buys you toys and a Stepford husband.

"Divorce is like an amputation—you survive, but there's less of you."

I looked at him, bending over a cocktail glass holding melted ice, knowing he hadn't come up with that himself. He glanced my way, still wearing the mirrored sunglasses.

"Atwood," he said, reading my mind.

The bartender alerted us that he was closing, so we dragged ourselves off the chairs and strolled back into the breezy night. In the gravel parking lot, a soft drizzle fell as we reached the convertible. Before getting in, Montero looked at me and said, "Be careful with Roque. He can make life miserable for you."

All the way home, I kept thinking about Roque's angry face and Micco's warning, and felt more lonesome than ever.

Seven

On the first day of classes, I woke up early. Still hadn't been sleeping well, and with the thought of facing students for the first time, it seemed pointless to stay in bed. I kept thinking about entering the classroom and bumping into the desk or becoming apoplectic—something embarrassing and stupid happening. Short bursts of nervousness and insecurity overwhelmed me, my body flushed and tightened with anxiety. I jumped out of bed and did some pushups, kicked the hacky sack for a bit and took a shower—one of several I learned to take during a typical day in this climate.

Over coffee and staring at the landscape, I wanted to review important items to discuss with students, but I couldn't. My mind wandered, my heart pounded at the thought of entering the classroom. So I decided to take a walk before my first class at 10 am. I threw on a blue, short-sleeved shirt and khaki pants, with the customary Top-Siders.

Outside, it was muggy and you couldn't spot a patch of blue sky. The campus bustled with cars streaming in, professors and students marching to their destinations, carrying briefcases and knapsacks. College police wore their special "colors," which included vibrant red berets sporting a small insignia of Cano the Coquí. They ushered cars to respective lots and assisted pedestrians with questions, their white-gloved hands waving, whistles blowing sharply.

As I walked closer to the main gate, I heard shouting and laughter that grew louder as I approached the entrance and the avenue—La Tirilla—that ran parallel to it. Older students—

51

"upperclassmen"—dozens of them, lined up on the sides of the gate, throwing flour, eggs, syrup, sometimes spraying dishwashing soap at the "prepas," or first-year students. Every time one got hit with an egg or a smattering of flour, an outburst of gleeful, taunting "ooohs" would rise from the gathered crowd. The more brazen ones would walk right up and smash the egg on the prepa's head.

Shocked, I tried to stay clear of straying particles. The hazed students walked stoically to class, cake ingredients settled on their heads and faces, a few crying. I tip-toed across slippery layers of egg yolks, whites and shells, and blue and green soap streaking the sidewalk as I headed toward my destination: the post office.

The overcast sky threatened rain, and I began thinking a walk wasn't such a good idea. But I had to mail paperwork to my parents' lawyer in the states. The college bordered the center of town, walking distance from the plaza, which typical of Spanish town planning had a Catholic church on one side and La Alcaldía, City Hall, on the other. Narrow streets crisscrossed without any logic, and people tried to walk on slim sidewalks, pedestrians bumping into the decreasing number of shoppers coming out of the stores in town. Most townspeople today preferred to shop at the malls.

There was a long line in the post office; it extended past the rented mailboxes and almost out of the building. One clerk attended to everyone. It didn't help that customers felt a need to talk to the man behind the counter about family and current events. I looked to see if any machines were available as an alternative, but no. All I wanted were a few stamps, and I had to wait for around thirty minutes, shuffling along the cordoned velvet ropes as if waiting to enter an exclusive nightclub.

An old woman started screaming about her son sending a package—did anyone have it? Anyone seen her son? Everyone in line looked away, making her invisible. I had lived in New York City long enough to know you don't make eye contact with weirdoes. But I felt sorry for her, saddened everyone else was icing her. In a metro area, with millions of people, neglecting homeless and crazy people was considered a survival tactic, but here, in a small town, it seemed cruel. I pitied her and she saw a chance, someone who obviously gave a shit, and I had a conversation on my hands.

She went on and on, I nodded, uttering encouraging filler words in my limited Spanish. She was off her gourd. The clerk kept saying, Doña Lili, leave the customers alone, go home. She turned to him and started insulting him for losing her son's package, then left in a huff, talking to herself.

I mailed my letter and glanced at my watch, alarmed my class was about to start in half an hour. I walked and breathed in the smell of wet dirt, felt the first, light raindrop. I sped up, walking like an Olympic marathon walker. The clouds cracked open and as I entered the college's main gates, I got drenched. Garbage streamed rapidly down the curb, dragging along eggshells and pasty flour balls in soapy water. Suddenly, a bright blue VW Bug stopped, and the driver's window rolled down.

"Need a ride?" A pair of green eyes looked over the slightly opened window.

I was stunned at the pretty, tanned face with the kick-ass smile and piercing eyes; a beauty mark at the base of her neck bordered her cleavage like a landmark. But I also felt stupid, standing there getting wet by the second, undecided. I said no, waving her along, more dismissively than I wanted. She yanked the stick shift into gear and smirked as to say, "comemierda," and sped off.

Common sense dictates you take an offer like that rather than getting soaking wet and offending someone at the same time. But she was a student, and I was new at this teaching thing. I didn't think it proper to fraternize with students in any way. Innocent me.

"You look like an animal that came out of the rain." Micco dropped David Mitchell's *Cloud Atlas* to review me up and down.

I went to the men's room and grabbed paper towels to dab myself, hoping to get dry before entering class. I took my shirt off and patted dry my underarms, chest, arms.

A knock at the door. I opened it to find Marisol holding a hair dryer. She stared at my naked torso.

"I'm sorry," I said, covering myself with the shirt.

"I thought you might need this," she said, smiling. I took the dryer and thanked her.

I dried what I could and ran out of the bathroom, wet areas dotting my clothes. I passed Roque, who had stepped out of his office to get a cup of coffee.

In my office, I went in circles trying to find materials for my Basic English class. When I had gathered everything I needed, I jogged to the classroom at the end of the second floor hallway in the Anonymous Building. Entering the classroom late, my heart pounded, my stomach tightened. I threw down the syllabi and other stuff on the desk, louder than intended.

We stared at each other, my students and I. They were prepas, some with flour streaked hair, runny egg yolk on their faces, green or blue dishwasher detergent staining the new clothes they'd bought for today, their first day of college classes. Their faces, at first a blur from momentary anxiety, became distinct, each one, as I dared to focus. The history of Puerto Rico in those faces. Light and dark complexions and everything in between: cocoa, tamarind, copper, butterscotch. Broad lips and noses; pointy, European beaks. Flaxen hair, lustrous Taíno hair, curvy and kinky waves.

"Prepa, too," I said, pointing to myself. Smiles, a smattering of laughter, but most of them had that lost I-don't-want-to-be-here stare. A few were at the point of tears.

Thirty-five students squeezed into a tight room with no air conditioning. The weather gets cooler, everyone kept telling me, but now it was August, balmy even after the downpour. As I called names, I tried to strike up a conversation with students. I told jokes to break the ice. Most of them didn't have a clue what I was saying. The typical response was "¿Qué?" What? Or to a neighbor: "¿Qué dijo?" What did he say? And then they giggled.

I tore a bunch of index cards from its plastic packaging, spread them out like I was doing a magic trick, one hand pointing to them. I scribbled a big rectangular box on the board to represent an index card and wrote what I wanted them to write on it. Micco had given me the idea with the cards, a way to get to learn student names. In his cards, he had written things like "la flaca"—the skinny one—or "tuerto" cross-eyed, "tetona," big breasted, etc., to distinguish students. I never went that far, but it did the job. The cards also helped keeping attendance, a mandatory chore requiring filling out one of many sporadic reports.

With completed cards in hand, I went around the room, calling names, asking questions in an English spoken for mentally challenged people or the deaf. Nitza, wh—a—t i—s Co-me-rí-o l—i—ke? I was surprised to get a couple of responses resembling English. I felt accomplished, even when they struggled, like I was getting something done. And I kept looking at their young, pimply, expectant faces, smiling unguarded, like they didn't have anything to worry about, not knowing the shit's coming down hard, not knowing they're clueless, not knowing anything. I had been like that only a few years ago. A student pointed to his watch, and I looked at mine—time over.

"Go," I said, waving a hand toward the door, and they ran to their next class, or to lunch, or to wherever English was not spoken here.

When my parents dropped me off at college, they had been crying. I could tell from their red eyes, although both claimed allergies. My mother had planned what seemed like months for that day. Made sure I got a mini-refrigerator and any other allowable electronic convenience, the top-of-the-line laptop, many socks and underwear, in the weirdest colors so as not to get them mixed up with another person's laundry. My dad gave me a beat up Oxford Dictionary that he had used in college. They both were proud but sad. I was their only child, and they must have sensed a twinge of old age approaching, of mortality. Without any sibling left behind, theirs was an empty nest come too quickly.

We went to lunch at a Denny's after moving me into my dorm. And they shared college stories. Mami had come from the South Bronx to Wellesley, a scholarship girl. She laughed when she told how she had arrived at the dorm with only two suitcases, mostly clothes. She had worked all summer and saved to buy dresses, slacks and outfits for every day, at a time when young people wore the same pair of torn jeans for a year. But she didn't have sheets for the bed, nor pillowcases, not even an alarm clock to get up early in the morning. The first week she slept with clothes as a pillow and her coat as a blanket. She had to call her parents and tell them to send a care package. Instead, and Mami always got teary-eyed when she told this part, they made another trip to Massachusetts, not an easy task because they didn't have a car and had to get someone to drive them. They brought her the needed items and more—Puerto Rican snacks, food and coffee, curtains for the windows.

My father smiled when Mami told that story, but never in a mocking way. He had it much easier. He came from a well-to-do family in the island. Business people, owners of the home decoration chain known as Decorama. "They sell fancy, over-priced junk," he used to tell me. But all those floral arrangements, picture frames, beads, candles and knickknacks paid his way through college. The Faltos sent him to study business and help run the family bric-a-brac trade. Papi never liked business, didn't have the heart or stomach for it, so he chose history instead and infuriated the family. He had to endure endless discussions about the real value of a college education, that it was wasted in pursuing studies not producing monetary gain. They didn't change his mind and had to be satisfied with the time he put in at the San Juan store during summers and Christmas breaks.

"He can write the history of the company someday," my grandfather would joke. Eventually, they would have forgiven and forgotten that entire episode, but then Papi met Mami at Columbia. As intelligent and accomplished as she was, the Falto clan saw my mother as a Nuyorican; in their eyes that meant a lower class, ghetto person. Shifty, not to be trusted, lazy and on welfare, always high on drugs. That's why every time my mother told that story, my father's eyes would sink, his entire face taking on the weight of years battling family disdain and disappointment.

I returned to my office and plopped down at my desk. Micco had his 11 o'clock, a British lit survey course with the few majors we had. Looking at his desk made me more depressed. He had postcards, a calendar of the impressionists, *New Yorker* cartoons, photos of the family "farm" in San Sebastián. A small crucifix taped to the back panel of the desk/bookshelf. An article on nuclear warfare—a constant fear with him along with threats of viral epidemics. He had a poster up with various types of small air-craft, since he wanted to learn how to fly one day.

My side was sparse, clean. A few composition books on the overhanging shelf with the sliding door. Not even a calendar, blotter or a cup to hold pencils.

I went into Stiegler's office, one door over, to ask if he wanted to go to the cafeteria for coffee. He had a radioactive sign on his door.

"What's that all about?"

He looked at me with quizzical hazel eyes, narrowing his auburn eyebrows. He pointed to the microwave inside the office, which everyone used. The communal microwave.

"I'm being nuked daily," he said in his squeaky voice. He opened his mouth, barely exposing tiny gray teeth behind the unruly mustache.

"Why not move it?"

"To where? I'm the new kid on the block, so they dump it in my office. Hey, maybe it should be in yours."

"Just move it out there," I said, pointing to the open unused area in front of our offices. He mused it over for a few seconds, scratching his chin.

"Roque may not like it," he whispered.

"Oh, come on," I said. I unplugged the machine and grabbed it. "Bring the table."

Together we installed the microwave in its new place, against a wall. It looked isolated surrounded by so much space, but at least it was away from any one person. Stiegler's eyes softened, a smile flew out from under the bush draping over his lips.

"You can't be too careful, you know," he said. I stared at him, confused. "There's some shit going on in this place," he whispered again.

"What the hell you talking about?"

"This is a cancer cluster zone—don't you know?"

"No, I don't."

"Baerga, upstairs in Humanities. Colon cancer. Giusti, Business; Huerta, Math, both breast cancer. Fernández, Spanish, lung; Robles, Accounts Payable, breast; Mercado, custodial, kidney, I believe. These are only in the last year."

"Probably coincidence."

"Coincidence, my ass! Man, this was a military base. They buried ordnance here, polluted the water supply, the surrounding environment—who knows how it's contaminating all of us."

"Oh, come on, Stiegler. There are students here."

His eyes widened like I was mad, or hopelessly näive, or both, then walked away, shaking his head. Perhaps I was being ingenuous, but Stiegler seemed to have a conspiracy theory for everything.

I had that coffee alone, and while sipping it in the noisy cafeteria, thought about the squatters. With classes starting, I hadn't given them much thought. But I had to do something, although what, I didn't know. Micco mentioned going to the police first, and there was a precinct just outside of the college, across La Tirilla, near the courthouse. I remembered needing a Certificate of Good Conduct to complete my file for Human Resources. This was a police check to assure the college I wasn't a chainsaw murderer or pedophile. Quickly, I looked at my watch and realized my next class was in two hours, so I decided to kill two birds with one stone.

Once I entered the precinct, I came across a mustached sergeant sitting on an imposing high wooden bench. His mustache seemed painted on. Sarge didn't look up from his newspaper. Around him his comrades laughed, loudly discussing the latest sports headline or the details of an action movie. A young handcuffed man sat by a wooden bench to the side of the front door, a stout, handle-bar mustached cop standing over him, struggling with a clipboard and paperwork. The young man's head nodded, and he mumbled. He was filthy, greasy, the stench emanating from his body unbearable.

I was standing at the door, the high bench and Sarge no more than five feet in front of me. I imagined offices to the sides somewhere and presumed cells, where the hand-cuffed man would soon go. But there wasn't much space or anything else for that matter in the front part of this precinct.

The cop pulled up the young man by the handcuffs and dragged him away to one of the hidden cells. I said "excuse me," to draw Sarge's attention. He lifted tired eyes to me and said with a voice weighed down by effort, "Yes?" as he reached for the clipboard left behind by the cop taking the homeless person away.

"I need a Certificate of Good Conduct," I explained.

"Form?" he asked, holding out his hand.

"Excuse me?"

"Where's the form?" This a bit agitated.

"Oh, I need a form?" A stupid question, I would soon learn, and Sarge's smirk confirmed it, or was it a response to my mangled Spanish? You need a form for everything in Puerto Rico, and "sellos." Get a form, buy the official "stamp" that meant you've paid for something and then go wait in line for eternity.

"Ask your Human Resources department."

I nodded, and he resumed flipping pages in his newspaper.

He saw that I hadn't moved. "Yes?" again, this time with a sigh.

I explained the squatters' situation.

He shrugged. "What do you want us to do?"

"Can't you get them out?"

His little eyes got even smaller.

"You need a court order to evict them."

I was wondering why Micco told me to come here, when Sarge swiveled around and reached over to the bins behind him holding all the forms, obviously all but the one for Good Conduct. Above the bins, and his head, hung a photo of the present governor. Sarge handed me the form.

"File a complaint. This will help begin legal proceedings." Speaking two consecutive sentences, while reaching for the form, tired him out. He began to perspire and breathe harder.

I uttered my thanks and waved goodbye.

He didn't notice. He returned to his newspaper and I stared at the legal size form—two pages long, back-to-back. I had to write the squatters' names? I didn't know these people—how would I get their names? Complainant's—that was me—parents and grandparents' names? The usual stuff: address, phone, social security number. Eyewitnesses? References from neighbors attesting to the defendant's conduct. Boxed spaces for the appropriate sellos to be purchased at your local "colecturía." This would take more time than what I had. I folded the onion-skin papers and exited the precinct. Walking toward me a lanky, droopy-mustached cop escorted a dark, hand-cuffed man.

I crossed the parking lot into the dirty, narrow street that twisted uphill into the network of streets leading to my hostage house, and which in the other direction connected to La Tirilla and the college. The municipal bus, ancient and noisy, spewed exhaust everywhere as it chugged into a stop. What if I can't get these squatters out of the house? I thought, waiting to cross the busy avenue. What if it takes me years and thousands of dollars?

For a moment, I considered calling Julia for help, but I just couldn't do it. During our weekly conversations, she would ask, "Is something wrong, René?" Tell me that I sounded stressed and worried. Was that mother's intuition? Or just my anxiety displaying itself? In between the "cultural field trips," we talked often and the topics were more frequently drifting away from the formal to the personal. Not always easy. How does one open up and let someone enter your private world who should have been a part of it from day one? Bizarre—to feel so distant from *your mother*—the person who carried and sustained your life for nine months, who labored to bring you into the world. The whole scene sometimes wore me out. It felt like therapy, and I didn't feel like talking to her about anything, never mind legal issues with squatters.

Roque called me before I could slip into my office and slump before my desk in despair. I thought he was going to make some comment about the morning's episode with the bathroom, but he ushered me into his office with a face more solemn than usual. He seemed exasperated; in fact, he sighed. But I sensed a smile behind it, like he was happy to have something on me, so early into the semester.

"Falto, these syllabi won't do."

"Why not?"

"You strayed way off the master syllabi. These are for courses I can't even recognize."

"Don't I have some say how I teach my courses?"

"Well, of course. But I'm trying to guide you toward a more effective pedagogy. I've been here a long time. I know our students."

"Are you saying they're too dumb to follow the content of these syllabi?"

"Don't put words in my mouth." He narrowed his eyes, his wing-like heavy eyebrows looking menacingly ready to pounce. "I can tell you from experience this will not work."

"With all due respect, Dr. Roque, please let me try. Let me do my job."

He sat back and pushed the syllabi away. Behind him, I noticed a small crucifix hanging lonely on the wall. "Suit yourself."

I slunk back to my office. Micco was warming something in the microwave. "Dead Man Walking," he yelled. Beside him, Stiegler waited his turn, frozen entrée in hand. He walked toward me, nervous.

"Was he pissed about the microwave?" he whispered.

"No, Stiegler. Go nuke away."

Eight

I first heard "God Bless the Child" blasting from Jeanie Caine's dorm room when I was a college freshman. Billie's raspy, mournful lyrics captivated me, held me hostage, as I was about to knock. As I entered the cluttered room, I felt like I had drifted into another era: a scene from an old black and white movie. Jeanie's taste ran to hip-hop and strong female vocalists like Mariah and Whitney. Who was this yearning woman singing the blues, sounding so affirmative but yet vulnerable? And why was she coming out of Jeanie's speakers like a sultry siren?

I found Jeanie on her bed, crying in a fetal position. Before I could ask her what was wrong, she waved me over to the bed and made me hold her tight. I held her for what seemed hours while she continued sobbing, my hand which she held to her face getting wet.

Jeanie's parents were successful doctors who had made the cover of *Ebony* magazine. They wanted her to take advantage of her very expensive education and become a doctor or lawyer—something "worthwhile." She wanted to live in Amsterdam and write poetry. She was always having fights with them on the phone. "They hound me something fierce," she said, "just to tell me the same old shit." So sometimes she would have these funks and play depressing music.

Today, I'm thinking about Billie singing that day, the chorus stuck in my mind. Back in college I couldn't understand Jeanie Caine. I thought she was selfish and spoiled. My parents and I never had volatile fights like she did with hers. None that would make me crouch in bed and whimper while listening to the blues. But then I didn't have parents like hers, until now.

Julia called to have lunch, another "together moment." I had grown accustomed to her presence, even enjoying my time with her, although at times I had to stop and remind myself, "Oh, this is my mother." The stories she told about cases, influential people she knew, celebrities she had represented, the ins and outs of the legal profession, the situations she confronted being a successful female attorney—it was dizzying and amazing. Julia was powerful and influential; the authority she wielded and the respect she earned scared people, especially men. She was also quite financially settled. The wealth didn't strike you until you saw it manifested in something concrete.

Julia invited me to her apartment in Miramar, the one-bedroom suite close to the law offices on the Milla de Oro in Hato Rey and the house in Guaynabo in a gated community that reeked of affluence and prestige. Both places were impeccably decorated by professional designers, with fine fabrics and colors enhanced with perfect lighting, and collected art appreciating in value every second you glanced at it. You can tell someone's rich when they don't think about the material things they own. An opulent item such as a Lladró figurine or a Steuben glass decanter blends into their everyday world.

You have a parent like this and you begin to appreciate Jeanie Caine. "And God Bless the Child" becomes your anthem too.

Around that time, I'd wanted to confess to Julia about my legal problems with the squatters and the conflicts at the college with Roque. Here I had a mother with this wealth of legal knowledge and experience who with one call could make Roque and the Riveras shit in their drawers, and I couldn't get around to asking her for help. I didn't want her thinking I was taking advantage of her guilt—not that she would have said that's what it was. But she tried too hard to please me, to compensate with little gifts, lavish meals and offers that I declined. She wanted to set me up at a studio apartment in the Condado, which I shot down. She wanted to buy me a car, nothing fancy, she said. I turned down the BMW

128i convertible, and she couldn't help smiling and shaking her head when I picked her up in a rental.

"I'm doing what any mother would do," she told me.

I thought, what, spoil your kid? You can't buy your son's love, especially coming from nowhere after so many years.

For my part, maybe not asking for help was too extreme. I mean, isn't that what parents should do? Give advice to their children? I had no one to turn to, but I felt strange asking Julia for anything, even legal advice. Mami and Papi were my parents in my heart and mind. To turn to her for anything was painful. It felt like betrayal. Still, she was my biological mother. And clearly she was trying hard to regain that role for herself. The truth was I needed advice badly. If anything, I had to tell her that I might be out of a job by the end of the academic year. I vowed that during lunch I would tell her everything.

But first I had to pick Julia up at work. The law offices of Garrutia, Matos and Bustamante were in a shiny skyscraper along the Milla de Oro, in Hato Rey, the financial and business hub of San Juan. She told me to park in her private space, since she had carpooled to work with a colleague. I drove the rented compact into the space tagged with her name. I got a kick out of the double takes that generated. This being the first time visiting Julia's office, I had no idea what to expect, but once the elevator opened onto the fifteenth floor—the Executive Floor—of the firm's headquarters, it hit me that my biological mother was a founding partner of at least a medium-size law firm. I passed the bevy of clerks, paralegals and typists in cubicles, all smiling and saying hello, and I approached Julia's secretary, a twenty-something with a vivacious smile. Before I introduced myself, she stood up, walked me over to the door and waved me into Julia's office.

"She's waiting for you," she said, with a wide grin.

Julia was at an enormous crystal desk, focused on some paperwork, her hair tucked behind her ears. She looked over her glasses toward me. I threw myself on the sofa, picked up a copy of *The Nation* from the coffee table. Behind her, through the large window, another row of buildings gleamed in the tropical sun. It was a big corner office, fitting Julia's stature, with all the expected amenities, including a small bar, but what stood oddly apart was a painting of a rustic Puerto Rican scene.

"Everyone's so happy here," I said. "Did you give out bonuses?"

"No," she said, returning to the paper in front of her. "I showed them your photo. They've all wanted to meet you." She looked up and laughed when she saw my smirk.

"Come here and give your mother a kiss at least." I went over and pecked her on the cheek.

"Let me sign these and we can go . . . I'm starved. You hungry?"

I nodded and waited as Julia went through her going-out ritual. She turned around a few times, gathered glasses, cigarette case, cell and threw them all in her purse. She padded her pockets, made sure her glasses were on her nose. On the way out, I asked her about the curious painting she had there depicting a wake for an infant.

"It's a reproduction of Oller's painting. It keeps me grounded."

On the way to the elevator, more smiles from the staff, and this time I couldn't help from blushing, knowing that I was the show.

"Some attractive women working here, wouldn't you agree?" Julia said with a sly smile.

"Yes, and single, I bet."

This sudden outburst of interest in me by Julia's underlings should have been a signal she was up to something. We arrived at La Trattoria, one of Julia's favorite eateries, and minutes into our conversation—mainly about the upcoming Thanksgiving family gathering in Lares—an attractive young woman joined us at the table. Yasmín Roselló, junior associate at the firm. She came over allegedly to say hello. "Come join us," Julia chirped, and she introduced us without batting an eyelash. Ms. Roselló extended a manicured hand as I sat there speechless. Of course, she was exceedingly good looking; uncanny, I thought, how in such a short time Julia would figure out my type. Ms. Roselló shook my hand and sat her long-legged, slender, well-shaped figure right across from me.

I hated that I liked Ms. Roselló, that I liked the way her brown eyes smiled, how smart she looked in a suit and how her graceful hands moved to make a point. I liked her, despite her being another career woman conflicted over marriage and motherhood. Our conversation, to which Julia occasionally, I would even dare say strategically contributed, flowed into sticky terrain. When I asked Ms. Roselló what law she practiced to make money for my mother, she answered, "mostly divorce." And this led to marriage, motherhood and grandchildren. The irony didn't seem to hit them.

"It's a cliché, I know," said Ms. Roselló, "but I feel the pressure." She smiled sheepishly.

"I think it's to your credit," Julia said. "To talk about it openly without sounding desperate."

"I'm sure you will be able to handle the pressures of motherhood and career," I said. "Look at my mother." I tapped Julia's hand. And she did that gesture of hers, when she probably wants to slap you and controls herself by twisting her neck and looking up with a smile.

"She could be your model," I added.

"Licenciada Matos is a great mentor in so many ways," Ms. Roselló said. I noted: loss of points for ass-kissing.

"I would love to have grandchildren," Julia said, laughing at me and Ms. Roselló.

I felt my face blush, and thankfully the food came at that moment and that subject dropped to the table like an unwanted side dish. *Yeah,* I thought, *perhaps you can be a better abuela than mother.* But it stayed in my head, like other thoughts better censored during the remainder of that meal.

I walked a tightrope between anger at her conniving maneuvers and genuine pleasure at having an unexpectedly delightful lunch date with an intelligent, appealing woman. What restrained me was the memory of that unfortunate restaurant outing in Lares, which I preferred not to repeat. So, I went with the flow and enjoyed the company of Ms. Roselló, who was, after all, an innocent bystander.

Ms. Roselló slid over a business card with her home number on it while Julia was in the ladies' room. I took it with a smile and a "thank you." I would never call her. She could be my soulmate, for all I knew, but I wasn't ready to accept yet another one of Julia's guilt-ridden offerings, this one more insidious than the others.

I didn't respond to Julia's chit-chat in the car. When I parked back at her building, I looked straight at her.

"What the hell was that, Julia?"

She rolled her eyes and clucked her tongue. "Is it so bad that I introduced you to a beautiful, ambitious young woman?"

"Did I ask you to pimp for me?" A stern look.

"Where do you get this mouth of yours?"

"That's what it feels like."

"Fine. I won't do it again. Live your miserable lonely existence."

"Hey, I'm doing okay, thank you."

"You don't look happy, René."

"Maybe that's because I'm not, okay?"

There was a moment of silence and then she went for the door.

"You know, I'm trying to do my best," she said, looking out the window, still holding to the door handle. "But I'm really getting tired of your hurt-child drama."

"Oh, really?"

"Yes," she said turning around, facing me directly. "Grow up, René. People make mistakes, everyone has to move on."

With that, she seized her purse and bolted out of the car.

Nine

It's a given that a single guy in a relationship must at some time introduce the girlfriend to the parents. At the point when we were quasi-living together (an arrangement involving personal tooth-brushes and a few articles of clothing burrowed away in one draw-er in each other's apartments), Erin and I decided to "share our happiness" (her words) with family. We didn't think much of it. Erin's folks were liberal New Englanders who only gave me a hard time for being a Yankee fan. Dinner at her folks was pleasant, full of good conversation and excellent wine. We both thought we had jumped over the biggest hurdle, because I had always bragged about how open-minded my parents were. And despite their polit-ical liberalism, Erin worried that her parents might harbor issues with her dating a Puerto Rican. She and I both knew progressive politics don't always immune people from fear of difference. So, we were both very happy when Erin's dad welcomed me to the family. Actually, it was scary for me because I realized that the meet-the-parents visit was this significant moment in a relation-ship full of expectations. But it was still a promising event. And we both kind of assumed that if the McMahons were on board, the Faltos would be a piece of bizcocho.

I told my parents that I would be bringing Erin to Thanksgiv-ing dinner, or La Cena, as it traditionally known in my family. I spoke to Mami, and the silence on the phone was deafening.

"Who's that?" Mami asked, finally.

"Erin, you know, the girl I'm seeing."

More silence, then, "Ay, Rennie, you know La Cena is a family thing."

"Mami, I'm serious about Erin. I think you and Papi should meet her."

"You planning to marry this girl?"

"I don't know—maybe. We haven't broached that topic yet."

"Well, when you decide, then you can bring her to La Cena."

"Jeez. What's with the formality? It's Thanksgiving dinner, for God's sakes."

"I don't feel comfortable with strangers in my house, Rennie."

"She's not a stranger to me."

"But she is to me."

"Well, I'm bringing her or I won't go. Mami, I've been over to Erin's parents' house, and they welcomed me with open arms. I can't believe you're acting this way."

She sighed into the phone. "This girl isn't Puerto Rican, is she?"

"What's that got to do with it?"

"Is she Latina, at least?"

"No, Mami. She's American, like the rest of us."

"Don't get politically stupid on me, okay. You know what I mean."

"Look, I'm just calling to tell you I'm bringing her along. You got a problem with that or not?"

After a few seconds of hesitation, she conceded. I hung up the phone in shock. Where was my liberal, open-minded mother, who talked freely with me about drugs, alternative sexual lifestyles, sex and STDs, and other topics most parents would prefer to avoid?

She must have disappeared into the ethnic meal she always prepared for La Cena. A Puerto Rican Thanksgiving is a hybrid of American and Boricua culinary tastes: a turkey covered with pepper and spices to approximate its otherwise bland taste as much as possible to lechón, or roast pig; it is accompanied by arroz con gandules, or pigeon peas in yellow rice; candied yams; pasteles, that is, Puerto Rican style-tamales in banana leaves; and potato salad, which must include heaps of mayo, eggs and, for that Spanish touch, red peppers and olives. The typical pies are served, of course, but it wouldn't surprise anyone to find some flan, tembleque or arroz con dulce as desserts.

Erin was amused by all of this, and she committed the biggest faux pas: she ate very little. Wouldn't touch the pasteles, nibbled at the rice, ate a sliver of turkey, and afterwards confessed to me, with a whiny voice, that she missed the traditional dinner. For some reason, that bothered me, and her finickiness did not go over well with either one of my parents.

They were both pleasant, but the conversation was thin, too guarded for a holiday meal. My usually garrulous parents, who loved to tease and laugh, and on these occasions were known to get up and dance to a salsa tune playing on the stereo, remained as reserved and laconic as any WASP family ever seen on television or film. Erin had this stupid, fake smile screwed on her face the entire evening, even as she picked through the food, setting the red peppers and olives from the potato salad to the side. I wanted to bang my head against the table at one point.

The only amusement for me, I hate to say, during the entire evening was watching Tío Bennie, the only other dinner guest, drink himself into a stupor, as he did every Thanksgiving. He wasn't really an uncle, but my parents had known him for decades and I grew up calling him *tío*. After his wife died and he sunk into depression and alcohol, my parents occasionally invited him to weekend dinners and holiday meals. He would drink like a mad man, chugging beer after beer, and at one point while sprawling on a recliner would start blabbering and then crying. Soon after, he would fall into a sonorous sleep, his jowls shaking from the jagged breathing.

"That didn't go like you wanted, did it?" Erin asked me on the drive back from Jersey. She had been quiet, staring out the window. Unusual for her; anytime I drove her car, she was super vigilant to the point that she sometimes made me so upset. I stopped and turned over the wheel to her.

"You think?" I answered.

We both laughed, but it stung me a bit. I felt bad for Erin, but I couldn't or wouldn't apologize for my parents. She wasn't exactly endearing herself to them. There had been some type of barrier in that dining room, where it came from I don't know. But I knew the silences and inability to converse freely went deeper than lack of topics. We were all liberal, well-educated, intelligent people, but something happened, and I did not know what.

I visited my parents a week later. They had not mentioned anything about Thanksgiving, even in our telephone conversations that followed. I filed the incident under lack of chemistry, but when I sat down for a cup of coffee, both of them sat down at the kitchen table, hands folded, their faces solemn like someone had just died. They wanted to talk, my father said.

"That young woman, Erin," my mother began. "She's a good person and whatever decision you make we will respect. It is your lives, after all."

"But," my father interrupted, "she doesn't exactly have the mancha de plátano."

This was the phrase for someone who looked Puerto Rican, or even Latino. So called because you can no easier rid yourself of your Puerto Rican look than erase a plantain stain.

"I told you she was white."

"White? M'ijo, she's like a walking bag of flour," this from my liberal mother. They both laughed at this.

"She's in dire need of some sun," my father added.

"This is racist, you know that, right?"

"Ay, please. We think she's all right. We're just having fun at your expense."

"But," my father again interrupted, "have you really thought the possible consequences of marrying someone not of your culture?"

I stared at them like I didn't know them.

"I can't believe both of you. Where does this come from and where's it going?"

"We're not opposed to you marrying her, Rennie. God forbid, we would never."

"But," my father interjected, "let's not be blinded to the differences and what they might mean."

"Like what?"

"Will she be willing to raise our grandchildren to know their Puerto Rican heritage?"

"Grandchildren?"

"Rennie," my father again piped up, "ours is an oppressed, colonized people losing its culture and history. We can't marry and blend and forget our roots. Where will we end up?"

My mother started crying, to my amazement. "Oh my God," she said. "What if they turn out to be asimilaos, ashamed of their Puerto Rican grandparents?"

"Then they'll be just like their father."

I snatched my jacket and keys and went for the door.

"You're not an asimilao!" My father blocked the door, wagging a finger at me. "We have both taught you about our history, our language, *your* roots. This is a Puerto Rican home, and we're proud of who we are, and we've taught you to be just as proud." The fierce look scared me—I had never seen it on my father.

I nodded and looked down. All I could say was "bendición."

"Dios te bendiga," they both responded, tired and despondent.

Ten

The older professors, the seasoned veterans with thirty years or more, tell me how little faculty members know about each other, even in a college where a tour of the campus takes less than fifteen minutes. How few friends they make in the course of an academic career. They become obsessed with work, with the petty, departmental dramas that lead to breaks from colleagues. The jaded college professor looks out of windows, isolated in the ivory tower of his or her own making. Too tired to extend a hand, too busy to notice or care about their struggling brethren, to chat with anyone other than a fellow committee member out of obligation and necessity.

I was a bit disappointed at their attitude, but I'd been there only a couple of months and that's how I felt sometimes. I knew few people other than those in my department, and even then, only a handful that I spoke to.

"Circulate, network," Julia would tell me. "You don't go out enough." A new worry for her: that I was becoming a recluse.

But the college was not conducive to socializing. Many professors taught and went home—all we needed to complete the factory feeling of the place was a punch clock. When news came about someone from another department who had cancer, it was like news from another front, or some foreign country.

"Migdalia Rosalbán," Micco said, "over in Business—breast."

Micco threw himself into his office chair. He was bothered in that half-agitated, frustrated way. Knowing Micco, he was not so much worried about poor Migdalia, but about being the next cancer victim.

"Don't drink the water," he said. I looked at him, surprised.
"I mean it," he added.

I recalled what Stiegler had told me, and I asked if that had any
bearing on what he was saying.

"Buried ammunitions—toxic shit—before the Army left," he said.

"Buried? Like right here on campus?"

"We might be sitting on top of it." Both eyebrows arched.

"Why would they do that?"

"What normal person understands the minds of fucking mili-
tarists?" he said with a smirk.

With that, he gathered his classroom materials and scooted out
the office, leaving me bewildered and a bit worried. He popped his
head back in.

"Are we still on for lunch?"

I stared at him and nodded, remembering that Micco had
agreed to drive me around to car dealerships. I had accepted that
in PR a car's a necessity, at times wishing I had taken up Julia's
offer to buy me a car. So I asked for Micco's help, and he agreed if
I bought him lunch.

Having lost my parents to fanatics with explosives, Micco's
information did not set well with me. Could any of that stuff
explode? Maybe it was an idle rumor, propagated by the island's
anti-militarists. You could not deny the unusual number of cancer
cases on campus, though. I remembered Stiegler's breakdown of
cases. Was Stiegler right? Were we all breathing or drinking some
carcinogen?

I peered out the window, down to the cemented walkways and
barriers in front of the Nameless Academic Building. And then farther south to the distant parrot green mini-mountains forming
part of the Cordillera Central, the Picos de Baná, flashing behind
the foamy clouds. Seeing this vegetation, in all its tropical wonder,
made it hard to believe that dangerous environmental risks lurked
so close by.

Owning a car would make me see the gradual degradation of
the landscape. Traveling the curving two-lane highways would
bring me closer to pollution, discarded refrigerators and stoves,
soiled Pampers and beer cans tossed by the roadside. I understood

that the greenness of the island, like so many other things in Puerto Rico, gave the people cover for destructive habits. Everyone on the island was bewitched, under a spell of ignorance and denial.

When I went with Micco to buy a car, these were not my thoughts, of course. I needed to get around, and the rickety buses spewing Co2 would not cut it for me. I once took the bus to Caguas—to transfer my driver's license—and the trip took forever and involved more chattering among passengers than I cared to eavesdrop on. I took the local bus rather than the express, which ran down the autopista, the three-lane superhighway. I got the panoramic route that gives you the shits every time the wobbly bus swerves around a mountain. That was enough to make me want a car.

After receiving my first paycheck, I decided to find a car. Micco volunteered to drive me around, promising to steer me away from shady dealers. We drove out to Caguas, the dealerships in Baná not worth it, according to him. Later I found out he took me to a cousin, who kept referring to each car I scoped as a definite "tumba-panty." In other words, a vehicle that would make the ladies drop their drawers. I ended up with a black, manual Civic—not high on the list of tumba-panties, but okay for my needs and budget.

Micco was unimpressed with my choice. He tried to convince me that women liked a man with a muscle car. This, from a short man with receding salt-and-pepper hair who happened to own a red sports car. In my new car, I followed Micco to the restaurant he had selected, an obviously upscale Italian restaurant in Caguas. It was an enjoyable meal, and I savored the food and the wine, even with the conversation about toxic poisons hidden under our feet.

With the rush to move from army base to college, no one had thought about any lingering explosives. The U.S. Army certainly did not inform anyone of any possible danger. And all the politicians wanted the afterglow of accomplishment and progress attached to a new college; they buried the facts about the ordnance. Stiegler had done some internet research and found some information on it. He handed Micco a file full of documents downloaded from government websites.

"The Army isn't hiding anything."

"What do you mean?"

"Fort McKenna is part of the FUDS program."

"Fort McKenna? FUDS?"

Micco sighed and wiped his mouth, impatient in having to bring me up to speed.

"Before the college, there was Fort McKenna, you know that, right?"

I nodded, although I hadn't known the name.

"Well, the Army still refers to it as Fort McKenna and it's on the FUDS list—Formerly Used Defense Sites. It's the Army's responsibility to clean up after themselves, and that program does it."

"Stiegler got this from the Army website?"

"U.S. Army Corps of Engineers—look it up," he said, pointing his fork at me.

"Holy shit. Why don't they tell people?"

"Puerto Ricans don't like knowing the truth—don't you know?"

"I'm beginning to see that."

"Well, it's not something you want to shout from the rooftops—who knows, maybe we never got the memo." He speared a clam and slurped it into his mouth, washed it down with wine.

"Stiegler told me the cleanup is supposed to have started a few years ago, but either they're doing it real secret like, or they're just bullshitting us, because I haven't seen any kind of movement in that direction." He paused for a minute, lost in thought. "Unless all that infrastructure construction they keep talking about isn't about replacing pipes."

"What are they cleaning?" I asked, drinking the last drop of wine in my glass.

"HTRW, hazardous, toxic and radioactive waste." Micco stopped cutting his veal and looked at me.

I stared at him.

"I'm not kidding—it's all there, check it out."

The bill arrived. More sticker shock looking at it than the prices of the cars I had checked out. I just gave it a tarjetazo—which in the local vernacular means paying it with plastic and adding to your debt.

The next morning I found Stiegler's folder on my desk. It was all true. And, worse, the "relative risk" level of the Fort McKenna site was deemed "high." How was it that no one knew about this stuff? Or if they did, no one cared enough to make a stink about it? But, then, what could one demand when the U.S. government was officially doing something about it? An article in the folder reported government agencies searching the waters off the coast of Oahu for hydrogen cyanide, cyanogen chloride and mustard bombs dumped there in 1944. A congressman said no one knew where exactly these munitions were and what their impact on health and the environment would be. Great, I thought. And that's Hawaii, a state.

Other articles and newspaper clips about contamination in Vieques—another mess. On one of our trips, Julia took me to "La Isla Nena," the popular nickname of the smaller island.

"The Navy would bomb targets on the island," she explained, "without any concern for the people or the fishermen, or the high incidence of cancer in Vieques."

I glanced at the placid turquoise water, trying to imagine it with destroyers blasting the beachhead.

"Then that stray bomb killed David Sanes, a civilian working for the Navy," she continued. "And ignited the national outcry that led to the closing of the base. Some of us had been working decades to close it down, or at least trying to get the Navy to stop their bombing exercises."

The Navy had resisted until the uproar escalated into persistent protests and media attention. They left but all the contaminants remained, along with the health risks and rising cases of cancer and other illnesses.

Marisol stepped into the office, holding student papers, a roll book and a textbook close to her chest. Today, she had put on less make-up, had her hair back to its natural color, up, and the effect was pleasing. Simple suited her, but she didn't know it.

"Listen, I have tickets to see Fiel a la Vega."

"Feel a whatsis?"

"Fiel a la Vega—a rock band. I was going with my friend, but she cancelled out on me. Wanna go?"

For some reason, I didn't believe this friend existed. I was not in the mood, but she gave me a pout and a few c'mons.

"Okay, why not? Hey, I got my new car. I'll pick you up."

"Let's do dinner before. I know a whole bunch of nice places."

"Sure, great."

She exited and I closed Stiegler's folder, which was marked with the radioactive symbol. On a Post-It, he had scribbled and underlined three times, "We are all fucked."

Working in the middle of a possible cancer cluster was worrisome, not what I signed up for, and I grew angry at the silence of the university's administration. I wanted to talk to the Rector, organize a group of faculty and students to get answers. These thoughts quickly dissolved. Squatters occupied my house, and I didn't have a clue how to get them out. The college, hospitable but alarmed at my lengthy stay in the "guest house," informed me that they could give me until the end of year, and then I had to find another place. Micco told me house rentals in Baná were hard to come by, apartments scarcer. I tried talking to the Riveras but to no avail. They liked the house, they said, and had no intention of moving out. They insisted they were being wronged.

It had taken me weeks to gather the necessary information requested in the grievance form. I called a lawyer and set up a meeting, and he agreed to meet me for lunch. I made sure it was in a fast food place. By now, I had become hip to the concept of cachetear, or "getting over." People seemed to glorify in getting something for nothing. No act of charity or favor seemed free; people always expected something. It would be rude to ask for this something—you had to know what you should offer if you were the recipient of the favor. If Micco drove me around to car dealers, then lunch was thrown in the mix, and from his perspective, it was almost a given that he would choose a pricey restaurant. Cacheteando. If this lawyer were to take his valuable time to see me—a client—I would pay for lunch. But he would eat hamburgers and french fries.

We met in a Fuddruckers, one of the fast food chains sprouting like weeds throughout the island. Licenciado Martirio Ledesma was waiting for me at the front entrance, as we had arranged. He was a squat man with a big gut, a barrigón, as they say around here; he had attached earlobes and thin, almost feminine, lips. Ledesma wore a plain, starched, white guayabera. No mustache—

and I immediately liked that. Micco had recommended him. He represented many of the faculty, having taught as an adjunct with the college before starting his practice. Micco mentioned that his English was impeccable, and that's what sold me. He extended a delicate hand, unusual for someone of his girth, I thought.

Seated in front of a turkey burger and onion rings snuggled in a plastic meshed basket, I skidded the manila envelope with the papers across the greasy table. Ledesma took a hearty bite from his Boricua Burger and dabbed his mouth with a paper napkin.

"What's that?" he asked.

"The official complaint."

He slid it back. "Hold on to it. We're not even close to that yet."

He smiled when he saw the puzzled look on my face.

"Sorry, my friend. But we must legally transfer the property to you first."

"And how long will that take?" He chewed and stared at me with a perplexed expression, a cross between impatience and surprise.

"Professor Falto," he dabbed his little fingertips on the napkin as he talked. "If we are going to make this work, you must be patient. These things take time; it's complicated."

"You don't understand. I'm living on campus and paying rent, and these . . . these lowlifes are living in my parents' house for free."

"They have rights, too," he said.

Again, the righteous, offended look of the insider, pitying me, the estranged one, who had lost his humanity as a Puerto Rican— how can you want to throw these poor people out on the street? What's wrong with you?

"Look, you can't go into a court in Puerto Rico with that attitude. The judge will not tolerate it."

"Well, maybe I should squat on the judge's property and see how he likes it."

Ledesma pursed his lips, took a swig of the colossal drink he'd ordered, and sighed. "Falto, just get me your parents' title, marriage certificate and your birth certificate. With those I can begin the inheritance process." He fingered a steak fry.

I had access to all my parents' papers now. Dad had left behind an organized file cabinet with every important document imaginable, including the infamous birth certificate which Julia had shown me. I thought about the lengths to which they went to keep this document from me, always providing any other alternative form of proof of citizenship which I had to present in person. They got me a passport, and faithfully renewed it, under the guise of its being indispensable for all the traveling we were going to do. And we did. By age fifteen I had several stamps on that passport, but I didn't know they had also obtained it to help them hide the truth of my biological mother.

"I can get those to you in no time—so this shouldn't take long, right?"

"We will have to announce the case in the national newspapers and wait a month." He waved the fry around, pointing to an imaginary map of Puerto Rico.

"Why?"

"In case there are other possible inheritors who may want to petition to disqualify you from the inheritance?"

"Disqualify me, for what?"

"There's a series of things . . . Most likely they do not apply to you, but we have to go through that process. It's the law."

"Of course, it is."

I saw myself on the streets, living in cardboard boxes, the Riveras walking by, laughing at my arrogance and naiveté. Maybe Julia should know about all of this, I thought. He inhaled the rest of his meal and left, leaving his card behind. I thanked him, for what, I don't know.

I remembered Marisol and the concert—I didn't want to call it a date. Hadn't really thought about it that way. But just thinking about that made me nervous. I just wanted to get out—in my new car, drive around, put some mileage on it, see the sights. Having a car was great, although I wasn't crazy about driving in Puerto Rico. Recklessness was the way of the road. It's as if you put mice into little cars within an enclosed box. Civility falters amid the chaos and absurdity of so many cars lined up without moving. I was in a strip mall in Caguas, another consumerist way station dotting the cemented island. Although I was only fifteen minutes away, I had to worry about making it on time because it was Friday and close to 3 pm; people would soon be taking off early from work and the traffic jams were legendary.

By the time I got home, it was time to get ready. Marisol told me she wanted to arrive at the restaurant around five, in order to have a "leisurely meal" and talk. You can't do anything leisurely when you have somewhere to go afterward. But these were her plans. I was basically tagging along, playing chauffeur. I showered, shaved, threw on some comfortable clothes, no cologne.

The dinner was fine, nothing out of this world. I can't even remember the restaurant or what we ordered. I think it may have been Mexican because Marisol must have drunk something like margaritas. She was vibrant, ebullient by the time we arrived at Roberto Clemente Coliseum for the concert. It was packed with a strange mix of young dudes sporting surfer wear, old long-hairs, women in hermetically sealed jeans and high heels waving their free curly hair along with the miniature Puerto Rican flags they carried. I understood the diverse crowd when I saw the two bands. The warm up band, Arlequín, played MTV sappy, pop stuff: their ballads, in particular, cloy and at times almost spacey. Fiel de la Vega was totally professional; you could tell from their faces—a bit worn and calm—that this was just another gig.

I could not capture all the lyrics; they were coming too fast for my limited Spanish. In important points, Marisol would bend over and shout a translation, one time getting close enough that I could feel her warm, boozy breath on my ear.

Then, the lead singer tossed his long ponytail back, sat on a stool and started playing his acoustic guitar. Marisol grabbed my arm, almost digging her fingernails into my skin, and brought me close to tell me that this was a great song. It was something about how no matter where you were, even on the moon, you would always be a Boricua, a Puerto Rican. A pretty song, but I could not comprehend the lyrics, which had the audience spellbound. They looked like zombies waving Puerto Rican flags, swaying to the numbing melody. On Marisol it had a different effect, or perhaps patriotism made her horny, because she gripped my thigh and started rubbing it. Another musician picked up a violin and started playing the sweet melody. Marisol put her two pinkies to her lips and whistled. Everyone, and I mean every soul in that venue except me, knew the lyrics to this song, and the concert became a collective communion of song, flag-waving, nationalistic intoxication.

The roar at the finish of that number was deafening, but more so was the reaction when the group began its hit song, "El Wanabi." Marisol grabbed me and took me out to dance in the aisle, along with others who had already broken ranks. Dancing everywhere, people clapping hands to the rhythm. Marisol shook her hips, made the red jersey dress sheathing her body electric. As her wavy hair dropped over her face, I had the urge to sweep it out of her eyes and kiss her. Maybe she read my mind because she threw her head back and laughed, then threw her arms around my neck, and to the music churned her hips against mine.

As I was driving her back home, Marisol told me to head toward Baná instead, and just when we were approaching the Baná exit, Marisol broke from her lethargic state.

"Keep driving," she muttered.

"Why?" I asked. "Just do it," she said.

And we drove another ten minutes or so. As we approached the Jíbaro Monument, Marisol directed me to turn into a dark parking area. She made me maneuver into a grassy area, some distance from the actual parking.

"What are we doing here?"

"Didn't you tell me you wanted to see El Jíbaro?"

"At this hour?"

"It makes sense after a concert like that; you'll appreciate it more."

Marisol grabbed my hand, threaded her fingers through mine, and guided me through the darkness, along the grass, up an incline, toward a fenced-in area. We reached the open gate and a cement walkway led to the monument. The area was poorly lit, but you could make out the two figures huddled together, atop a massive rectangular marble pedestal. We climbed up the stairs leading up to the two figures: a woman, hair tied back in a bun, sitting with a child; a man standing, hand on her shoulder, holding a hoe, staring into the distance. The immediate resemblance to

Grant Wood's *American Gothic* was unmistakable, to me, anyway. These faces could have come from the American Midwest.

Marisol took out a penlight from her purse and shone it on an engraving on the northern panel. In a respectful, serious tone she translated: "The jíbaro is the man of our land, cultivator of our homeland, genesis of our race and authentic expression of the Puerto Rican experience."

Then she walked to the southern panel, and again translated: "The jíbaro has always been the symbol of our collective identity, the synthesis of the virtues of the Puerto Rican people."

"And what about her," I kidded, but she didn't get my attempt at a feminist joke.

Marisol was lost in the moment. Silently, she turned and headed down the cement stairs, and headed back to the car, lighting the way with penlight in hand.

I felt bad she had taken the time to show the monument to me and I had left unmoved. How could this mass of stone and a few overblown words bring out such a somber demeanor in anyone? I stared at them and saw a woman lost in her child's gaze and a man with tired, sad eyes.

When I returned to the car, Marisol was seated, staring ahead, twirling a strand of curly hair. I sat down and was about to start the car when she put her hand over mine. Her eyes glistened; they looked down once and met mine again.

She glided across and kissed me. A soft kiss, a peck really. She must have seen something inviting in my eyes. She kissed me harder, and I could not resist. I could not say no to her, not then and there. She climbed on top of me, slipped off her underwear, unbuckled and lowered my pants and underwear, and breathlessly told me to adjust the seat. I did, with one hand, as the other bunched up her dress.

We made love like two high school kids on the last day of summer. Her passion kindled my dormant desire, and by the end, the Civic was rolling as if on water. Her last words, when she reached orgasm, resonate in my head today as when they broke the black stillness of that cool Cordillera night.

"Dios mío," she screamed, "¡qué vivan los nuyoricans!"

Eleven

My familia consiste of Mami, Papi, sester, Magi, brodels, Tato y Axel, me, this server, and the dog Sashi. Mami has 42 years. Papi has 45 years. I biggest in famili. Than come Magi, Tato, Axel. We live in the camp in Ciales. Papi work en a factoría Mami dame of house. We not rich not poor. I like my house. Have my proper habitation. My famili very united. Like go to movie and famili things. Organize party for all famili, much cousen, aunt, oncle, abuelos, much fun. Reunite over much food to celebrate be together . . .

I could not read any further. I had read these compositions for hours, and it was like transcribing ancient hieroglyphics. My eyes were becoming crooked, blurred from the strain, my head throbbing from the effort and anger. Anger because these students had received English instruction since the early grades right through high school. Anger because I could separate the best compositions from the abysmally bad, and upon investigation find that the former lived in the best, fenced-in neighborhoods, their parents were most likely lawyers or doctors, and each one had attended a moderately priced private school. Those students having attended the expensive privates were now at an Ivy League school stateside, or if they had ended up here, were taking Honors English. And, why, of all things, did I assign them to write on family? Even the most unintelligible scribbling pulsated with family love that came across as a birthright.

Outside, a misty rain was coming down. I usually ran in the evening right before dinner, rain or shine, but I loved running in this type of weather. Running in the rain, I get some thinking done. The slapping of running shoes against rainy ground is like a thinking metronome. I jumped into my shorts, a Mattingly Yankee T-shirt, laced up my spanking new Nikes and headed outside.

Although small, the campus had enough acreage for a good run. There was a wide oval area used by some of the college's teams as a temporary field. The real field was in construction going on five years. I was just starting, not even completing my first lap, when I saw the young, green-eyed woman who had offered me a ride. We had bumped into each other on campus a few times, once at the college hangout. She had just finished her run and held that reflective pose familiar to runners: head up, hands on hips, breathing hard. From behind, she looked wonderful. Her tight shorts outlined a shapely bottom tightened by exercise. She had the youthful legs of a runner, muscular and without a trace of cellulite, tanned a hue darker by the sun. Her strong legs were sculpted down to thin ankles hugged by athletic socks and New Balance running shoes.

My intention was to say hi and move on, but she smiled. Like an idiot, I stopped moving forward and ran in place staring at her radiant face. Today, perhaps because of exercise, her green eyes appeared vibrant. She had her hair up in a ponytail, accentuating the bronze, flushed oval face.

"You like running in the rain too, huh?"

"Love it," I answered, a little too excited.

I kept running in place, the rain misting us both.

"You don't mind getting wet?"

"I like wet," I said.

She laughed, and I felt like a bigger idiot.

"Wet is good," she said, smiling.

"Should get going," I blurted and waved stupidly as I took off.

I made my laps and passed her a few times as she walked her last laps to cool down, when I noticed Marisol sitting on a cement bench under a large willow tree. She waved and I walked over to her.

"You're a good runner," she said.

"Oh, really, and how would you know?"

"I ran track at the high. You have good technique."

I nodded, bending over, breathing hard. "Why you out here?"

"I love sitting here and thinking."

I sat next to her a bit tired from my run, having pushed myself extra hard the last few laps. We talked longer than I had expected or wanted. I learned her parents were first wave Cubans, those who had the money and pull to emigrate and leave Castro's Revolution behind.

"They were young and had few family ties. They could escape. We ended up in New Jersey," she said.

Her father, a chemist, decided to take an opening in Wyrling's Puerto Rico plant, when the island was becoming a haven for pharmaceuticals that took advantage of corporate tax breaks. Marisol wasn't happy with the move. She had friends back in Jersey, a feeling I understood well.

"I hated it, all of it. I loved Jersey, my school, our house."

She rebelled, but she was alone, because her mother fully supported her dad. Her siblings, a brother and a sister, were younger. Her brother was born in the island. They didn't suffer the feeling of foreignness that Marisol, as an estranged English-speaking Cuban born in the States, encountered. The taunts from other kids, having to master Spanish, being marginalized.

I wanted to ease her mind, so I told her about the issues between my parents' families. My parents' dreams of returning, not unlike her own parents.

At this she shook her head and curly hair: "No, Rennie, it's not the same. Your parents could return. They just had to jump on a plane."

"And you think it's easy to do that?"

"You don't live with all that anger and frustration that Cubans have to deal with. It's not the same."

I let it go, sensing her own anger and frustration.

"Doesn't matter, anyway," I said, "they never made it back."

When she asked me why, like so many when I tell them, a light turned on and her jaw dropped.

"Yes, that horrible, media event."

Her head dropped. "Life's so fragile," she said.

For some reason I felt like a schmuck. Like I had used the information to one-up her in some slimy way. I felt ashamed but also strangely relieved. I got up to leave but our eyes met again.

"Gotta go," I said.

"Can't you stay a little longer."

"Sorry, a stack of papers is waiting for me."

She nodded, and I left. I turned around to take another look at her, and she was looking at me.

"You should get out of the rain," I yelled.

But she stayed sitting on the cement bench, swallowed under the shadow of that gigantic moss tree, looking out toward the rain, falling harder now.

Dr. Roque called me in to what now seemed a weekly event for both of us. So far, he had criticized my syllabi, informed me about students complaining about my grading, warned me about hanging out with students and anything else that he could pin on me.

"Professor Falto, what are you wearing today?"

I looked at him—had he gone blind over the weekend? I scanned myself, while sitting in his hard office chair.

"Jeans, shirt, shoes," I laughed.

"This is not funny. We have a dress code at the college."

"Really," now understanding his point and not liking it at all. "I wasn't aware of that."

"Well, that's why I'm informing you."

"Why now?"

"Most professors have the good sense to know in a professional setting one dresses professionally. In your case, I'll notch it up to youth and inexperience."

I scanned him. His professional attire consisted of typically disheveled, tacky polyester pants, a too tight, short-sleeved shirt and sandals. And as usual, on top of his head, that helmet of gelled hair. Today, he wore white socks with the sandals, and his aftershave reeked.

"Please make an effort, Professor Falto," he said in a sing-songy way that made me want to screech.

"Do you expect me to wear suits in this weather?"

"Of course not. But the jeans must definitely go. How about putting on some socks? You're not 'hanging out,'" he said making air quotes, "with the students. You're their teacher and need to instruct them in more ways than the subject matter. Maintain a business tone in everything you do."

"Aha. Will I receive a salary increase to cover this new wardrobe I need?"

He looked at me, exasperated.

"Didn't think so," I said.

All day I checked out my colleagues' fashion sense. Stiegler with his wrinkled shirts, stained baggy pants and Brashers. His unkempt wild mustache invariably spotted with crumbs. If the weather dropped to near chilly, I bet he would break out his flannel shirts. Apparently, Roque considered this mountain man attire professional enough. Juan Cedeño with his Hawaiian shirts and too tight, pleated Dockers. Carmela López with her drabby grays, blacks and whites, looked like she belonged in a convent, not a college. Lately, Freddie Rivas dressed in all black. Professional? Maybe, but it seemed better suited for a mortuary. Micco varied. On most days, he could look sharp; but on others, he came in unshaven, frazzled, his clothes appearing to have been sprung from the hamper.

And Marisol. Today, she looked exceptionally fine. A cream-colored summer dress, gossamer-like material, the kind that in the sunlight you could see through. The top of the dress crisscrossed her breasts, accentuating them, and the hem fell at the knees exposing muscular calves. She had lost weight and had been working out. A new haircut, short and wavy to the neck, completed the makeover.

She saw me staring at her and smiled. I was standing next to the coffee machine, drinking a cup. She was talking to Rita Gómez— who always looked professional, but everyone commented she overdressed—and saw me checking her out from the corner of her eye. I smiled and did a turnaround back to my office. And as I knew she would, she excused herself from Rita and headed straight to my office.

Before talking to her under the moss, I had been avoiding her since the Jíbaro Monument. She called me a few times at home searching for explanations, and I tried as best I could to convince her that our lovemaking that night had been a monumental mistake (a pun she did not find funny). We were colleagues and this created problems. We both let our guards down that night, and yes, it was pleasurable, but wrong. Now, here she was again. Standing in front of me, looking super sexy, seeking answers I could not give her.

"Falto, why are you tormenting me?" She whispered this as she closed the door behind her.

"What are you talking about?"

"I saw you looking at me, practically undressing me."

My God, I thought, was it that obvious? I opened a textbook on my desk.

"I was just admiring your dress."

Her lips puckered into a smirk. She came over to me, turned the chair around, and, with her hands on the armrests, corralled me in it. Her coffee brown eyes, the same ones that closed in passion that night, now stared at me defiantly.

"Stop pretending you're not into me."

I shifted back in my seat. It took tremendous effort not to swing it into position and repeat the performance from that memorable night. She smelled great, had that glow of a desirable woman who knew what she wanted. But I held my hand up, as if to say, "No más."

"I'm not." We were both whispering now.

"That wasn't just sex, Rennie." She came closer, cleavage suspended in front of me. "Deep down, you know that."

I didn't want to answer her. Her hold on the chair loosened; she stepped back.

"Just go out with me again."

I could have continued having fun with her, because how many times do you have fantasy-satisfying, hot sex? But it wasn't right. She seemed to want something deeper, much more committal, with the right person, but I wasn't that guy. I did not love her, and to think of loving her made my heart ache. I should have been

upfront with her, but she looked so vulnerable. So I did the immature thing and ignored her, kept reading the book in front of me.

She came at me and grabbed the book.

"You're an asshole," she said and backhanded the book across
the office. She walked out, slamming the door.

In the days that followed, Marisol rarely talked to me, hardly ever
looked my way. When she did, to discuss something professional,
she had this distant, frosty face that couldn't conceal the anger.

Iglesias, a senior faculty member, once told me that academics
fight ferociously over everything because all they can fight for are
crumbs. And even before you can fight over those crumbs, you
have to jump through hoops just to get at them. The second visit
to Roque's office in the week dealt with conference money. A professor, especially a junior one, should develop professionally, and
therefore should make an effort to attend and give papers at con-
ferences and other professional activities. I had a paper on ESL
writing accepted at a conference. I was looking forward to traveling to Chicago and meeting with other writing professionals.
Roque rejected my request for funding.

"You haven't finished writing it, have you?"

"Well, no . . . but . . . "

"Money is tight, Professor Falto. Next time you want funding,
have a completed project." He closed the manila folder with my
proposal and request.

We both knew that was bullshit. Very few people ever wrote an
entire paper before submitting an abstract to a conference. Roque's
determination to make my life miserable was starting to worry me.
Before I had thought he was one of those grumpy, demanding, but
perhaps deep down lovable academic types. As he persisted, it
became clear he just didn't like me. Then Micco told me to watch
my back. Evaluations were coming up.

Fear is a great motivator. If Roque were after me, I had to make
sure he had nothing on me. That my performance showed an
assistant professor working hard at improving his teaching and
scholarship. I returned to the conference paper, to finish it, but
kicked up my hacky sack instead.

Twelve

Marisol left me a present in my office: a candle that Micco said looked like a phallus. And when you looked at it carefully, he was right. It was an aromatic candle that was supposed to relax you, make you feel sexy and "lovey-dovey." That's what she wrote on the card. Besides an apology for getting angry at me earlier. Maybe it was really a votive candle.

About the same time, I met with Ledesma at his office to sign the papers transferring the house to me. That was the proverbial good news, followed by the bad. Even though the house was now mine, I could not serve the Riveras with an eviction notice.

"Why not?" I asked, confounded.

"Because you don't have a legal standing for eviction."

I practically jumped out of my seat. He held out one of his delicate hands as his face turned to the side in a sign of impatience.

"They didn't owe you money; they owed the past owners of the house."

"Who, by the way, were my parents."

"That does not come into play. The property has been transferred to you. You cannot end a tenancy of which you are not a part of, contractually speaking. Your parents also didn't initiate an eviction process after several months of non-payment. That doesn't help your case."

Great, I thought. Just like my parents to feel sorry for squatters. The infamous "ay bendito" plaguing Puerto Ricans. That phrase is uniquely Puerto Rican. Since being on the island, I don't know how many times I've heard it used in varying situations, always expressing a sense of sorrow or feeling sorry for a person or thing. But it also expresses resignation that nothing can be done to alleviate the sorrow, the pain, the suffering. A Puerto Rican says "ay bendito" in solidarity with the sufferer's inertia.

I just sat there and sighed, with this profound sense of frustration and powerlessness, feeling with every minute more Puerto Rican.

"So, what now, Ledesma?"

"We'll present your case with the tribunal and see what happens."

"You don't sound too sure."

"The worst possibility is the court gives the squatters more time to move, if they have a valid reason. We need to check up on them a bit."

That meant I had to dish out more money. Whatever my parents had left to me in cash was going down this deep hole in my attempt to secure the one major item they had left me. I signaled "go ahead" with a nod.

"Have faith," Ledesma yelled as I walked out of his office.

Yeah, right, I said to myself.

A few weeks later, I found another gift from Marisol in my office. A copy of a Georgia O'Keefe flower painting, the one that looked like a vagina.

"Many of them look like vaginas," Micco reminded me. Then, he went on about O'Keefe in startling detail and with great knowledge of the painter's biography.

"How do you know so much about O'Keefe," I asked.

He hesitated, then said, tight-lipped, "My father." O'Keefe was one of his father's favorite painters. Then he said, "Not for the greatest reasons," smiling.

It was such a strange smile that it caused me to look at him perplexed. Usually, Micco drops the subject. If you don't get what he's saying, he won't bother to explain it for you. But this time, he looked embarrassed, as if he needed to, or wanted to, explain.

"My father's a perv, what can I say."

Again, the puzzled look on my face, this time with a mix of shock and incredulity.

"You heard right," he said, and then proceeded to narrate his father's sexual addiction, how he came to the realization one day that no one woman could satisfy him forever and within a week had moved out of the house, leaving his mother, sister and him stupefied. He was angry and confided in me that to this day he has issues with his father.

"He left me at a vulnerable time in my life, and I still resent him for it."

He told me all of this within the few minutes between classes. And I was grateful that both of us had to attend to classes. Afterwards, I think we both realized the awkwardness of that conversation. For sure, I thought Micco wished he hadn't given me that personal tidbit, until I found out others in the department knew. Julia even knew. In fact, within academic circles, many people in the insular bubble called Puerto Rico knew, because Dr. Montero, professor of philosophy, was a renowned and esteemed scholar, until his call for a Neo-Hedonism brought his career spiraling into ridicule. He told his family how sorry he was, but he had to follow his inner instincts. Sobbing, he hugged him and her sister, but Micco's mother did not want to look at him. After the divorce, Dr. Montero used his life savings to move into a commune in New Mexico, where reports and complaints of wild orgies and bacchanalian parties in the desert surfaced often.

Surprises. They come out of nowhere, like the wonderful news that I was going to be "visited" by Roque and the Gang of Three, the more informal name for the Performance Review Committee, that body of tenured, senior faculty in charge of determining whether you are worthy of teaching at the university level or are better suited for other employment. I understood that they needed to review my performance, but I wasn't keen on the blitzkrieg nature of the visit. They would not tell you when it was going down, so at any moment they could swoop down and do their damage. That's how I saw it; that's how I felt it. What, I asked, if you come on one of those crappy days we all have. They didn't care to provide me with any type of decent answer. They had tradition on their side, years and years of doing it this way. And they were not going to change "the process" for some super young punk from the States who knew nothing about how things were done here in La Isla.

I refused to let them visit me. I argued that they should allow professors the maximum opportunity to do their best; if it was a scheduled visit, the professor had no, or minimal, excuses for bad performance. But that fell on deaf ears. I would have turned to a union if we had one. The so-called Association of Professors had been trying to change this policy for decades. But said association had zero power. According to the Puerto Rican Superior Court, professors were considered part of management and therefore had no standing as workers to form a union. The association, therefore, collected dues, threw fabulous parties and managed to secure benefits for their members only when the Congreso de Obreros Universitarios, the union for non-faculty workers, went on strike and won a major benefit that had to be given to everyone.

I informed the Committee I would not let them in my classroom. I would close the doors for the entire review period. But, then, that was madness, assisted suicide with Roque pulling the lever. I asked if they could at least tell us, not just me, but the others undergoing this cruel process, the weeks of the visit. "We always do that," they answered, smugly. They were also gracious enough to provide the newbies like me with the form they used, as if it were a crib sheet. I looked at all those boxes, waiting for check marks, and felt like I was being squeezed into them. Did I have to teach to the form? I asked, trying to be ironic, but the remark did not elicit a smile.

A few days later, I found another one of Marisol's gifts on my desk. A German, Galileo thermometer, or a thermoscope. As soon as Micco saw it, he looked at me and we both laughed. For those who have never seen this contraption: it is long, about fourteen inches, over five inches in circumference, with a flat, round base and a tip that resembles the end of a condom. It's a thermometer that works on the principles of weight and density. But the blatantly phallic quality of it made us laugh, but also made me wonder out loud to Micco if Marisol understood that or if it were some unconscious thing at work. This one came with the cryptic message: "Saw this and thought of you."

These gifts were starting to creep me out. I did not like these little subconscious, erotic presents appearing in my office. I returned
all of them with a note telling Marisol that I appreciated her gesture but there was no need. I accepted her apologies, gave her,
again, mine for being an asshole, and told her for us to move on.
I also told the department secretary, Nitza, to not let her into my
office nor to take her gifts there, which she did not appreciate.
Nitza was a big romantic and thought giving such gifts was a
grand thing and, consequently, returning them was the height of
rudeness. She told me that Puerto Ricans didn't do that type of
thing.

"Don't sweat it," I told her, "most people don't think I'm Puerto Rican, anyway."

Marisol did not respond well to my returning the gifts. My
"rebuff" of these gifts, she told me, was "heartless and insensitive."
Giving gifts, she said, was her way of moving on. Marisol returned
to the brain-freezing stares and monosyllabic conversations.

Weeks later, on a humid, rainy day, the committee marched into
my classroom. I was prepared but nervous. The students, I think,
were more nervous than I. At first, they clammed up worse than
usual as the three somber faces stared at us from the back of the
classroom, trying to look inconspicuous.

"We try to be quiet and blend," said Carmela López, when I first
protested against this type of intrusion. Now, her tired spinster
face stood out like a gargoyle stuck to the white drywall, along
with her two partners, Iglesias, who came the closest to blending,
given his teen-like stature and demeanor, and Foley, whom I had
seen only at departmental meetings. Apparently, doing performance reviews was a task that he relished or took seriously enough
to show up. His penetrating blue eyes unsettled me the most.

The students' willingness to help me overwhelmed me. Even
those who had rarely spoken in class raised hands and tried to
answer a question, read a passage or contribute something to the
discussion. These were simple exercises, basic English, but that
day my students in that class seemed heroic in their efforts. I
thought the class went extremely well, and two of the committee
members agreed. Carmela López did not. She gave me low scores

for not following up on questions, organization, even "lack of respect" for students, citing my joking with a student that anyone in the classroom that day, including the student who laughed, understood to be teasing. Then Roque executed his "Chair's Visit" and rated my performance "unsatisfactory," writing extensively on each item.

"Clearly a hatchet job," Micco told me.

With the committee going 2-1 in my favor, and Roque's evaluation so adamantly against, an outside committee made of professors from other departments had to evaluate me. I was vindicated by the students' evaluations, all of them excellent, despite a handful of complaints about hard grading. Student opinion only matters as far as how it can be used. If it is glowing, like mine, it would matter if Roque shared it and wanted me to stay. But since he wanted to rid the department of me, the students' evaluation of my teaching was chalked up to their naiveté, or that they identified with my youth or had underdeveloped critical thinking.

I awaited this third visit, which would make or break me. This had happened too fast, and I had no plans. What to do if my contract were not renewed? It never occurred to me that I could be dismissed after one year. I didn't want to live off Julia, and what would she think about my losing this teaching job? She would be angry for not confiding in her. She was trying hard to win my trust, and my secrecy on this would raise doubts.

Then, the students went on strike. A political strategy inherited from the sixties, the student strike was now considered passé in the States. In Puerto Rico they had become so commonplace that everyone anticipated a few days off during the school year for them. Some faculty scheduled trips, personal events or medical appointments during these breaks. A strike's length depended on the issue. Tuition hikes would take months to resolve. Our students paid the lowest tuition anywhere in the United States, something like $50 a credit, half of what others paid at the privates on the island.

You had to give credit to the students for their organizational abilities and enthusiasm, though. They turned these strikes into festive parties. Soon you had dozens of young men and women in front of the college playing congas, timbales, güiros, maracas and other assorted Latin percussion to the established repertoire of protest golden oldies. There had been rumors about this strike—there are always lingering whispers. The students were upset about a new college attendance policy that threatened the "beca," the local name for the Pell Grant, the federal funding that almost every student in Puerto Rico received. If they were not attending all their classes, the "beca" would also be eliminated. A substantial amount of students had grown accustomed to using the "beca" for anything but college. In my short time in the college, I had witnessed a steady acquisition of "beca" shoes, "beca" parties and even "beca" cars. This infuriated me when I saw a well-dressed student, having received the "beca," still without the classroom text.

The students wanted the absence policy to remain the same, which would give them time to receive their "beca" and spend it as they saw fit. Student leaders met, decided and wham: ¡Huelga!

I was teaching one of my classes, when I heard the chanting coming down the hall. The syncopated rhythms of the percussion, the clapping of hands, felt like a Christmas parranda entourage coming our way. But it wasn't Christmas, so we knew it was the strikers. Students in the class gathered their materials and stuffed them into backpacks, waiting for my signal to leave. The marchers arrived at my door, parked themselves outside, stopped the music and started chanting. One of the leaders charged into the classroom and gave a little speech to the rest of the students, declaring an official huelga, and then proceeded to disable the chalkboard by smearing it with cooking oil. The students looked at me. The student leader was agitated that they were still seated.

"The college is closed," she yelled.

I signaled with my head to go and they proceeded out of the classroom. Some students joined the conga line shaking down the hall. Others, I presume, would go to the beach. The more diligent would use the time to catch up or study for a big exam.

I found their cause self-serving. But I didn't care. Like the others, more than other colleagues, I welcomed the time off to think about my situation. At the guest house, I uncapped a beer and sat by the porch to look out toward the mountains. The sunlight was bright and enticing.

I have a new car begging for mileage, I thought. I rushed into the bedroom and tossed some clothes into a carry-on. Midway through the packing, I picked up my cell and dialed Marisol. After the gift incident, we had been having a series of long telephone conversations, and by now I had her on speed dial. Just as fast, I cancelled the call. It scared me to think she was only a quick dial away, that I could call her to invite her on a trip without first considering the possible consequences. No one would know us beyond the college campus, I thought, not thinking about the more serious situation: we would be alone, relaxing somewhere, catching rays half-naked in a tropical setting. Just thinking about it aroused me.

We both agreed to a friendship. We kept our distance, ran through our schedules, and when we bumped into each other in the hallway, it was a quick hello and goodbye. I was finding it harder to do, especially when she looked especially stunning. Later in the evening, during the marathon phone conversations, we would spill our feelings like it was therapy.

When we arranged an outing in San Juan, we always hoped someone from the college would not spot us. That was not impossible. A good amount of professors, including Marisol, lived in La Losa, the nickname given to the capital, which literally translates to "tile," the fancy, ceramic kind, of course. Micco always mused how in Spanish it can also mean gravestone.

Most of these professors hated teaching in Baná, which they considered similar to a soldier being sent to a remote outpost, or doing missionary work in the interior of some God-forsaken third world country. They complained about the long drive, and had their chairs devise special schedules so they only had to come in two days a week. They looked down their noses at the institution, the students and the town, kept their eyes and ears open for resignations or open positions at the central campus, the alleged crown jewel of the system situated in Río Piedras, just outside San Juan.

Hanging out in San Juan always meant a risk of bumping into one of these snooty professors, something we both didn't want.

Roque would get on my case for this, too, if he found out. We made sure that we selected a secluded club or greasy spoon that these people would never think of patronizing. Even then, we kept our eyes open. All this so we could dance together, laugh a little—just have fun.

Roque had me wondering if I was cut out to be a university professor. Maybe, he was right, I thought. "If you want to write," he told me, "then do and don't teach," paraphrasing Bernard Shaw. Did I want to work in this type of hostile environment? He would always be on my ass, and the tenure process runs seven years. Seven years of hell, I thought. He had me running scared. Right then, in early November, with the campus shut down by strikers, I just wanted to pick up and leave to somewhere quiet. We were on a tropical island with renowned beaches I had yet to visit. But suddenly I wanted to go with Marisol, to sit on the sand with her and see her run into the water in a bikini. See her smile in the radiance of Caribbean sunlight.

Dialed, cancelled, dialed, cancelled. I wanted to spend this time with her but was afraid to be alone with her. The idea of making love to her again made my heart race, but frightened me. I visualized us together by transparent, turquoise water, spread out on a colorful beach blanket, listening to soft tunes, while our bodies absorbed and exuded heat.

I dialed again, almost losing my breath when she answered.

"Hey, you up for a road trip?"

Thirteen

My mother told me the coquís sing like crazy when it's going to rain. "They're asking for rain," she said, giving a look which meant "stop whining and go to bed." But I kept hearing them, kept thinking I saw their little bright eyes staring at me through the darkness. Their persistent chirping, rhythmic and soothing for others, to me seemed like an alarm clock's loud ticking and made me uneasy. After kissing me, my mother rearranged the mosquito net to make sure there were no openings. That summer throughout the island, dengue had struck and caused fatalities. The grown-ups talked about it in that hushed, serious voice they use to talk about bad things. It was the really bad dengue, the one that causes bleeding all over your body.

Tossing and turning, putting the pillow over my head to drown out the chorus of coquís, I kept going over our trip to Puerto Rico. It was supposed to be a big deal, my first trip to the island, and special for my parents, since it was their first visit together as a married couple. Right from the start it didn't go well. Before we boarded the plane, my mom had told my dad that she would not set foot in his family's house. Although sad and upset, Papi understood, so he gave in to Mami's wishes.

The plan was for my father to take me to meet his family. My grandparents hadn't seen me in years, and some relatives had only seen me in photos, a situation generating gasps when discussed by my father's family members. Later, my mother would take me to meet her grandmother, my great-grandmother and other relatives in Lares. Meanwhile, she would stay at the suite in the hotel part-

ly owned by Papi's family. She was going to read Vargas Llosa's latest novel and get some sun. My father said nothing. On our way
to Guaynabo, he spoke only as he pointed out the sights like a
tour guide: El Morro, "one of the Spaniards' great engineering
feats," the Normandy Hotel "shaped like a ship," Muñoz Marín
Park, Oso Blanco "where they put the bad guys."

The Falto house was a mansion to a kid accustomed to living in
apartments at that time. It had more than one bathroom, comfortable furniture, fancy pictures on the walls and the best thing: a
pool. That was the coolest. I told Papi I wanted to stay with his
family, and everyone around the table sipping drinks looked at
him as his already sun-burnt face turned redder. Abuela Isabela
thought it was a good idea. Why should he have to travel all the
way across the island and up mountains, she said. This is his vacation; he should have fun. My father looked at her. She tightened
her lips, rolled her eyes and waved the issue away.

We had a big lunch, with roast suckling pig, lechón. I met all
these relatives I didn't know I had. Some of them called me a yanqui and made fun of me because I couldn't understand Spanish.
Abuelo Enrique kept shaking his head about that. Your mother is a
Spanish teacher, he told me, "tell her to teach you Espanish." He
thought that was a big joke and waited for everyone around him to
laugh. His breath smelled like whisky and cigars. When he laughed,
his round face lit up, and he stroked his crescent mustache as he
sipped another drink. On his wrist, he wore the biggest gold watch
I had ever seen. He always wore guayaberas, but I didn't like them.

We went to the big mall, Plaza Las Américas, after that feast at
lunch. Papi thought this was a huge deal, this mall. We walked
around and it looked like the largest mall I had ever seen, bigger
than the ones in Jersey, even. There were so many people there, all
dressed up like they didn't need any more clothes. Papi wanted to
buy mom something, but he stopped at a bookstore that looked
like it had been hit by a hurricane. Unshelved books everywhere,
stacks piled up against walls, a few books on the floor. "I prefer
this bookstore to the chains," he said. I was getting bored, and
noticed a toy store across from us. Being a typical tween, I was
more concerned about action figures than reading, so off I went in

search of Darth Vader. My mistake was not telling Papi, who after a few minutes noticed I was gone and freaked. He had the security guards searching for me, and I thought he was going to call the FBI. It was embarrassing. I felt like a dork, and he was angry at me, but also gave me a huge hug when I answered the page and went to the first security guard I spotted.

Mami found out and raised hell. "You go off to La La Land," she yelled at my father, "when you go into a bookstore. Jesus, Juanma, learn to be a bit more responsible when it comes to your kid."

That really pissed off Papi. He went off about how he was a good father. And they went on like that for a while.

A day later I found myself in a car with both parents, climbing up these freaking mountains, travelling to meet my great-grandmother, Doña Aurelia, better known to the Sanz clan as Mamá Relia. At first, Mami was going alone, to let Papi spend time with his family. But at the last minute, he decided to go with us. At one point, we had to stop for me to throw up because the ride was so curvy. When we finally met Mamá Relia, she looked ancient to me. She must have been close to ninety and looked like a mummy. With her gummy mouth and few teeth yellowed by chewing tobacco, and her loose, wrinkled skin, she scared me. Close to her, I smelled tobacco and rubbing alcohol.

"Kiss her," Mami whispered at me. A difficult thing to do, and on hesitating, she secretly pinched me to do it.

Lares was boring, too quiet for me, and with little to do. I was ordered to go to the basketball court to play with the neighborhood kids, as my mom caught up on family gossip from her aunts and cousins who had dropped by with huge pots of food. These kids were not any nicer than my own cousins. They looked at me like some foreigner, which I guess I was. I couldn't speak Spanish, and they were jealous over my pricey clothes and sneakers, so after a while they ignored me. When I returned, my mother told me she had a treat for me. She took me into the town's plaza, like any other I had seen in PR during that summer. But in Lares' plaza, there was a little ice cream shop that sold the craziest types of flavors: rice, beans, guanábana, among other strange tastes. I asked for the weirdest combo, because I was beginning to dislike this place and everything Mami thought was cool. Garlic and avocado, I think, and enjoyed it to my surprise.

The ride back was hell, worse than having to puke, because Mami and Papi kept fighting. They started arguing over history, the Grito de Lares, the rebellion in that town that started the war for independence and why it failed. My father at one point reminded Mami that he was, after all, the historian in the family. Then, somehow, they got into it over the Madonna incident, which happened the year before but was still a hot topic in the island. Madonna had grinded her crotch against a Puerto Rican flag in a concert she gave in San Juan. The locals were outraged. The Puerto Rican Senate passed a resolution condemning her "lasciviousness." The leader of the Puerto Rican Independence Party called it "an infamy without parallel in the history of our country." Papi agreed, but Mami thought Puerto Ricans had more serious issues to worry about. If people don't respect your flag, the symbol of the patria, you have nothing, my father yelled, banging the dashboard. My mother looked at him like he was crazy.

"Juanma, please, like Ricans here really care about the *patria*," she replied, placing a mocking emphasis on the last word.

"What do you know about being Puerto Rican," he said, and that's when they really started yelling. Stuff I couldn't understand, or maybe I just tuned it out. I kept looking out the window at the houses lining the curving road, the green vegetation surrounding us, the limestone rock high above us, trying to spot other kids my age along the landscape.

I remember silence after that. In the parking lot, in the elevator and in the luxury hotel suite, there reigned a scary quiet that made me hide in my room until I heard something, like a small dog whining. I opened my door and looked across the suite's living room toward my parents' room and saw my father leaning his head against the door, sobbing and saying things that only my mother could hear. He slumped against the door like that for a few minutes, until my mother opened the door and let him in.

Fourteen

We passed the Jíbaro Monument, and I couldn't hold back from smiling. Marisol saw my big-ass grin and punched my arm. I was in such a giddy mood that I would have smiled even if Roque himself had presented me with my dismissal letter. Sitting next to me, Marisol listened to Yankee Daddy's "Gasolina," which she took out of a portfolio full of CDs and popped into the car CD player. Her bronze legs propped up on the dashboard, she rocked her feet and toes to the beat as she sang the refrain. The song became our road anthem.

She had not hesitated when I called. "Give me an hour to pack and get to Baná," she said, and then we were off.

We entered the autopista heading south, agreeing on the direction without any sense of destination. Soon, the highway broke through into the drier landscape of the leeward side of the Cordillera. Not desert like Death Valley, not even close, but for a tropical island where mostly everything was flush green, the sparse, yellowish flora appeared foreign. Marisol explained how despite its small area, Puerto Rico had two phosphorescent bays, a rainforest, karst topography, caves, wildlife refuges and biosphere reserves. I looked at her surprised, and she told me that in college she had entertained the idea of majoring in geology.

We rode past patches of uninhabited areas that added to the desert feel. Occasionally, we'd see a little house way up on an isolated, elevated alcove and wonder who the hell lived there.

We approached Guánica after noon, both hungry, so we exited the highway and decided to lunch somewhere along the little town's malecón, or boardwalk. At an outside table, we ate a crab taco each, sharing a Medalla beer. The smell of the ocean wafted across the curving cement strip that constituted the boardwalk, and bright sunshine cascaded down on everything. Toward the water, fishing boats scurried off into the horizon, sailboats lingered on the turquoise expanse.

Noontime during a work day, and the place was empty. It had the peace and serenity that only remote vacation spots can have. I glanced at Marisol and saw in her sunglasses my own shaded reflection staring back. Then the tropical landscape was broken by a hideous sight: a big boulder surrounded by rusted, iron gates. I moved forward, looked over my sunglasses. Marisol saw me and turned around.

"It's just a landmark," she said.

"Of what?"

"Where the Americans landed in 1898."

I wanted to see it closer, so Marisol gulped the rest of the beer and we took a look. It was some sort of commemoration of the event, a Plymouth rock-type of idea. This was where the American soldiers set foot to invade the island of Puerto Rico. It was a large coral boulder with the date September 16, 1898, and the words "3rd Battalion, U.S. V Engineers" carved on it.

As we walked back to the car, I turned around and saw how ridiculous it looked, jutting up from the ground, surrounded by an old, grated railing meant to protect it, from what or whom I wasn't sure. Certainly, not from the seagulls and pigeons who had had their way with it. It looked like an ignored eyesore.

The boulder made me think about the invasion, made me revisit in my mind the status issue. I asked Marisol where she stood.

"Statehood," she said.

I looked at her a bit stunned; many professors were pro-independence.

She read my face and smiled. "I know. I should be a pipiola, right?" she said, referring to the name for those in the independence party.

"Frankly, I have no opinion on the issue," I said.

"You're probably the only Puerto Rican alive who doesn't."

We both laughed.

As we drove into the lower elevation, the Caribbean sea appeared, warm and welcoming.

"How can you be so sure, Marisol?"

She threw her head back on the seat, looked out toward the foothills. "In my heart, I think it's the best thing."

"To become part of the nation that invaded and colonized Puerto Rico?"

"The U.S. has been nothing but good to me and my family. Why should I hate it?"

After Guánica, we headed west to the famous Phosphorescent Bay at La Parguera. After arriving, we parked the car in the lot of the Vistamar Hotel. We looked at each other with a "what now?" type of look. All sorts of thoughts began running through my mind. As we faced each other, the moment crackled with sexual energy, but it felt awkward. Two co-workers with a lot of R&R time on their hands, headed for a hotel suite located in a romantic, tropical setting. And we had already discussed sharing a room, out of financial necessity.

The woman at the desk did not question our being together, or give us any type of snarky looks. As we entered our room, Marisol mentioned that lots of young couples used these rooms, especially during the weekend. "What does the hotel care? For them, money always trumps morals," she said.

Now, I would be lying if I said thoughts of passionate love-making had not entered my mind as I checked out the full-size bed. But I wanted to remain faithful to the idea of non-committal friendship. Hours of chatting on the phone led us to a compromise. We could hang, but out of respect for my feelings—for Marisol, my commitment phobia—ours would remain a friendship without any sexual contact. That was the plan.

Vistamar Hotel must have been built in the sixties. The rooms were clean and comfortable, but held that worn-out, threadbare look. The walls could have used a new coat of paint, and the bathroom had small hexagonal tiles. The view was spectacular, though. From our balcony, we could see the pool below and the Caribbean Sea farther out. As soon as Marisol saw the pool, she wanted to go down for a dip and dug through her carry-on for her swimsuit.

"Come on, move it," she said, running into the bathroom to change.

I was putting my few clothing items away when she came out in a yellow bikini. I had to smile and shake my head. She looked at me with playful eyes and laughed.

"That's cruel," I said, taking out my toiletries.

"Put yours on," she said, pouting her lips and folding her arms. I nodded my head, opened a drawer and with two fingers waved my trunks.

"Just hurry up," she said, throwing herself on the bed.

When I got out of the bathroom, I did not want to look at her eyes. From the corner of my eye, as I scrambled to put my carry-on away in the closet, to fumble around for the room card key, my wallet, I could see her checking me out. We had not seen this much skin on each other until now, not even that night in the car. I felt exposed and put on a tank tee. I turned to tell her, "Okay, let's go," and our eyes met for that one instant. Hers were dreamy and locked in on mine. Mine probably showed evasion, anxiety, maybe even fear.

She stood up and straightened her bikini top. "Okay, let's go." She kissed me on the cheek and patted me on the chest.

At poolside, I could not keep my eyes off her. She had a knock-out figure, and the yellow bikini looked fantastic on her tanned skin. She loved the water and kept diving into the pool, coming out with that bikini wet, squeezing her hair dry like a towel. At one point I had to turn on my stomach to hide my erection.

"Take off that T-shirt, Rennie. It's too hot." She practically tore it off me. "Let me put some sunscreen on you."

Her hands on my body felt good as she spread the cool lotion over my back and shoulders. As I turned over and she started to spread some on my chest and stomach, I held her hand to stop. She smiled a crooked little smile that made me desire her more. I had to jump in the water, finally. But she jumped right in to splash water on me and minutes later put her arms around me.

The tropical sun took its toll, and after a few hours and beers by the pool, we returned to the room and crashed out, too tired to think about anything but a nap and doing nothing more serious than spooning. When we awoke, it was dinnertime and we had to make arrangements for a boat ride if we were to see the phosphorescent bay. As soon as you come into the area of the hotel, a bunch of boat owners hold signs to try and get you to sign up with them. Marisol told me to ignore them because she already knew the best tour guide.

We showered, separately, and made our way down to Joey's Boats and signed up for an 8:30 ride. That gave us enough time to eat dinner, and we both dug into our seafood and tostones. A band, Combo Guasua, had finished its last salsa set, and recorded music starting piping in hip hop and reggaetón. Marisol's face lit up, her lips reciting the rap lines floating from the speakers.

On the drive, I found out how much she really loved this stuff. We had left the radio on a station featuring reggaetón and Latino hip hop tunes, much to my dismay. She seemed to be rolling with it, so I didn't ask to change the station, although I was getting a headache from the tiresome rhythm. Then the music lesson began.

"Hip hop isn't just 'a black thang,' you know," she informed me, righteously. "Some of the best MCs and DJs of the early period had black-sounding names, but they were really Puerto Rican."

She riffed off some bona fide "classic" (her word) hip hop groups—her favorites being NWA, A Tribe Called Quest, Run DMC—and then she explained, what seemed to me, the whole history of Latin hip hop and reggaetón. By this time, I had spazzed out, but she was so into it, I couldn't tell her to stop. To my disappointment, she began whipping out CDs from her green portfolio, to better illustrate some of the points she was making. She played Vico C's "Saboréalo."

As the song came on, she laughed. "I used to dance to this every time it played on the radio. Went to his concert in 06 . . . Awesome," she said, punching my arm to accentuate both syllables.

"Oh, my god, you have to listen to this," she said, and played me "La Recta Final," translating the words, which admittedly were powerful and politically conscious, something I usually don't associate with rappers. As Vico C continued in a tone that seemed angry, no matter what he rapped, I wished the lesson were over; it would have been a good moment to stop, I thought. But she moved on to Wisin y Yandel and "Rakata" and "Abusadora."

"They're from around Cayey," she said, with pride, which was close to Baná.

The duo's voices were beginning to grate on my ears. Why do rappers try to sing when most can't? And the rhythm, it felt like someone beating on my head, a Latino version of the Chinese water torture. "Pam pam pam," yelled Wisin y Yandel; *pam pam pam* went my head.

Of course, there was no way in hell I would have told her that. I was so embarrassed to confess that my teen soul had been nourished by grunge, alternative and a little heavy metal. That the only rap I ever listened to was by the Beastie Boys (when I eventually told her, she mentioned that one of them was Rican). At that moment, I would have rather listened to Rage screaming in something like "Take the Power Back," or even Chris Cornell's wailing vocals. Even Nine Inch Nails pounding away. Shit, I started getting nostalgic for something mellower like Soundgarden's "Black Hole Sun." Or some Radiohead—"Karma Police" would suffice.

I looked at Marisol sitting there, by my side, and those lyrics from "Creep" about being a creep and weirdo crept into my head. And as the breeze played with the palms outside, I kept hearing the Red Hot Chili Peppers singing about flying away on that zephyr. How sad, she would probably think, this dude, so assimilated, listening to all that white shit. Her face turned serious as she slid Tego Calderón into the player.

"You know, this music helped me get through high school." She laughed, shaking her head a bit. "It was so hard moving here, Rennie. The kids, especially the girls, hated me. Called me all kinds of names. I had more fights that first year than I could remember."

She caressed my hands on the table. "But I identified with the Nuyoricans, and we would dance to hip hop while on breaks, and that kept us tight, our little group."

We finished our meal and as we each enjoyed the last glass of wine from the bottle I had ordered, the taped music blared on.

Daddy Yankee's "El Ritmo No Perdona" came up and a few couples started dancing the perreo, or "dog dance," but the way they contorted into various positions a more likely name would be "doggie style." Marisol caught me mesmerized and asked if I wanted to dance. I hesitated, but she took my hand and soon she was rubbing her booty against me, extending her arm backwards around my neck and up to my hair. I tried to keep with the rhythm, thinking pure thoughts as she bent over and gyrated her tush. At one point I had to smile and look away, whispering at her, "I can't believe you." She laughed, of course, and proceeded to shake her shoulders and breasts at me.

Outside, the low clouds had overpowered the last dint of blue, a slither of orange seeping through a sepia sunset. It was a perfect night for a ride on the phosphorescent bay. A quarter moon provided minimalist light, and when we had finished our dancing and headed for the launch area, it was pretty dark.

Our guide, Toño, met us with a hearty smile, effervescent handshakes and pats on the back. Six other passengers stepped into the long motorboat, which probably held no more than ten. Besides Marisol and me, there were two other couples—honeymooners from Minnesota and an older married couple from Florida. An older gentleman, a retired biology teacher from New York and a young woman from Ciales rounded out the explorers onboard. Toño welcomed us in heavily accented but understandable English, gave us the mandatory safety instructions, which included making us put on life vests, and then maneuvered the craft away from the pier and into the silent, black night.

The boat cut a swath of bluish-green luminance as it puttered forward. We all oohed and aahed at the sight; a few of us dipped a hand into the warm water, to immerse it in the incandescent light provided by those flagellating tiny organisms in the water. Toño explained the science behind it, in that tone guides use after having given the same information countless times. Then, he took us into deeper water, but not far from shore, and cut the motor. In the stillness, he agitated the water with an oar, then took an empty plastic container and gathered some of the water so we could see it up close. We passed the container around, shaking it to see how the water glowed when we did.

Near the end of the tour, Toño took us closer inland and invited us to swim if we wanted to, as long as we did with the life vests. It was shallow enough for anyone who wanted to go in, and they had told us when we signed up that we should wear our swimsuits if we did. Most of us made a move to jump in, except the elderly couple from Florida. Even the retired teacher seemed enthusiastic for a dip. He took off his shirt, replaced the life vest and jumped in. He was in good shape for an old guy and soon he was cutting through the water in sharp strokes, the glow of the water surrounding him. The honeymooners went off to themselves and they kissed and hugged as the water bounced around them. The Ciales woman, gazing at the starred-filled sky, floated in what seemed a sea of stars.

Marisol and I were the last to jump in. In the water, she put her arms around me and kissed me hard. Surprised, I saw her take off and swim a few laps, stopping to tread water and look at the luminescence she was creating.

"Isn't it amazing," she yelled back to me.

"Yes, it is," I said.

Farther ahead, I saw a young woman nearer to the shore. She was no more than twenty feet away from me, yet in the radiant water and quiet of the night, she seemed farther away, lost in an eerie aura that I could not enter. The water's bluish-green incandescence made her face glow more than usual, and when she smiled I thought she was the most beautiful woman I had ever seen. She waved at me, and I recognized her—the Green-Eyed Girl. I floated in the water just staring at her. She laughed and swam back to the shore of the little island where a group of students had huddled around a campfire.

Toño returned us to the pier, on the way picking up plastic six-pack holders and floating bags. I marveled at how beautiful the bay looked, despite how hard Puerto Ricans tried to pollute it.

It had been an exhilarating outing, and both Marisol and I felt the adrenaline rushing through our veins as we headed back to our room. Around us hordes of young people yelled and screamed in various drunken states. Marisol recognized some from the college, but others were most likely from the area.

"Don't worry," she told me. "They're too drunk to remember anything."

Some were dancing, most of them laughing and having a good time; the more unfortunate puked against walls or lay fetal positioned on cars. It looked and felt like Spring Break.

We went upstairs to our room, showered and changed. I almost asked her to join me in the shower—it was faster after all—but decided against it. Marisol put on a sheer, white jersey dress that hugged her body. The whiteness of the gossamer material made her tanned body stand out more than usual. I stared at her applying her lip gloss, putting on big earrings.

The hotel dance floor was packed, the atmosphere charged with youthful energy. As night morphed into a new day, and my head buzzed with the alcohol we were consuming, I began to notice how other men scanned Marisol's body. I've always considered jealousy a petty, possessive attitude, but I could not help myself. Even as I danced with her, they scoped her vertically, zoomed in on her butt or breasts. Perhaps if I had not drunk as much as I did, perhaps if I knew for sure at the end of the night she would lie naked against my own naked body, I could have laughed away their looks.

At one point, returning with Marisol's Cosmopolitan, a guy was practically nuzzling her neck as he tried talking to her. Her laughter made me angrier. There is nothing more awkward than standing in front of a guy hitting on a woman you're with while you're holding two drinks. I felt like an idiot, a schmuck, a pendejo. It could be mere conversation, but your testosterone and macho pride magnifies the situation, makes you feel like you have barged in on something much more lurid or sexual. Where is the "Dear Abby" for guys on stuff like this? Holding two drinks, like some servant, makes the situation even more demeaning. I know all this sounds immature, but that's how I felt. Perhaps the pent-up hormones had kicked in, I don't know, but seeing this guy, who was attractive, bending over that close to Marisol was too intimate for my liking. Knowing what was going through his mind, making her laugh, it made me feel powerless, like she was slipping away and I could do nothing but watch and feel whatever sense of manhood I had left seep out of me too.

The guy had this smirk that invited a punch in the face. You could tell by his Christian Dior shirt, by how he spoke, by his sense of entitlement and self-worth, that he was a blanquito, the vernacular on the island for upper class and snobby. By now, I was immersed in a thick, stewing anger. When he saw me with the drinks, for the benefit of Marisol and his friends, he made a crack about "our" drinks finally getting here and how slow I had been.

"Your drinks?" I responded, "Sure," then threw them both, along with plastic cups and straws, in his smug face and nice polo.

It was fortunate that Marisol and the guy's friends had been in control, so the scuffle was more separation than fight. I had lost my cool and felt terrible, but just as easily I would have gotten pleasure out of beating the crap out of that guy.

Marisol grabbed my hand and dragged me out of the dance floor and toward the elevators and then threw my hand away out of anger.

"What the hell was that?" she asked, pounding the floor button on the elevator, glaring at me with such a disgusted look that I held my head down in shame.

"He was hitting on you," I said, sheepishly, folding my arms.

She laughed to herself and shook her head.

"Well, he was," I said.

She sprinted out of the elevator. I followed, shuffling my feet, sullen and upset at the guy, at myself.

The night was hard getting through. I sunk into a chair by a corner of the room, watched as she changed into shorts and a tee, heard as she brushed her teeth and did all those things women do at night to stay beautiful.

Right before she slipped under the light bed cover, she stared at me and said, "That was really stupid, Rennie."

I nodded, said softly, "I know."

"I can take care of myself, okay?" After a few minutes she shot up and said, "And, by the way, what difference is it to you?"

She turned off the light, and I remained seated in the same chair, in the dark, the moonlight straining through the window and settling on my body.

As I watched her fall into deep sleep, my eyes sweeping the bed-covers outlining her body's curves, my buzzed mind ran images of our entangled nude bodies making love again.

I stood up and walked over to the balcony. Below, the empty pool gleamed blue under the lights. Farther away, the sea was a blanket of darkness. Besides the occasional distant drunken voice laughing or a car burning rubber, the night was serene.

I now regretted bringing her along. Yes, I deeply regretted making a fool of myself, too, but the incident with the blanquito would not have occurred if I had come alone. Maybe that's what I needed, some alone time to think through all the shit that was coming down on me. But then I thought about the trip here and the fun we both had. Just talking to her was great. Somehow the situation seemed abnormal, unnatural, though. How could we share one room, intimately close, wanting each other, and not get it on? It was insane. It was self-inflicted cruelty. But if we gave in, then what?

I did not know if I could stand kissing her, touching her and not make love to her. On top of everything else, it just seemed to add more weight to all my problems. I began to regret coming to Puerto Rico. Why did I bother? What was there for me here?

She stirred in bed. I turned around and saw her get up on her side. She squinted at me.

"Rennie, come to bed."

I stripped to my underwear and jumped into bed with her. We spooned, my face cradling her hair and neck. She smelled clean and floral, and inhaling her made my skin tingle. I wanted to kiss her so bad. I tightened my arm around her, pushed my hips into her butt and became aroused.

"Behave," she said in a drowsy voice mixed with a little laugh. I laughed into her hair and tossed back on the bed, my fingertips on my chest feeling my heart beating.

Through the night we turned, flipped and flopped, until on one cycle we faced each other. She caressed my cheek and bent in to kiss me. A lingering, soft, wet kiss. From there, our bodies went on automatic, moving in third gear, coasting speed; our passion, fluid, prolonged, graceful.

Outside a young woman sang a muted, drunken bolero, and in the bathing moonlight, we fell into a sweaty, naked embrace.

Fifteen

No one knows for sure when the annual Thanksgiving Family Reunion started, although members from the older generations venture different years. Thanksgiving dinners, always an occasion for the Matos Canales clan—Julia's family—to gather kept growing in number, to the point that the holiday dinner soon evolved into an "event," and before you knew it, flyer invitations were sent out, then emails, to every conceivable relative along the various branches of the family tree announcing the important details for the reunion. At times, family from the States, or South America and Spain, attended. The number of attendees grew, but one tradition remained constant, and that was to rotate the locale every year. This year Hacienda Colibrí, in Lares, was the site, and I headed out to this family property for the second time within a year.

I received a direct, verbal invitation from Julia's parents, my biological maternal grandparents, the first time I had met them. They had chided Julia for "hiding" me. Don Marco and Doña Cruz knew about me but kept silent as to the background of my birth, claiming, perhaps truthfully, that they themselves did not know the entire story. I had been on the island for months, and Julia finally got around to presenting me to them, and for this they were very upset. We drove up to their house in Guaynabo, and at the doorway Julia stood, head hung low, arms crossed, as they gawked at me for minutes and then hugged me. My grandmother held my face in her delicate hands and looked at me with her amber eyes full of tears.

"Dios mío," she said, "he looks so much like your brother Miguel," she said to my grandfather, who examined me with tilted head.

"I was thinking the same thing," he responded. He came over and also embraced me, surprising me with the strength his slight body possessed.

Julia had inherited his eyes, my eyes, equally deep set and piercing.

"I'm not going to welcome you to the family," he said. "Because you were always part of our family."

I just nodded down toward the floor.

"Welcome, home," he added.

When I informed Julia I was bringing Marisol along, this notice was met with some silence, then the question, "Why?"

I didn't want to get into mother-son type conversations with Julia. It bothered me, especially when it came to issues dealing with women I dated. I told her Marisol was my date and that was that. I don't think she was concerned about RSVPs and if there was going to be enough food. My grandparents had told me to bring anyone I liked.

"Don't worry," said my new grandmother, "where two can eat, three can eat," citing a popular refrán, or saying.

In a moment of weakness, I had let it slip that Marisol and I were getting a bit more serious. Julia had met Marisol only once and afterwards suggested she was "mature" for me. "The Cradle Robber," she would joke when referring to her.

More seriously, she asked, "Are you sure she isn't desperate? You know, tick tock."

Maybe there was a grain of truth to this, but those thoughts were dissipating, because I just liked being with her. And what difference did a few years make, anyway? And something I would never tell my biological mother: Marisol confirmed everything any young man had ever praised about a more experienced woman.

On turning to the inclining drive leading to Colibrí, we were met by parked cars lining the sides of the narrow road, a sure sign there would be no parking up hill. Marisol pointed to an empty available space, which I managed to squeeze into, and we walked up to the hacienda. She twisted her arm around mine and held me tightly, at times playfully pulling me down or squeezing my butt.

We reached the house, walked up to the first floor, which had several huge, shutter-type wooden doors, most of them closed. On entering the only opened set, wider than the others, we walked into the salon, where a trio of rattan rocking chairs faced each other. Above, an eighteenth-century iron cast chandelier, electrical sconces now substituting burning candles, swung with the afternoon breeze settling into the high elevation. Inside, there were touches of the hacienda's past, photos of coffee harvesting, a large wooden pilón, a mahogany dining table for ten, an enormous, heavy dish display and other antique furniture. We peered through a locked glass door into a large refrigerated wine cellar, full of bottles stacked neatly on rows of wooden racks. The kitchen retained its original spaciousness, but it was obviously modernized and well-equipped to cook for many mouths.

Marisol went to the bathroom, and I roamed around the house, exploring in more detail sections I had scanned or missed entirely during my previous visit. In one of the parlors, I came across an entire wall of photos, dozens of them, some which had that unmistakable sepia color connoting history. On closer inspection, I realized they were family photos. My family. People I could not name or place if my life depended on it. I squinted and stared, looking for a sign of recognition, resemblance, anything bordering on a connection to these framed ghostly figures. A gallery of nondescript types in unflattering attire who did not appear willing or capable of smiling. Some, I finally noticed, had the striking Matos eyes, which even in a static picture, from decades ago could demand and hold your attention.

"That's the boring branch of your family, Rennie."

I turned around and Doña Cruz was standing at the door, all five feet of her. She was wearing capri pants and neon green sneakers. Her hair set in a chignon. "Hola, abuela," I said, and her amber eyes lit up. On my visit to their home, she was not pleased that I did not call Julia Mom. When Julia had left the room, she looked at me sternly and told me so in crisp but heavily accented English, and then she whispered, "What you call your mother is your business, but if you know what's good for you, you better call me abuela."

She had been an elementary school teacher, a very strict one who never resorted to any physical punishment to gain her students' respect. Julia tells of a time that her mother became incensed over a teacher's paddling a student. After lecturing the colleague and realizing that she could not convince him to change his ways, she simply walked away. But the male instructor made the mistake of mocking her as she headed for the door. Doña Cruz turned on her heels, walked to the man and slapped him hard with the back of her hand, making his lip bleed. Asked about the hypocrisy in this act, she defended herself by saying that he was a man, not a child, and then added, "I was not going to let him ridicule me in front of colleagues." A few days later, his paddle went missing. He accused her, but nothing could be proved. Years later, she became the superintendent of schools in the district and forced the man into retirement. The paddle came in the mail, with his first pension check.

"These are mainly Marco's family. Sad group, don't you agree?" I nodded.

"Now, my family, there you have the real characters." She pointed to a photo of a stout man with laughing eyes. "That was my father, Jorge Canales, your great-grandfather. Fought for independence, first against the Spanish then the Americans. In his last years, founded orphanages throughout the western part of the island."

She pointed to the woman next to him. "My stepmother. A good woman, but not very loving."

She looked up, searching the wall. "My mother," she said, her voice fading as she continued searching for a picture. "There," she pointed to a portrait of a slender, young woman with a sad face. "Get it for me, Rennie."

I retrieved the photo, set in a beautiful wooden frame. She dusted it off and held it lovingly in her hands.

"She died of tuberculosis when I was two," she said, and forced a smile. "Your great-grandmother." I nodded and mumbled, "Thanks," not completely knowing why.

Through the photos, she introduced me to other members of her family. An Uncle Paco who ran off to sea and never came back, the camera capturing him looking away, distracted; a somber Manolín, months before he joined a circus; Aunt Matilde, demure in a frilly dress, who eventually turned to men's clothing and chewing tobacco; a brother, David, manufacturer and distributor of "pitorro" or Puerto Rican moonshine, mugging it up for the camera. He went off to Korea and got killed. Before leaving, she showed me a photo of Miguel, my grandfather's brother, and my resemblance to him was indeed uncanny, scary almost. Except he was much better looking.

"He was the youngest, un enamorao, a skirt chaser," Abuela said, "until he found the love of his life, who destroyed him."

"What do you mean?"

"He lost her and drank himself to death."

I leaned forward to get a closer look at Miguel, trying to find insight into that type of self-consuming passion.

"That's the past, Rennie," she told me as she hooked her arm around mine. "Let's go meet the living, okay?" She turned off the lights in the room and shut the door.

Downstairs, the music erupted. A trio had been hired; the older folks had decided on the music, much to the disappointment of the younger members of the clan. They set up quickly and began their repertoire of ballads and up-tempo oldies. During the breaks a DJ was promised to play hip hop for the youngsters. The music inaugurated and invigorated the activities. Where before folks wandered about, huddled in isolated bunches, now the music brought people closer to the center, where a large tent harbored long tables. The caterers stepped up their activity, shuttling heavy trays of food to the waiting Sterno burners. To the side, a pig roasted on a spit, to the amazement of the children. Nearby, one of the cooks attended to a big vat full of boiling oil, in which a turkey was being fried. Family dogs were brought along, the younger ones excitable with the commotion, while the older canines escaped to a shady corner.

Abuela led me to the balcony, from where we had a good view of the activity.

Round tables and folding chairs laid out on a wide clearing accommodated the approximately sixty people in attendance. Behind a sturdy bar, two young women moved like dervishes taking orders, mixing, lining up shots of Bacardi and Barrelito, uncorking wine, throwing ice in glasses, popping beer bottles. A photographer roamed around, cameras hanging from his neck, snapping pictures and joking with his subjects. He avoided bumping into the videographer, who didn't enjoy competing for shots. Both gravitated to a skinny young man in cargo pants, presumably a cousin, holding a parrot on his forearm. Video Guy told Camera Guy to hurry up and take his stupid pictures so he could work. The latter, less serious and having more fun, said something humorous and dismissive and snapped away.

The bird, a twelve-inch beauty, flapped its green wings and preened itself, stretching its neck and head feathers. Its eyes, encircled in white and peering over the red band above its beak, looked on quizzically at everyone staring at him. It was an iguaca, or Puerto Rican parrot, a critically endangered species.

Abuela noticed that Don Marco was sipping beer. "That man is going to kill himself with his bad habits. He shouldn't be drinking."

She went off after him, urging me to come down. I wondered if I could ever begin to connect to any of these people below— people whose genetic material I partially shared—in any meaningful way. So many of them, family yet strangers. Marisol interrupted my reverie as she slid her hand under my T-shirt and ran her fingernails halfway down my back. She joined me in a moment looking down at all the movement.

"It's a circus down there," she said. "Let's get something to eat, I'm starving."

Heading toward the food tent, Julia grabbed me. She had drunk a few glasses of wine. "Do you mind if I borrow my baby for a minute?" She directed this to Marisol, but didn't wait for an answer.

"Get me some food," I yelled back to her as Julia dragged me to meet her siblings.

This first encounter initiated a series of unfortunate introductions. "This is your nephew," she said to Tere, the youngest, living in Barcelona with her husband, the banker; and Justin, an accountant like his father, who relished every bit the role of eldest son. They looked at me like a specimen, pulling back their craned heads while nodding in agreement or in a dumb affirmation of reality.

Later, Julia told me she had prepared most of the closest relatives. This would account for their lack of surprise, but what their faces expressed was a mystery. The siblings did not necessarily look pleased or dismayed; their expressions mostly resembled bored indifference.

"Buenas," said Justin, and then added something like welcome to the family, while extending a hairy, pale hand.

I stared at his bespectacled pale, stubbled face and his little, crooked teeth as he smiled. "Gracias," I answered and walked toward the food.

Julia grabbed me again. "Wait, I want to introduce you to other people."

"Can't that wait, I'm famished here." She smirked and relented. "I'll tell them to go say hi where you're eating."

Great, I thought, meeting the family hordes while trying to enjoy a meal. "At least he's tall and good looking," I heard Tere say as I walked away.

Marisol had set me up with a hearty plate of food. We were both hungry and started digging into the food. The drinks, and perhaps the sun, had us a bit buzzed, and we were enjoying each other's company.

And then the steady procession of family members began. First, Don Marco came over and almost squeezed the food out of me. Slaps to the back pushed me forward, and if Marisol had not held on to me, I would have fallen. He had this deep, donkey-type laugh, that Marisol imitated all through our ride back and had me cracking up. Then came the uncles, aunts, some of whom just found out about this mysterious grandnephew. They welcomed me but, even with my young age, I knew that on the drive back home they would gossip—or in the local vernacular, pelar, peel poor Julia, who drank another glass of wine, talking to her parents. A conversation with few words. Both grandparents stood stiff, arms crossed. She looked so alone. Suddenly, I didn't think this was some torture I had to endure. Poor Julia, I thought.

The older cousins, who came over with their spouses or significant others, threw languid stares at me, made empty promises about hanging out, traded cell phone numbers, all a shallow show of familial solidarity. For the teen cousins, I had become a novelty. I was the main attraction in an otherwise dreary, traditionally boring event that they were expected to attend ever year. They asked unabashedly stupid and ignorant questions like if I lived in a ghetto or if I had a girlfriend, with Marisol sitting next to me. Or comment something along the lines, "Wow, this must suck for you. I would die." I wondered how politicians kept up with meeting so many people, kissing babies and such, grasping so many strange hands. I was exhausted, drained. I was so glad that Marisol came along. She grounded me, made me laugh, told me to take it all in stride—deja que te resbale, she quipped, "Let it all slide off you."

After meeting Juanco, the cousin with the parrot, and his attractive girlfriend, Marisol took advantage of the interest that Iggy the bird had stirred and grasped my hand. We ran off into the wooded areas behind the house. Earlier she had spotted a small creek and wanted to show it to me. We ran like children down an incline toward the bubbling water.

Out of breath, we threw ourselves on the ground.

We stayed like that for a while, peeking through the branches to get a glimpse of sunlight, the heat on our faces feeling wonderful. The gurgling of the creek soothed us, made us drowsy.

Marisol sighed, and said, "This is fabulous." Like two blind lovers, our solitary hands searched for each other and clasped.

"This is kinda cheesy," I said, and we started laughing.

She let go my hand and swatted me. "It's romantic," she said, fake pouting, still laughing.

I turned to her and kissed her. She bent at her waist and grabbed the back of my neck, returning the kiss. She pulled me on top of her, my face buried in her neck. I breathed in the mix of perspiration and floral soap. Just when she wrapped her legs around me as we continued kissing, a gaggle of children stomped toward us, screeching. We jumped, startled at the screaming and running but also embarrassed.

The grandchildren and some of the teen cousins led by Juanco were rambling down the hill toward the creek, and us, their heads up to the sky. Juanco, in particular, was frantic, trying to run forward with his gangly legs, looking back and yelling at his girlfriend, who was crying. He kept looking up, and I realized Iggy was not with them.

"The parrot ran away," I told Marisol.

"Oh, no, your poor cousin," she said.

"Poor Iggy," I said.

We both started scouring the branches, and soon we joined the posse looking for Iggy. A few minutes later, a few of the older folk came down to search.

I spotted him on a low branch of a ceiba and pointed to Marisol. Iggy bobbed up and down on the branch, whistling and making strange sounds. I told Marisol to get the others and tell them to be quiet. "Don't do something stupid," she said with a worried look on her face.

"Don't worry, I'm an expert tree climber."

"Are you serious?"

"Just get the others."

I had been climbing trees up to my teen years, and although rusty, it wasn't a hard tree to climb. I loved sitting on a branch on a cool day. Mami would tease me and called me monkey boy. I took my shoes and socks off, secured a good footing and pulled myself up to the branch, which was no more than ten feet from the ground. A sturdy branch, one that could support both bird and man. I sat at the edge closest to the trunk.

Iggy kept bobbing, but less so now, his quizzical eyes staring at me. I didn't move, trying not to scare him off. "Hey there, Iggy," I said, in that sing-song way one talks to a baby. By then, a crowd had gathered below, their eyes gaping at me and Iggy. Juanco looked like he was crying, his hands wrung together in prayer-like fashion. His girlfriend, distraught, stood behind him, biting her fingernails, her eyes red and raw.

"I know," I whispered to Iggy, "they're assholes." I tried to soothe him, patted the branch beside me, lay my hand on it. He approached me cautiously. When he was close enough I patted his neck feathers with two fingers, and he let me. I put out my wrist and he stepped up onto it, as he was obviously trained to do. I caressed his feathers, soothing him with my voice so as not to fly away again. I could have stayed up there with Iggy for a while. It was peaceful and isolated. The wind blew away all our worries.

I had no plan how to get down a tree while holding on to a bird. Luckily, one of the uncles had the intelligence to get an extension ladder from the house. I took off my shirt and managed to cradle Iggy in it, while they shot the ladder up to the branch. Juanco climbed up the ladder and took down the bird swathed in my shirt. The crowd cheered, surrounding Juanco and Iggy, and off they went back to the festivities.

I sat on the branch for a few minutes. Marisol climbed halfway up the ladder.

"Ingrates," she said, "that little snot didn't even thank you."

I shrugged my shoulders. "Why don't you come up?"

She gave me a dirty look as she hugged the middle of the ladder. "Come down. Let's go home."

That was the best thing I had heard all day.

We walked back, arms around each other's waists. My shoulders and legs ached a bit, and I had to admit my tree climbing days were over.

When we returned, I received my shirt back, which now had Iggy's droppings. A little souvenir to say thank you, traitor, I guess. Julia came over with a tied dye T-shirt she had found somewhere and handed it to me. Iggy was now in his cage. Julia told me Juanco worked for the DRNA, the island's natural resources agency, and thought it would be cool to bring one of the parrots to the family reunion.

"For the kids," she said with a smirk, "but it was all to impress his girlfriend." The girlfriend wanted to hold the bird and, once on her wrist, she panicked when the bird started pecking at her arm. When she screamed and shook her arms, Iggy took off.

"You saved Juanco his job," Julia told me. "I'm very proud of you."

"I did it for the bird," I said.

She nodded and wrapped one arm around mine. Mari had gone to get some leftovers for the road.

"You don't mind if I steal you away from your babysitter for a while, do you?"

"Come on, Julia."

Laughing, she steered me into the shade under a Royal Poinciana, and then stared at me. "Okay, all jokes aside," she continued. "Where's this going with Marisol?"

"Why does it matter to you?"

She exhaled, looked up, returning that heavy gaze on me. "Seriously, René. How can you ask me that?"

"Ah, jeez. I didn't mean you don't have the right . . . "

She shook her head vigorously. "I'm asking because I'm concerned. Is that wrong?"

"No, no, it's not." Glaring into those eyes was like staring into a mirror. "It's kinda nice, actually."

"René, I know it's hard to have a mother come out of nowhere. I get that. But it's hard for me, too," she said, tapping her chest, "to have to *earn* a son's love, *every day*." She stood staring at me with a confused, pleading face, her hand now on her hip.

"I'm good with Mari, okay?"

"Okay, but don't think age doesn't matter. It does."

I didn't want to hear it, partly because she was probing into an area I had visited several times. But Mari and I were in a good place. Why spoil it with these gnawing thoughts?

"Thanks for bringing me to the reunion," I said, trying to change the subject.

"If I hadn't, your grandparents would have skinned me alive," she responded, laughing, pushing back a loose strand of hair. "But, I'm glad too," she added, holding my hand, squinting into the setting sun.

"You know, meeting all this family, I thought it would change something."

She sighed, her back sliding down against the tree trunk, until she sat. I sat down by her, and we both glanced back at the crowd of relatives milling about.

"They say you can't choose your family," she said.

"I don't mean to complain or anything. I just thought finding them would, I don't know, give me some insight into myself."

"It doesn't work like that, m'ijo." She tossed her hair and wrapped her arms around her knees. "I was always the black sheep in this family."

"Really?"

"Oh, yeah. The rebel, the political activist, the feminist. The law student who got knocked up." She ripped a handful of grass and tossed it. "My parents thought I was starving for attention, but I was just living out my restless life, my way."

She put her hand over her eyes. The ranks among the relatives were thinning out. You could hear goodbyes, the slamming of car doors, the ignition of car engines.

"Roots can ground you," Julia said, quickly turning to me. "But they can strangle you, too."

"The photo gallery was cool, though," I said.

"Sure. Family history fills the gaps," she said, shaking her head. "But in the end, it's just a bunch of dusty pictures of dead people, René."

She gripped my hand tight.

I nodded.

The evening sun shot orange streamers across the sky. Led by Justin, my uncle, a few relatives picked up guitars and four-stringed cuatros and entertained the others. Before that, the classically trained Matos and Canales crew showed off their expensive music lessons with a Bach fugue here or Mozart sonata there. During one of the musical numbers, Cuco, a German Shepard, sat down to chew on something resembling a curving bone. His owner, a cousin third removed, took it from him with some struggle. The strangeness of the artifact intrigued those gathered, and speculation began as to whether it was human or not. Magi, a cousin twice removed, and a graduate student in archaeology, wondered if it was a piece of Taíno hip belt used in ceremonial ballgame which the Indians played.

"It's clearly not a bone," she said, although Wiso had another opinion.

"Who cares about the Taínos," a drunken distant cousin yelled. "All they gave us was barbeque." Laughter. Someone yells, "Not a bad idea right now. I'm hungry."

Magi wrapped the artifact in a towel, stashed it in her bag. Wiso whined, and she rewarded him with a leftover piece of turkey.

Julia asked me to stay with the few family members who remained a bit longer, but I declined. We hadn't packed for a longer stay, I said, glad that we hadn't thought of bringing a change of clothing, something we usually did on our outings.

I ached to leave and started to kiss my grandparents goodbye, when the photographer declared time for the family photo. Of course, I felt obligated, so I promised Marisol we would leave right after that. It was a burdensome production. First, to cut down numbers, telling non family people to get out of the frame, then trying to squeeze everyone into the shot. Even with his panoramic lens, he had problems. Finally, he had to go on the balcony to take several shots.

We gave our goodbyes to everyone present. Just when we started the car, an older female cousin appeared on the balcony. Waving her hands, she yelled, "Aunt Luz did it again!"

Julia laughed and peeked into the car. "Every year Aunt Luz takes down the photo of her sister, Blanca, from the gallery and hides it somewhere on the property." She shrugged. "It's a long story," she said, and with that joined the others in what had become the inadvertent traditional family scavenger hunt to find the purloined photo of Tía Blanca.

We waved, both of us happy to leave. But Marisol made me stop at the Lares Heladería, where she had the rice and bean ice cream combo, and I just had strawberry. We wanted to rush back because the work had piled up, now that the strike was over and classes had resumed. But as luck would have it, we hit a traffic jam on 129. An angry motorist had shot a cow after he had hit it. Both his car and the dead bovine blocked the roadway, and he refused to move his car if he was going to be charged for killing the animal.

"I was trying to put it out of its misery," he kept yelling. But he was having a hard time convincing the officers, who thought his true intention was revenge for the damage it had done to his Mercedes.

Sixteen

Normally, at three o'clock on a Friday, I'd be home or in the car with Marisol riding a blue highway hugging the side of the Cordillera, heading to one of our hideaways. A beach tucked in some cranny of the island or a favorite bar or restaurant lost deep in the interior. Anywhere but in my office. But there was nothing normal about the last week of Fall semester classes. Craziness creeps in everywhere. Colleagues review rosters, prepare final exams, evaluate student essays they should have returned a month ago. All of this while attending to the various meetings and responsibilities that pile up at semester's end. And everyone is dying for classes to end, to go home and rest from mental and physical exhaustion, to enjoy the holidays.

Meanwhile, students deemed M.I.A. came down from the hills begging for some "consideration."

"Who are you?" I asked one, not facetiously.

The student then proceeded to tell me his life story, the problems had, the troubles seen.

A young woman cried, tears streaking down her face because she "just can't fail this class."

"But you only attended the first week of classes," I said, shocked.

Another came in with her parents for support. "My daughter is a good girl," the mother affirmed.

"I'm sure she is, Señora Estofona, but she is not a good student," I replied, pointing to the missing quizzes, tests, assignments, the rather poor record her good daughter had accumulated.

"Ay bendito, profesor," I heard a lot. "Consideración."

Yes, I considered you to be an awfully irresponsible individual with big cojones who had no business entering a college classroom. That's what I would have loved to say, but I didn't. I smiled and wished her luck and told her I would take it under consideration, noting in my mind the big F she was going to receive.

After dealing with students and grades, I then had to deal with Roque. After grades were posted, performance reviews were reported, the results of the evaluations and the recommendations that would be sent to the Institutional Personnel Committee. A Friday afternoon before the Christmas break, Roque scheduled me last. Deciding to do the adjuncts ahead of me, something that Micco told me was unprecedented.

Before my appointment with Roque, Stiegler came out of his office, smiling broadly and gave me a double thumbs up. Tenured, and not up for promotion, Micco was nowhere to be seen.

One of the adjuncts walked briskly by. It wasn't a picnic for them either. Some needed this job, along with two other jobs at local colleges, to make ends meet.

My thoughts were interrupted by a skinny young man with skeletal cheekbones. I recognized him as Martín Costa, a student who brought religion into every discussion we had on any subject and drew crosses on his exams and papers for good luck. The students disliked him and rolled their eyes almost in unison every time he took the floor. He was forever cheerful, which made it worse. He threw his Pollyannaish smile at me, and I asked if I could help him.

"No, I came to give deese," he said, handing me religious material.

"That's okay, Martín," I said, giving the brochures back to him.

"You take, read, good for you."

"You should give it to someone who will read them. I'll just throw'em in the trash can, honestly."

At this he looked at me perturbed, a bit bothered. This was his latest attempt to convert me, to convince me that my soul would go to hell unless I accepted Jesus, and he liked me too much to let that happen to me. Touching as that was, I told him he needed to respect everyone's individual position on religion. That in a university, diverse opinions are the norm, or should be.

Here he was again, this time with reading material. He rattled off all his religious jargon in that soft, preachy tone, and I just could not take it anymore. So young and so smug, so arrogant in his dogmatism. Normally, I would let him talk himself out and thank him for his concerns, claim to be busy and wave him out of my office. But today was not a normal day. Soon I had to face Roque and his pasty, pockmarked, glaring face, relishing what he would have to tell me.

I raised my hand for Martín to stop. "Let me ask you a question," I said.

His face lit up, excited that he had finally reached me, that I seemed interested in the possibility of conversion and salvation.

"Are you planning on being up in heaven?"

"Sí, to be with our Lord Jesus."

"Well, you know what. If you're gonna be there, I don't want to be. Now take this stuff off my desk and get out."

Stunned, he grabbed the religious pamphlets, but before leaving me, he turned around and said, "I will pray for you."

"Great, you do that."

I felt bad as soon as he left. That was uncalled for, I thought. Even if I just couldn't take him anymore. I was going after him to apologize, when Nitza called me to tell me Roque was ready for me.

I entered the sterile office and sat down on the opposite uncomfortably hard chair. He sat there, hands folded on the desk, a concerned look on his face. He cleared his throat a couple of times, took a sip from a bottle of water. I sensed that he was not enjoying this, found it unpleasant, and that gave me fleeting hope that he retained some sense of humanity.

"How are you today, Professor Falto?"

Why did these rituals always begin with an attempt at civility?

"I could be better."

A vague smile, and he opened the long green cardboard folder.

"Well, you know we have had some discrepancies in your evaluation."

He stared at me, and I nodded. He seemed prepared to go into some long justification. I already knew his methods, having spent more time than I wanted in that office, listening to him talk and talk.

I stopped him before he could begin. "Doctor Roque, please just tell me the Outside Committee's results."

Narrowing his eyebrows to construct that charming unibrow, while the edges spread out ready for flight, he slid the paperwork toward me.

"I see that they recommended renewal," I said with a smile. "Unanimously."

"That's their opinion. My recommendation is to terminate your contract."

"Well, I guess we have another discrepancy of opinion." I looked at him hard. "What now?"

"This case will go to the Institutional Personnel Committee. It's in their hands."

"That's it?"

"You can write a rebuttal to my recommendation if you want. You have a week from today to do so. Good luck." His lips pursed, he stared at me defiantly.

I stood up to leave.

"By the way, Professor Falto . . . " he signaled for me to close the door I had just opened. I did. "Your little relationship with Professor Santerrequi . . . " He shook his head, his fingertips tapping on his lap. "Ill-advised."

I bent over the desk to face him squarely.

"I came here to discuss my performance review, Doctor Roque, not my private life. Are we done?"

"She's deluded this is going somewhere. Be honest, be a man and stop playing with her."

I didn't know what to say. The audacity shocked the hell out of me. I just shook my head and stumbled out the office, slamming the door as I did.

The music woke me up. I had fallen asleep reading. After leaving Roque's office, I sat down to write that rebuttal to his recommendation. This was my first sentence: *Dr. Roque is a vicious, ignorant, biased asshole and his recommendation cannot be taken any more seriously than his wardrobe.*

I thought it best to stop there and give it a little distance. Perhaps all the tension was more than I could handle. I felt exhausted, anxious, yet somewhat relieved to put down on paper what I really thought, even if I would not use it.

I dozed off again. And the music, festive and loud, broke me out of it. Marisol had told me about the lighting of the Christmas tree. A big event, everyone turns out. I thought it was a bit late to light up a tree, relative to the States.

"Christmas goes on longer here," she told me. The Christmas spirit lasted until mid-February, in fact.

I had nothing to do, so after throwing some water on my face and brushing my teeth, I walked over to the little plaza with the fountain in front of the administration building. Every year they decorated with lights the same tree, an enormous spruce that the Army had planted decades ago. Earlier in the day, I had seen groundskeepers on a hydraulic lift doing the honors.

There was a substantial crowd when I arrived at the site, a short distance from the Guest House, where I still uneasily resided. Most of those gathered tended to be students. There was a smattering of professors, many staff, administrative people and their children. I didn't see Marisol, who would have had to drive from San Juan, or any of the other English faculty.

The highlight at this year's lighting was the Tuna de la Guácara, a musical group organized at the college almost at the same time as the founding of the institution. Forty-something years later they had become an institution themselves, recording many records and giving concerts all over the world. This year, they had decided to celebrate their success by coming home. Their specialty seemed to be Puerto Rican Christmas tunes, which ran from the religious to the bawdy. They were draped in their traditional yellow capes—in the Spanish style, I'm told. It was a big group and they appeared in stride, clapping hands, playing guitars and other stringed and percussive instruments, putting everyone present in a party mood.

They stopped, and the rector waddled to a little podium made tinier by his massive presence. He gave thanks to the group and said a few words about tradition, yadda, yadda, yadda. He turned on the switch and the tree was magnificent. Such a minor thing, and I felt warm and fuzzy inside. I thought about the happy Christmases in Jersey. My parents went all out and, being an only child, I was spoiled rotten. My heart ached, and I missed them so much. Will this ever end, I thought. This inconsolable pain, this inexpressible loss, only needing a memory to light it up like this Christmas tree.

"Pretty fine tree, isn't it?"

I looked to my right and I was surprised to see Foley, who had crept up on me from somewhere out of the amassed bodies.

"Yes, it is—great lights."

I stared at him and if I stared hard enough, I could see right through him. He sure was pale enough. How, I wondered, could anyone live in the tropics and not get some shading of sun, a little bit of brown. It was chilly out, as it often gets in Baná during this time of year. Being at a higher altitude, the town gets cooler at night and early in the morning, although rarely dipping lower than the mid-sixties. Coming from the New York City area, I just didn't see the need for a jacket or sweater in this type of weather. Foley had on a light, hooded windbreaker. But, then, he didn't perspire.

"Not Rockefeller Center," I said, "but it'll do."

For the first time, I saw his stark, blue eyes twinkle, and he smiled, not a bad one either. He had great teeth, intense white and even, not small.

"Not a very fair comparison, is it?"

I shrugged. "I suppose."

"You're going to drive yourself crazy, you keep comparing—it's a different world, Falto. Take it from me. I've been here for over twenty-five years."

"And why are you telling me this?"

He was surprised at my question, doing something like a double take. His head slanted and his grin turned into a disbelieving

smirk. Like he was giving me pearls of wisdom, and maybe I was
being swinish.

"Well, for starters, because you're having real problems adjust-
ing, aren't you?"

"That the official line?"

He grabbed my elbow and pulled me under a nearby tree, dis-
tancing us from the nearest group of people. He glared at me, his
steel blue eyes locking onto mine. When he did this, his entire
demeanor changed. He became another person, somebody who
got your attention and maybe inspired fear despite being average
height and slight of build.

"Look, I'm on your side."

He stared at me again, and for some reason I believed him. I
nodded and he let go of my elbow.

"Roque has it out for you, no doubt about that," he said in a low
voice, turning his head to make sure no one was around. "But it's
so blatant, it's pathetic, and he doesn't have enough people on the
Institutional Committee."

"How do you know?"

"Because I'm the chair of the committee," he said with his nice
smile. "In fact, he's becoming a bit of a nuisance." He put his
hands in the windbreaker's pockets and looked up at the brilliant
tree, toward the tuna which had gathered again for one last song.

"Just don't worry about it," he reassured me. He was about to
walk away.

"Foley," I yelled. He turned around. "Why?" I asked.

"Why what?" he said, leaning in toward me from the distance.

"Why are you helping me?"

He smiled even more broadly, tugged at his ear. "It's the American way, isn't it?" Then, he got lost in the crowd.

The music continued playing, way after the tuna had packed
and left, piping out of gigantic speakers supplied by the college,
and it flowed into the next week, and the next, until every day
blurred into one long, ongoing party.

Meanwhile, I struggled to write my "defense." That's what colleagues called it. "Rennie, how's it coming along, tu defensa." As if
I had been accused of some charge and needed to clear my name

and reputation. As if I was some criminal and needed to defend myself.

>*Illustrious Members of the Most Respectful Institutional Personnel Committee, I am innocent of all charges that have been levied against me by this administrative tyrant, Dr. Roque, who clearly has lost his mind after being dumped—and who can blame her—by his ex-wife.*

Foley's words served as comfort, but I didn't know how much weight they held. What if Roque swayed enough members of that committee—my academic career would be shorter than some Hollywood marriages. It seemed so unfair. I was beginning to like the students, feel like I was making a difference, actually teaching them.

>*I throw myself at the mercy of this Honorable Committee—the students' evaluations speak for themselves. Have a heart, people. Isn't this evaluation supposed to help me become better?*

I was struggling with la defensa when Marisol called to remind me about the big Christmas bash. Every year the rector threw a big party. No matter how bad the economy and the financial state of the institution, there was always money for partying.

"In the time-honored Puerto Rican tradition," Micco would say. "Baile, botella y baraja," or "dance, bottle and cards." Attributed to a Spanish governor, it was like his official governing policy, the idea being to keep the natives happy and distracted so they wouldn't rebel.

Marisol sensed my hesitancy. "Oh c'mon, you need to get out." True, I thought. "What about the defense," I said.

"How long can that take to write?"

>*Honorable Committee Members, I write these short lines to beg for more time to write my defensa—thanks to my girlfriend, whose name I must keep in secrecy, given the ridiculously conservative attitudes . . .*

Juanqui y Los Muchachos were in full swing when I arrived at the cafeteria, the site of the college Christmas party. Marisol and I agreed to come separately, even though it appeared as if everyone in the college knew about us. The band played a lively merengue, which got people up to dance. The dance floor was packed with faculty members "brillando la hebilla," or "polishing the belt buckle," as Mami used to say. Weird seeing intellectual gray heads dancing. Surreal, like an old episode of *Twilight Zone*. Everyone decked out in their best, the women had spent hours at the "beauty," and the men had dusted off their suits and ties. Lots of satin and linen running around.

I spotted the English table and Marisol. Our eyes met, and she gave me that little twisted, wicked smile of hers, which meant "happy to see you" and "you're looking good." I dislike suits but the occasion called for it, so here I was wearing the only one I owned, a tailor-made suit picked up on one of the family travels to Milan, and a skinny tie, because I hate the fat ones. Mami persuaded me to get it done.

"When will you get this opportunity again," she said. She got me on that alone, but it didn't hurt that she offered to pay half. That was a few years ago, and it fit me well.

I had to admit I felt great, despite all the crap coming down on me. Tonight, I thought, I can forget about Roque—who fortunately sat with friends somewhere else—and get lost in baile, botella y baraja.

"You should wear suits more often," Marisol said, pulling my tie, as I sat down next to her.

I laughed. "I'm already dying to take this one off."

She bent over and whispered "Okay, later I can help you out of it."

I grabbed her hand and took her to the dance floor, me, the once apprehensive dancer. I had become better since hanging with Marisol. My spastic feet tapping had evolved into more fluid, rhythmic steps.

"There's hope for you, Falto," she teased.

I complimented her on her dress, a full length, red formal with a low-cut back. The silky material clung to her curves like a novice driver on a mountain highway. "Splendorous" was the word that came to my mind.

The night floated along, one merengue after another, from salsa to cha cha, one conversation after another, drink following drink, and then the moment of zen came when, seated around most of my colleagues, I realized that during the course of the evening I had heard gossip about everyone seated at the table. Freddie had connived in winning a system-wide grant to study theater in Cuba, although he did not teach the subject and certainly not theater in Spanish. The truth, I was informed in a whisper, was he had a lover living in Cuba, and this was a way to get back to him.

Micco, according to the grapevine, had gotten one of his undergraduate girlfriends pregnant. Roque insisted that Micco had the habit of sleeping with female students. When this came to me, disgusted, I almost approached him, but Marisol told me that it was a complete fabrication. Roque, she told me, had the bad habit of spreading malicious rumors and ugly gossip without evidence. He had marked several professors on campus with this gossip already.

"He means well, to protect students in the college, but he gets carried away."

No shit, I thought.

Rita Gómez didn't come, a rarity, because although shy and demure, she loved to dance and party and never missed an event. She had made me promise her a dance. The word was that she had taken ill.

Talk of infidelities, corruption, crimes and misdemeanors. Departmental intrigues, institutional failures, dirty college politics. And so it went in the world of the humanities. It had become stifling in the cafeteria, what with all the talk and people, so I stepped outside for fresh air. I sat on one of the cement benches, legs crossed Indian style, and watched three students kick a hacky sack around. I was about to stroll over and ask to join them, when Marisol strode up to me.

"What you doing out here?"

"Just getting fresh air."

"You could have told me. I thought you'd left."

"Sorry, couldn't take all the b.s. flying around in there." She nodded and sat down next to me. "Speaking of bullshit, you know what Roque told me?"

Marisol sat down next to me. "What?"

"To stay away from you."

She looked at me, stunned.

"Yeah, you heard right," I said.

"When was this?"

"During my performance review." My eyes bobbed up and down, watching the guys kick around the footbag. Basic stuff, delays, one of them trying to do a flying inside.

"That prick."

"Said you're deluded to think this is going somewhere—that I'm using you."

"What did you tell him?"

"What else? To mind his own fucking business."

Her eyes widened.

I laughed. "Well, not exactly like that. I had my work mouth on."

There was an extended moment of silence—never a good sign. She picked at her dress, staring at the ground. The guys had a good round going without dropping the bag.

"Yeah, he's nosey," she finally said.

They dropped it, and then came the usual cascade of shouts and laughter.

She stood up to return inside, then did a turnaround, like she was lost. I jumped up and grabbed her arm.

"You know what? I think I'm going home," she said, looking at my arm holding hers.

"Whoa," I said, "what's going on?"

She went inside, retrieved her purse and passed me on the way back to her car. It seemed like a mile to her car in that silence. Her mood had changed, and I couldn't help thinking that anywhere Roque's name popped up, it was like a toxin, contaminating every-thing and everyone.

"Mari, did I do something wrong?"

I went to caress her face, but she held my hand and started to cry.

"Hey, what's the matter?"

"Nothing, that's the point," she said. "Nothing has happened or will happen with us."

"Don't say that, c'mon. You letting Roque get to us?"

"It's not about Roque, dammit. It's you, it's you."

I was looking at her looking at me with those big brown eyes, all teary, and minutes later I was wondering what the fuck had happened. The evening had started out great and suddenly I was hearing all this negative stuff.

"What do you mean, it's me?"

"It's me, too."

"Mari, you're losing me here."

"Pedro is right—I'm fucking deluding myself."

"No, no. We've come a long way."

"Long way to what, Rennie? And, where are we going with this?"

How could I answer that? I didn't know the answer to that one. I just didn't. And maybe I didn't want to answer. Didn't want to be pushed to answer.

Silence at the most inopportune times is a death warrant. She slipped into the car, slammed the door and drove away.

> *Dear Committee Members, due to an unforeseen development, I beseech you to please bring down on me the harshest punishment allowed by this venerable institution. Quartering seems particularly and metaphorically appropriate at this time. . . .*

Walking the streets can be an antidote for the blues. After Marisol drove off, I went back and gulped a whisky with soda. I'm not the guy who's going to sit and drink all night because his girl's gone—not that guy. But I needed a jolt. Then, I had to walk, somewhere, anywhere, didn't matter as long as I moved toward something and away from everything.

My meandering took me up hilly Altavista, past the hospedajes, the private buildings housing students, the closest thing to dorms in the area. It was quiet, with the kids gone for Christmas break. Or wasted, watching mindless films, or becoming numb playing video games, who could tell? It was late, but I had lost track of time, had no watch and didn't care to know the time. But it felt late.

I spotted the corner that held my parents' house. The house was brilliant with Christmas lights and ornaments. Cheap, tacky-as-hell, bought at a bargain basement. I could not find solace in their tackiness. Could not find satisfaction in laughing at their stupid attempt at festive happiness. Because they were happy. Squatters, yet they had the audacity to fix up the place like they had a right to it, a right to domestic bliss, a sense of home that they could adorn and decorate.

Their inside lights were off and their battered Corolla was gone, so they were off spending their government check on more Christmas cheer—anything but paying their rent.

I ran to the side of the house facing the corner, jumped up and grabbed a fistful of lights. They came down, crashing to the ground. For good measure, I stomped on them, delighting in popping them into a pulp. Down came the twinkly small lights, the Three Kings ornament, wishing I had a sledgehammer to smash the entire house down. Lights turned on across from me, and I started to run down the steep hill, stumbled and tore a hole at the knee in my pants, cursing the Riveras under my breath.

Who knows how many winding side streets I walked before finding one I knew. Hobbling now, my knee hurting. A young woman walking in front of me turned, startled. She clutched a canister of pepper spray. She saw me and relaxed. Green-Eyed Girl.

"What happened to your leg?" she asked, looking down at my torn pant legs.

"I'm okay," I said. "You're out late."

"Yeah, coming back from a party. You mind walking me back to my hospedaje?"

"Sure, if you don't mind me limping along."

At her door, she thanked me, and I said "no problem." She hesitated and told me she could help me with the knee, but I said not to bother, I was close to the Guest House. And she glanced my way, sending that look any guy with decent radar can read. Any other situation, it would not have been easy to turn her down. She, too, looked splendorous in her mini skirt and high heels, her hair dazzling around her stunning face, her green eyes crackling with unspent energy and passion. Oh, so easy to get lost there, I thought. To get lost and forget myself in this young woman's desire, that bronzed body, soft and voluptuous.

I grinned stupidly. "Good night," I said, struggling on my descent to La Tirilla. From where I stood, the campus Christmas tree shone brightly and lonely.

That night it was easy to say no. Because with every pained step I took, another answer kept surging in my head, and with such pain I knew it had come too late.

Back at the Guest House, I replayed a message from Julia. A long one. Her voice a bit slurred. In the background, upbeat voices and music. The office party she had invited me to. She called to invite me for Christmas dinner.

"Just you and me." The phrase laced with loneliness and sadness.

I called back to accept. "I'd like that," I said. "Just you and me, Julia."

Seventeen

The Christmas ball was huge, and clear, more like a crystal ball to my young eyes, although much lighter. I held it in front of my eyes, panning it, and through the open areas that did not have the special silver trimming, I could see through it, getting a kick out of the blurry, distortions of my mother and grandparents, and everything else in their apartment living room. It was like looking at circus mirrors.

"Okay, Rennie, give me the ball," my mother said.

I handed it to her, carefully, because this was one of the early Christmas decorations my parents had bought together to celebrate the holiday as a family, after I had been born. Mami put it in a prominent area of the tree, a big beautiful fir. I liked closing my eyes and breathing in its piney scent that blended with the smells of the pernil and other holiday foods drifting from Güeli's kitchen to make that Puerto Rican aroma of Christmas, so distinct and memorable.

It was probably a week or so after Thanksgiving, the traditional time to trim the tree. Mami was decorating the tree by herself, while Güeli cooked half the menu of any criollo restaurant. Papi had gone to buy beer and ice. Buelo Wiso sat in his recliner, watching TV and drinking a Budweiser, complaining how it would never be as good as Schaefer. He would never help Mami with the decorations, but liked to tell her about the bald spots.

"Allí, put one there," he would command.

"Why don't you get up and put it yourself, Pa," my mother would tease.

"Eso e'cosa de mujeres," he responded.

Mami would look at me and smile, then whisper: "Guess drinking beer and sitting on one's fat behind is man's work."

I'd giggle and look at Buelo's buttocks spreading across the recliner with the duct tape patches.

"Don't be talking about me to the boy, Maggie."

"You know we love you, Pa," she said and hugged him as he remain seated, his tattooed arms reaching back to embrace her from behind. His tats mesmerized me. He had served in the Navy and emblazoned across his right forearm ran the letters, U.S.S. Wasp, the carrier on which he had spent a good portion of his naval career as a mechanic. He had a dragon on the other, a cross and a heart with a knife on his right biceps—who knows what other parts of his body held ink. These were not the modern types of tats you'd find in studios—which Buelo Wiso considered "mariconadas," or "faggotries." For the longest time, I thought he was referring to puppets on a string when he said that. His tattoos were traditional, done in blue, with perhaps a dabbing of red.

Those Navy days were long past. These days, Buelo liked to sit and drink his Budweiser in his Schaefer mug, watch a baseball game, or oddly enough, bullfights televised on the Spanish channels. He sat quietly as the procession of horses with picadors poked at the bull, and whatever followed until the matador came into the ring. And even then, he appeared unmoved, as the matador made his passes and finally killed the bull. Perhaps he'd make a snarling comment about the little Spanish "puppet's" too tight pants, but he reserved outbursts for when a bull would have his day and with a brutal thrust throw the poor son of a bitch ten yards. Then Buelo's fat torso would rise a bit, his massive buttocks edging on the recliner, his right hand snapping its fingers like Puerto Ricans tend to do in amused excitement, and he'd yell in glee, he'd celebrate the bestial victory, however temporary.

But usually, Buelo would sit, a toothpick clinging out of his mouth, his big forearms slung over his round belly, and with wide eyes and an innocent voice comment on things.

"He loves to provoke," my mother would say.

"And he's an expert at it," my father would add.

Buelo and Mami had a long running feud over the status issue. He was pro-statehood.

"He's a pathetic pitiyanqui," my father would say.

My mother, who often said worst things regarding her father's American chauvinism, would defend him then.

"He fought for his country, Juanma, like many Ricans in that generation. What else can you expect?"

"His country?"

"Ay, please don't start. If Puerto Rico had a navy, then we could talk, awright?"

But when Mami and Buelo got into it, it got ugly. They would scream and she would throw things, not against walls to smash, and never at her father, but perhaps a book slammed on the table, a ratty sofa pillow hurled across the room. He'd point a sausage finger, tell her never to set foot in his house. Poor Güeli, used to the fights, would leave for the supermarket or cocooned herself in her bedroom to watch the novelas. In a soft voice she would beg for peace, but father and daughter wouldn't listen. They were in that loud, tit for tat, rapid fire, forget dialogue, it's a matter-of-who-can-yell-the-loudest-over-your-opponent Puerto Rican mode.

"Ay, Dios mío," Güeli would say, sighing. Then under her breath, uncharacteristically, would say "Jodía política," fuckin' politics, and head back into the bedroom.

As a child witnessing these verbal battles, I never quite understood the content. Only the often repeated words entered my consciousness: "estadista," "independencia," "pitiyanqui," "comunista." When he got patriotic, he would argue in English, and I'd pick up a few sentences. Things like, "Without the U.S., Porto Ricans would still be eatin' bananas and shittin' in letrines." Or, "You should get on your knees and thank the good Lord you are an American." But it would calm down, both combatants moving to a corner, distracted by something else, yet you could almost see the fumes emanating from their heated heads.

It depended on his moods, I guess, plus the amount of alcohol consumed. Buelo was not an alcoholic, but during special occasions he'd slam down a few, and he was not a lovely, charming drunk. And anything could incite him, get him going. That day, I remember looking at all the trimmings, the multi-colored lights with which Mami had circled the tree—all the decorations, each having a singular, significant importance. Being six or seven years old, I blubbered out something about Santa bringing me a gift I wanted badly. Don't remember what exactly, probably never will, but I do remember as if a camera had closed up on Buelo's face, my grandfather's eyes withering, his enormous presence withdrawing, back into the sofa, his upper lip snarling.

"Oh yeah, Santa Clos?" he said.

"Yeah, Buelo."

He pouted his lips in that snarky way.

"I don't think so, nene."

"Why not?"

He pushed himself toward me, an effort that made him breathe heavier, and put his face as close to mine as possible, his breath smelling of beer.

"Because he don't exist, Rennie, that's why."

My mother stopped midway in circling the tree, silver garland hanging in her hands. Her eyes fixed on her father, who had a full-blown sneer on his face. And he took a sip of beer. An exchange of words, harsh, and they were off. Güeli even screamed at Buelo.

"What do you mean, Buelo?" I screamed, now crying. "I've been good."

When I started crying, my mother slapped my grandfather on the arm hard. Buelo got up, and Güeli got between them.

"You respect me," he yelled.

"Right now, it's really hard, Pa," my mother said. They reserved the hardest things to say in English.

I didn't care about their bickering. I wanted to know then and there if or not the man in the red velvet suit would be bringing me that special present.

More yelling, and I was crying out loud now. What had I done? The words did not register for me.

"What does 'exist' mean, Mami?" I asked.

"Your Buelo is just playing with you," she said.

"Stop," he screamed. "Tell the boy, Magda, tell him the truth."

My mother looked at him, amazed, her eyes, I remember so well, blazing with anger, perhaps even hate at that moment.

"No more lies, m'ija," Buelo was saying, out of breath now. "He deserves to know."

More words in Spanish, flung at Buelo like knives, as Mami squeezed me, now crying in her arms.

Güeli shaking her head, stood up and said something to Buelo, in the most solemn tone I had ever heard her speak. She pointed a finger at him and left him with his head down, cradling his hands in front of him.

Minutes later, he told my mother, "Nena, I'm sorry." And then he began to cry.

Watching that tattooed man, weighing over 250 pounds, weeping with such fervor, scared me out of crying. I still see him in that battered brown leather recliner, the tears falling off his nose, his head down, an arm extended as a peace offering to my mother. My mother took his arm and held it up to her cheek, and she bent down and kissed Buelo on the head.

"Buelo, don't worry, Santa's gonna bring you something too," I said.

And he looked at me, hugged me hard and kissed me.

"Yes, he will baby, and he better bring you something, or I'll kick *his* fat ass."

José Feliciano's "Feliz Navidad" came on the radio, I smelled Buelo's Old Spice aftershave, saw Mami sniffling, wiping her nose on her red Christmas sweater, and I felt better that Santa would bring me that present. From the kitchen, Güeli started singing the lyrics, and out floated a cloud of heavenly aromas stemming from the kitchen, her hands holding fresh coquito mixed and put back in the rum bottle to serve it from there. I felt so warm, surrounded by people I loved, surrounded by sounds, smells, memories, the sort that come back stronger than ever to haunt you.

Eighteen

Licenciado Ledesma had a tic which signaled bad news. I had met him enough times to pick this out: a rotating of the right shoulder, accompanied by a little clearing of the throat, which prefaced the unwelcome information he was going to lay down on you. Reassuring in a way, a sign of a person with a conscience at least, who hated delivering news that would make his client irritable and unhappy. For a lawyer, that was the closest he could come to being virtuous.

His secretary led me into his modest office, and he stood up. Right away the shoulder got moving and the throat started making noises as he extended his manicured hand out for a handshake. He had phoned, left a message on my cell, and I was happy to receive it because I thought the Riveras had been evicted. Two weeks ago in this same office, I had signed a barrage of paper making me the legal owner of my parents' house. Ledesma handed me the deed with a smile.

"You're now a property owner and a Puerto Rican taxpayer. God help you."

I didn't know about Hacienda, the tax department, but as his secretary gave me the latest tax bill, I thought it could not be worse than the fleecing I was getting from the licenciado. But I paid happily, thinking the big mo was with me.

"We'll initiate an immediate Demanda de Desahucio," he had said. At my puzzled face he translated: "Eviction process."

I could not believe the judicial system was finally taking my side.

"It's pretty straightforward from here," he added, leaning his big torso forward, his demure hands coming together in a somber gesture of gravitas. "Recently, the Puerto Rican Legislature amended the process, which now should take no more than two weeks. The Riveras will have 10 days to leave, once they are served with papers."

"My heart bleeds for them," I had said. "Don't let the door hit your fat asses."

Ledesma had frowned at my remarks and told me he would contact me when it was all resolved. So, finally I was summoned, thinking resolution, but here was Ledesma rotating his shoulder like some overused major league pitcher and clearing his throat like he was trying to dislodge something stuck to the back of his adenoids.

He had me sit down, asked if I wanted coffee, not a good sign coming from an attorney who bought his suits from Sears. I just stared at him. In our budding attorney-client relationship, he had become accustomed to my impatience and the facial signals that said, "Just give me the fucking bad news."

"There's been an unexpected development," he said.

"Oh, do tell."

Not missing a beat, used to my sarcasm, he informed me the Riveras had acquired a legal aid lawyer to represent them.

"I thought you said this was straightforward."

"These two are good at what you Americans call, 'milking the system.'"

"So, what are you telling me?"

"They're like professional squatters and will use the legal system to keep living in a place as long as they can."

"But there was an eviction process, right?"

"Process, Falto. You said it. And the process allows them to present their case."

"But I own the house, and they are not paying rent. How much of a case can they have?"

"Well, technically, the rental contract was not between you and them. Their case is not between landlord and tenant. They have recurred to *interdicto posesorio*, or at least their lawyer has, alleging that since your parents became deceased, there was a period when no one legally owned the house and they were in possession of it and thus have a claim to it."

My look must have been amusing to him, because he chuckled. I was certainly not in a jovial mood, but the absurdity of the situation and his reaction made me laugh too. And we both kind of laughed for a few seconds until we could do nothing else but sit in silence.

"I can't believe this," was all I could say.

"It's a frivolous argument, Falto. You have to understand that it has no legal standing, but the court must hear it and juridicate. They are just buying more time."

"Great. Meanwhile I'm living in a guest house, and they're entrenched in the house that represents my parents' retirement dreams."

Ledesma pursed his thin lips, his eyes saddened as he stared at the legal paperwork in front of him.

"Sad but true, amigo," he said, nodding.

"Well, do what you have to do and get them out."

He stood up and stretched out his hand. He stared at me more seriously than ever before.

"These are bad people, Falto. You will have your day in court, trust me."

I shook his hand, paid the secretary the hefty bill and walked into the cool, bright January morning, feeling violated and used.

Walking back to the Guest House from Ledesma's office, it hit me how quiet and desolate the town was. The students had departed for the Christmas recess, the losa professors back in their precious San Juan, the area faculty visiting family somewhere else on the island or the States. La Tirilla eerily silent, El Pub, the college hangout, closed. A relative ghost town.

Back home, I threw on a tee, laced my running shoes and jogged until I lost track of the laps, falling on the bench under the giant moss tree where I had talked to Mari that day. Sweating, breathing hard, I lay back on the cool concrete bench and peered through the tree's leaves, thinking about Mari, wondering what she was doing.

After the blow up in the parking lot, she called and apologized, but I couldn't get her to see me. She wanted time to think, she had said. No, she had said "needed." And then she added, "You should do some thinking, too." I ached to be with her. That basic fact trumped any other thoughts, and I'd let that carry me anywhere she wanted me to go. What else was I supposed to think?

Birds chirped on the tree above, and suddenly I hated that I could hear birds singing. I was the only person on campus, except for the guard at the entrance of the college. My colleagues had gone off traveling somewhere, an inspirational idea. I headed back to the Guest House and started packing a carry-on. After a quick shower and slipping into cargo shorts and a clean tee, I roared away in the Civic, heading east to Fajardo.

There, I parked in the lot at the Ferry Terminal, bought a ticket to Culebra, an island that friends, colleagues and even Julia praised for its beauty and tranquility. The ferry was similar to the ones crossing The Narrows in New York City, the trip longer. Upon entering the town of Dewey, the views of the coast were postcard gorgeous, with the sea reflecting shades of varying blues, the sky a clear powder blue. I had not made reservations or thought about it, so when I entered the Hotel Kokomo, right off the dock, I hoped there would be a room available. "Tiempo muerto," the desk clerk said, meaning literally, "dead time," but signifying "slow season." She handed me the cardkey to a pleasant, clean room.

The next morning, I drove to Flamenco Beach and was amazed to see my feet so clearly through ocean water. What a slice of paradise, I thought, as I felt myself melding into the white, spotless sand. My thoughts became scattered with every stabilizing beat of my heart, until mental effort glazed into "nothing matters."

An Australian I met during dinner recommended snorkeling near Luis Peña, one of the many keys off Culebra. Swimming near the coral reef, along striking, colorful tropical fish, I faded into pinks and opals, time and place. When I surfaced, a fellow snorkeler pointed to a manatee about a hundred yards from us, the massive beast gracefully diving in and out of the water.

My last night in Culebra, at Flamenco, my reverie was broken by laughter. A young woman ran barefoot on the beach, dressed in a formal gown, the train dragging across the white sand. A man in a tux, equally barefoot, pant legs folded up to the knees, caught up to her and wrestled her to the ground. She screamed and laughed as they both went down, and they tussled, kissing drunkenly until all I could hear were the waves splashing onto the sand.

I returned to Baná tanned and rested, but restless. The Spring semester would start in a week, and I had not heard from the Institutional Committee about my contract. I was not looking forward to more battles with Roque, and I could not keep Mari out of my mind.

The day after my escape to Culebra, I sauntered over to the college post office to pick up mail and encountered Micco, himself tanned, although presumably from a bottle. He was sorting through a mountain of mail he had thrown on one of the side counters. He spotted me with my copy of the *Atlantic* and a couple of bills.

"How do you manage to receive such a small amount of mail?" he snarled.

"I don't have as many friends as you, Micco."

There was an awkward silence, and I thought he was losing his wit and sharp tongue. But he looked at me with disturbed, sad eyes.

"Rita Gómez is in the hospital," he said. And I knew where this was going.

"When?"

"She found out a few days before classes ended, and she has really deteriorated, Rennie." He continued looking at his mail. "Some of us are visiting her at the hospital tonight."

"Count me in," I said. He nodded as he threw a handful of brochures in the garbage.

"Eight o'clock. HIMA in Caguas."

I had not known Rita as well as I would have liked. She taught Business English, and I did not really have any common ground to start a conversation. Right before she became ill, though, we had a few coffees together, short conversations in between classes when you're drinking your coffee and you chat. Her English was hard to understand at times, but everyone agreed she was a dedicated and effective teacher. Short and thin, she came across as timid, but Micco called her "una mosquita muerta," someone who seems to be timid, but once you knew her better, you realized she was pretty slick. Once she felt comfortable with you, she became animated and funny. At one dinner party, she got a little tipsy, pinched my butt and spent the rest of the week apologizing. Now, she was one of the increasing number of cancer cases at the college no one wanted to discuss or link together—she was part of this "growing coincidence."

I was not prepared to see Rita in the hospital. My last image of her was of a smiling petite woman, holding a coffee cup telling a bawdy joke, and then running off in her spike heels to cover her Bus Com class. Now, she lay still, tubes coming in and out of her body, a wool cap covering her bald head, her sunken face sallow, her teeth protruding, her breathing troubled.

The cancer was claiming her, and we all knew it would not be long before fully owning her. At first I could not look at her. I could not look at my own parents' mangled bodies, preferring to bury them without seeing them or touching them one last time because I would not recognize them and the horror of having to see them in that state would overwhelm whatever grief I had, would swallow any words I had to say farewell. But like the others, I went over and grabbed Rita's cold hand, and she squeezed it, and I wanted to cry. Her way of saying goodbye, I knew. I kissed her forehead, but could not say spirited, empty words, like the others. In our short conversations, I began to sense that we had that in common, a b.s. detector; we both saw the world cynically and shared a black humor that other colleagues could only shake their heads at. She and I both knew she would not get up from that bed. With tears in my eyes, I just said, "Love the cap." And she squeezed my hand harder.

In the hospital cafeteria, while drinking coffee, I told Micco something had to be done.

"Like what?"

"I don't know, Micco, but fuck, this is getting ridiculous."

"Easy, Junior, I'm on your side."

"It might be a coincidence, but the college should take a more active role."

"What are they supposed to do?"

"How about they secure our safety, Micco?"

He nodded, and sat back on the chair. After a few minutes staring at my coffee, I told him I was going to organize a committee of faculty, employees, students and community people.

He shrugged a shoulder.

"I'll start by contacting the Congreso leadership," I added.

At this, he leaned forward. "They're agitators, Rennie. They don't think through issues."

"They get results. We'd have zero benefits if not for them."

"Junior, don't mess with things you don't know about."

I looked at him, a bit quizzically. "Don't you think something should be done, Micco? You could be next."

He was a morbid hypochondriac, the type of person who asked you how a particular mole looked, or if his tongue looked weird, a man who obsessed over nuclear warfare. The thought obviously bothered him. He drank the last drop of coffee in his Styrofoam cup and stood up to leave.

"Will you join us?"

"Let me think about it," he answered.

That was Micco saying no way. Typical, I thought. Complaining about the situation and not willing to get off his ass and do something. Typical of him, typically Puerto Rican. His non-reaction pushed me even more. The college had to at least entertain the possibility that something may be happening on the campus. The radioactive material was there and, although the Department of Defense was doing something, the college community was being kept in the dark and people were getting ill at an alarming rate. We deserved explanations and answers. First thing in the morning, I would contact the Congreso leaders to form a special committee.

On my way out, I bumped into Mari. I had not seen her since the Christmas party. She, too, had been vacationing. Her usual bronze skin had acquired a copper hue. She had let her hair grow and now it curled around her face wildly. She pushed her sunglasses to the top of her head, something I always found sexy, and her eyes shone big and bright.

We gave each other awkward hellos, I informed her of Rita's situation. We then fell into that sad silence reserved for when someone you know is dying and words are futile and superfluous.

"You look very relaxed," I said.

"Been doing some thinking and I'm in a good place."

"I've been thinking, too. But you want to see Rita. We'll talk."

She stared at me, not knowing exactly where I was coming from, because I myself didn't know how to express what I was feeling. I was willing to talk, though. Anything to see her again.

"Sure, we can talk." She waved, and my eyes followed her walking away.

Later that night, I received a call from Julia. She had found out about my situation with the squatters and was upset that I had not asked her for help.

"Don't worry how I found out," she responded to my inquiries. "By now you should know this is one tight island. And lawyers talk—a helluva grapevine." She sighed, and her voice cracked a bit when she said, "Rennie, please, don't shut me out."

"It's my problem."

"But, damn it, I can help you. On this one, I can actually help you. Why do you refuse to reach out to me?"

"How can you say that? I'm here aren't I?"

Silence on her end.

I wasn't in the mood. I was tired. Images of Rita kept running through my head. Anger started creeping up my body. Mari's tanned face staring at me, half interested in what I said and maybe I was reading too much into it, but there was a spark of hope in her eyes.

"Fine, Julia. Help me in any way you want."

"My goodness, René, don't ask as a favor to me. I am just being a mother who cares, not someone trying to gain points."

I exhaled. "I'm sorry. Yes, it is getting to me, these squatters. I don't know if Ledesma is in over his head."

"Martirio is good, but it doesn't hurt to give him a bit more help. I'll call him. You sound tired, get some rest."

Before she hung up, she asked about Mari. Normally, I would be evasive, but after this conversation, and because I needed to talk to someone, I told her about our current situation. I expected her to say move on, or get a younger girlfriend.

After a pause, she said, "Love's hard to come by, René."

"Excuse me?"

"No seas bobo," she said.

And she hung up after throwing a bendición and some kisses my way.

A week later, when the second semester began, I went to the department office to pick up mail on the first day of classes. There was a letter from the Institutional Personnel Committee, which I tore open. They had recommended reappointment, a one-year renewal on the tenure track.

When I finally got around to writing the defensa, I had kept it short but real:

Dear Committee Members:

I am a first-year professor. I accept that I need to learn more about my students and how to teach. But my dedication and commitment to them cannot be questioned. The student evaluations speak for themselves. The remarks of the other Committee members speak for themselves. I ask that Dr. Roque and the Institution support my efforts to improve by giving me formative criticism and opportunities for development.

Sincerely,
René Falto Matos

Micco questioned the brevity of my rebuttal. He thought I should respond to every single point made by Roque and Carmela López. But when I sat down to write it, I was exhausted, despondent over losing Mari, and I felt the entire thing was so much bullshit. I wasn't going to validate their criticism by responding to it.

I guess my words had some sway with the Committee, or Foley's had more.

I turned to go into Roque's office, not to gloat but to make sure that he was aware of the committee's decision. I wanted peace with this man.

"He's not there," Nitza said, a bit bothered.

"He didn't come in today?"

"No, Doctor Roque has taken a leave for the semester."

I didn't believe her. I opened the door, and the office was bare of all Roque's possessions, minimal as they were. Not even the crucifix. The office looked like no one had ever occupied it.

Nineteen

He appeared at my office door like a ghost, almost transparent, furtive and quiet. I flinched as his blue eyes locked into mine. He didn't even laugh or smile at my being startled; he was probably used to making people jump.

"Jesus, Foley, can't you knock or something."

"The door was open," he said, pointing to it and speaking in that tone he always used, soft and self-assured, as if everything he said was obvious and understated.

"I'd like to invite you to dinner."

Now he smiled, those perfect white teeth gleaming. Was he trying to be charming? He stood at the doorjamb—why he didn't just come in I don't know. Dressed in his typical suit and tie, he carried this aura of authority. Arms crossed, he stared at me with those hardened eyes, waiting for an answer.

"Are you asking me out on a date, Foley?"

No smile. "I'd like to talk to you about a few things, and I find it more pleasant over drinks and food, rather than here."

"Oh, so, you're going to tell me some unpleasant things?"

He crossed the doorjamb, made a sound that sounded like a chuckle and put his arm on top of my file cabinet.

"Why do you have to bust my chops? It's an invitation to drinks and dinner."

"To discuss important matters?"

I thought he was trying to restrain himself from rolling his eyes. He kind of bit his lower lip and looked away.

"Let's just call it a friendly dinner, shall we?"

I laughed, loving that I was apparently pushing some buttons. "That sounds ominous, Foley, I don't know."

He bent into me, his eyes now turning a darker hue as his eyebrows closed in, all traces of a smile gone now.

"Listen," he whispered, "don't fuck with me. I'm too old for games. I'm telling you we should talk, okay?"

There was something in his voice, confident, full of urgency and import, that intimidated me. And those eyes, which he should have insured as tools of whatever trade he was plying. I had been slouching in my chair, and I raised myself a bit, as if the eyes and his hard stare had lifted me up.

"That sounds serious, Foley."

"Enough with the formality. It's Jake, call me Jake. And, yes, it's on the serious side. But," and here he paused, smiled.

At that moment I entertained the idea the man may have had schizoid tendencies.

He added, "That doesn't mean we can't have a pleasant date."

Smug with his little joke, he turned around to leave. "Seven p.m., my place, this Friday," he said with his back to me and raising his finger in the air.

"Is it about Roque?" I blurted at his back, which made him stop, look up and exhale.

He turned to me, his arms akimbo now, looking at me amused, but, I could tell, also bothered. He was about to speak but then turned around and shut the door.

"You received your letter, right?"

"Yes, and if you had anything to do with that, thanks. But where did Roque go?"

He seemed exasperated. I was asking too many questions. He pulled Micco's chair and plopped himself down, straightened his tie, knitted his fingers on his lap and slouched toward me.

"You're a real pain in the ass, you know that?"

I was going to protest, but he held his hand up, eyes closed. It looked like I was giving him a headache to boot.

"Sometimes you should just go with the flow, Rennie. Be thankful you received a renewal."

"I am grateful. But it's strange that he disappeared. Is he okay?"

He tugged his ear and smiled. "Magnanimous of you to worry for him after the shit he pulled on you."

"I don't like him, and the feeling is mutual, I'm sure, but I don't wish him any harm."

"You're a good kid, Rennie, and I say that with earnest affection and no disrespect. I could wax on how you remind me of myself when I was younger, blah, blah. But bottom line is you're a wise-ass, and I kind of like that. But that can land you in trouble."

"I sense a preview of Friday's discussion."

"Yes, we'll hold on that. As for Pedro . . . " He looked out the window and then back at me, that creepy grin on his face. "Let's just say that he had cultivated enemies who had serious capital on him, and they cashed it in."

"You're losing me."

"Well, your friend and ex-officemate, for one. He had some information on Roque's credentials. Doctor Roque isn't a doctor. He managed to get hired and promoted without a doctorate."

"How the hell?"

"The university system at its finest. He had enemies, for sure, but loyal friends, too, and they helped him get in, didn't even check the credentials, and when everyone called him Doctor Roque he never corrected anyone. For all those years he kept it a secret, clearly in violation of institutional policy and regulations."

"What's going to happen to him?"

Foley reared back and laughed.

"Absolutely nothing. In fact, he's getting a sort of promotion. They'll transfer him to the main campus, where they are above following institutional policy and regulations. And for now, to avoid the obvious embarrassment, he gets a paid leave."

"That's ridiculous."

"Well, it's their problem now. If someone sues for any reason based on his lack of credentials—a student he fails, a colleague he recommends not to renew—they'll have a case on their hands. You get my drift?"

"Yes, I do," I responded, grateful for the information, but feeling slimy at having it and knowing how it emerged. "And you say Micco's involved?"

"He finally played his trump card."

"Why did he feel a need for one?"

"I'm sure you've heard the stories about Micco's student love interests and how he allegedly treats these women."

"I heard they were rumors."

"I don't know, Rennie, really. But we know the remarks were coming from our now departed colleague. His divorce turned him so bitter it showed on his face every day. He was becoming rigid and intolerably self-serving. He had to go."

"So, it comes down to revenge."

"Oh, come on, it's always more than that, isn't it?"

"From what you tell me that's what it sounds like."

He stood up to leave, but stared at me with a face that flashed a combination of amusement and pity for my naiveté.

"Micco is more ambitious than he lets on. Everyone has an agenda."

"What's yours?" I asked.

He stared at me for what seemed an eternity. "Well, now, what fun would it be if I told you? I think it's more productive if you asked yourself the same question."

With that he walked out and in the hallway shouted, "Seven p.m., Friday."

Since I set foot on the campus, Foley had said no more than a few friendly words to me, mostly cursory stuff, and now he was inviting me to his house for drinks and dinner. It didn't make sense, but he had been instrumental, I know, in helping me retain my job. Minimal gratitude compelled me to attend. But, what did this man want?

My gaze landed where he had been sitting so regally, Micco's previous chair, now vacated along with the desk. All the stuff on his work area had been transported to the chair's office, where Roque once dwelled and terrified everyone, especially me. I now found his arrogant self-righteousness and hypocrisy unbearable. Colleagues had often told me how hard he was on instructors who didn't meet his demanding standards and how he played a strong hand in getting them dismissed. He had once said his happiest days were working as a Peace Corps volunteer. He should have gone into social service instead of academics and saved many people hassles and aggravation.

Now, Micco was the new department chair. Everyone was shocked; no one thought he was the type to want an administrative position, the chairmanship of a department, much less of the English Department, widely reputed to be the worst, with the most argumentative and rebellious professors. From Foley's comments, it seemed as if he had been positioning himself all along. Kind of bittersweet not having Micco around. No one had claimed the desk, so I had the office all to myself, but it sometimes made me feel lonelier and more alienated than ever. In a strange way, I missed his obnoxious comments and off-putting innuendos, his corny jokes delivered in that terrible British accent. It's like a ragged pair of smelly sneakers you know you should throw out but still keep, only because they are there and keep you in a comfort zone.

Reminiscing made me realize that I hadn't congratulated Micco on his new position. At the office I signaled if the new chair was in and Nitza waved me in as she typed away. Nitza was fond of Roque, one of his few admirers and supporters. Ever since his departure, she seemed more ornery and smiled even less.

I rapped on the open door to his office to get his attention. He seemed earnestly at work, shuffling papers—a rarity, that he appeared at work, that is.

"Hey, Junior, nice to see you. What can I do you for?"

I sat down on one of the hard seats, one of Roque's legacies.

"You need to get rid of these seats, my man."

"I'll take it under advisement. How you doing?"

"I'm great. Just dawned on me I haven't congratulated you on your new job. So congratulations."

He bowed his head and gestured taking off an imaginary hat.

"Didn't think you had it in you," I said, looking at him in what most have seemed like bewilderment and repulsion. He glanced my way, not certain how to take my words.

He pointed for me to close the door so I kicked it shut with my foot. He threw himself back on the new leather chair, considerably more comfortable than the Spartan one preferred by Roque. Micco's face turned sullen, even nasty, his lively eyes narrowing on me.

"Don't judge me. You don't know how long I've dealt with that troglodyte. I know Foley told you, I can tell." He bent over the desk and moved toward me. "So fucking shoot me," he whispered. "Pedro was getting out of control, abusive. Your case was the proverbial last straw."

"So you did it for me, that's sweet."

"You can joke. But some of us actually did think an injustice was being committed in your case." His seriousness and indignant sneer shut me up.

"He had promised your position to a friend, and when he was blocked, he took it out on you."

He tapped a pencil on the desk, the only sound in the room for a few seconds. "But this," he said, pointing to the desk emphatically, "was also an opportunity, and I took it."

Shrugging his shoulders, he added, "I'm a shitty teacher, Rennie, I know it. The students and I are better served with me in administration, the only place to make decent money in this racket, anyway."

I stood up and extended my hand. "I'm glad for you, then, that you found your true calling."

He shook my hand and then, in his irritating fake Brit accent, told me, "Now, get the blazes out of my office and don't let the door hit your bum."

I was about to turn and leave when Micco reminded me about Rita's funeral, which was tomorrow. In the midst of Roque's disappearance, my renewal and Micco's promotion, we had received the inevitable news of Rita's passing. Micco had been at the hospital, in the unit's waiting area, as her most immediate family gathered to say their last farewell.

The funeral was in Fajardo, Rita's hometown, where she also had lived in a gated community. She used to have special schedules, and drove from Fajardo to Baná, a considerable distance, but she always told us she didn't mind because her hometown was so beautiful it was worth it.

Julia called me and surprised me by telling me she would attend the funeral. Rita's family and mine had had dealings with each other, business and friendly, for decades. One of Julia's partners owned an apartment in one of the many exclusive condos in that coastal town and offered it to her for the weekend. It was a roomy apartment, so she invited me to stay there and, shockingly, asked me to invite Marisol, which I did.

I didn't think Marisol would accept, but I think we were all devastated with losing a colleague. Most of us had rescheduled classes to take a few days off. We all needed rest, time to reflect. Being by the ocean would help the healing process, for me, anyway. Marisol felt the same way, and I think she sensed we needed to open up again and talk. At least, that was my hope.

We drove in separate cars to Fajardo on a cloudy day to commemorate Rita's life and lay her remains to rest. The parking lot at the Sabadell Funeral Home was full, and we had to park on a side street. We walked single-file like strangers on the narrow sidewalk leading to Sabadell.

The funeral home had three capillas, or small parlors. All three were full, so that the respectful in attendance would spill into the lobby to congregate and talk, cry or munch on the snacks and beverages offered by the establishment. We entered Rita's capilla to a standing-room crowd. Almost everyone in the English Department was in attendance. Glaringly absent was Roque, who apparently was too embarrassed to make any public appearance, even to pay respects to a colleague. According to Micco, Roque had voted against Rita's tenure due to her "badly accented English and weak academic background."

Dutifully, we approached the casket to pay our respects. It's always amazing how funeral cosmetology can turn a pallid, drawn-out face into one with color and a placid and peaceful appearance. Rita, I thought, we'll never dance again. I touched her cold hand, in which they had wrapped a rosary, and said my last farewell to the body that had once contained the essence of Rita María Gómez, a woman who seemed to love life so much and was given so little of it. We gave our condolences, the "pésame" in Spanish, to her parents and other family members who received them in that vacuous, tired way, after hearing it so many times.

Marisol and I moved to the little room in the back to listen to a reverend give a homily. Rita, I knew, was not a very religious person, but she was not one to take any particular stand against it. She attended church with her parents, who were very religious, more for them than anything else. She believed in a higher being. But the preacher surely was the parents' doing. He spoke in that gentle fashion so common among preachers and so soothing to the grieving. Rita's parents sat up front in cushioned armchairs set out especially for the most immediate members of the grieving family. It struck me so odd, and sad, to see older folks mourning the loss of a child, even if like Rita, she was approaching forty. The rest of those congregated sat and fidgeted in rigid, blue velvet chairs.

These ceremonies are always drawn out; people stand to speak, to reminisce, eulogize, and maybe they take too long because they don't want to let go. Micco spoke on the department's behalf. His words were curt and centered on how devoted Rita was to her students—I couldn't help sneering. Rita had no such notions about being an unselfish, martyred teacher; she worked hard at being the best teacher possible, but like most of us had no qualms about complaining about student laziness and the hopelessness we all felt at times in a thankless profession that paid badly.

The preacher led everyone in prayer, and I turned and saw Foley seated by a corner, eyes closed, deep in prayer. I don't know why that shocked me, but it did. Even Julia, who I finally found in the second row, impeccably dressed in a black pantsuit, had eyes shut and was mumbling something. While everyone bent heads in prayer, or pretended reflection, I glimpsed at Marisol and thought how lovely she looked in black, how her bronzed calves looked spectacular in her high heels.

I had thought the prayers would bring an end to the ceremony, but a young woman stood up in front of an upright mike. The resemblance to Rita was striking: the same almond eyes, the evenly shaped slender nose, the shiny black hair. She mentioned how "Titi" had always loved this song she was going to sing for us, how whenever it played on the radio she'd raise the volume and sing out loud. "Although not very well," she added, drawing nervous laughter from us.

Then music played, and she sang Lee Ann Womack's "I Hope You Dance." She sang it beautifully, and later we learned that she was studying voice at the Conservatory in San Juan. The prayers had not moved me, the scene itself had not. But that young woman, looking so much like her aunt, singing that song so powerfully, while we listened enraptured to the lyrics as if they were our friend and colleague's parting words to us—it moved me to tears. Over in the corner, Foley bowed his head and, when he looked up, his eyes were red and two tears trickled down his cheeks. Quickly, he wiped them away with one hand.

As she sang the refrain, I saw Rita dancing, twirling in her graceful way, her head back in laughter, tossing her hair.

Then, when she reached the part about not settling for the path of least resistance, I had to exit the room, wiping with a palm the tears, choking on my outrage and anger. So wrong, so wrong, I kept thinking.

I straightened up as Foley walked out of the door. He looked at me, smiled and grabbed me by the shoulder.

"Come on, have a drink with me," he said.

"We have to go to the cemetery."

"Not for about half an hour, they said." He stared at me, head lifted, his arm resting on my shoulder.

"Humor me, I'm Irish. There's no wake unless there's drinking."

We headed to a little corner bar, signaling to Micco, who, afraid of crowded rooms, surely had walked out before the stirring rendition of the song. He tagged along, and the three of us were soon plopped on stools, sipping scotch—the only drink fit for mourning the dead, according to Foley.

Into the silence, we scattered reminisces of Rita, the usual funny stories, the lasting memories that would keep her alive for us. Literally a hole-in-the-wall, this was the type of bar where men came to pick up a beer on their way home. We held three of the five stools. A small TV had a daytime soap on, an odd choice, given the virile clientele, but then what else could the bartender put on when he did not have satellite access to sports? The bartender was a short guy, who was insulted when we expressed surprise he had Glenlivet; he served our shots as if he were a bartender at the Hilton. In the background, merengue and bachata music was thumping. We hunkered over our drinks in silence, feeling, with unequal intensity, the buzz of the scotch mingling with our sadness.

And then out of nowhere, Foley recited something, in some guttural language. Micco and I stared at him, like he was possessed, and maybe he was. He chuckled.

"How that time has passed away, dark under the cover of night, as if it had never been!"

"Okay, buddy, time to leave," Micco patted him on the back.

"Alas for the bright cup!" he responded, raising his shot glass, laughing. "Alas for the mailed warrior!"

He was bent over, laughing, holding his sides.

"Are you okay, man?" I asked stupidly, loopy from the shots, the heat and the funeral.

He shooed me away with his hand, and after a few deep breaths, collected himself. You couldn't tell Foley had that laughing episode as he walked erect, somber, back toward the parking lot.

He got into his Saab to join the cars lining behind the hearse. Julia shouted for me on the other side of the parking lot. She was standing by Marisol who, crossed arms, looked my way. Micco asked if I wanted to drive with him, but I told him I'd ride with Julia and Marisol.

On the way to the cemetery, it started to drizzle. The radio played pop music, and I asked to turn it off. Both Julia and Mari agreed out loud, and we sat in silence for the rest of the slow ride.

At the burial site, Rita's father almost fainted, and his two sons had to hold him up, then sat him down by his wife. The light mist continued, umbrellas sprung open, the last words and prayers uttered, as everyone placed a flower on the casket before the crew pushed it into the family granite mausoleum.

A small crowd gathered around the niece with the voice, congratulating her on the song, the gift she had, wishing her well on what appeared to be a surefire career. The rest of us dispersed, heading to our automobiles, and our lives.

Twenty

Julia drove us back to the funeral home, where Mari and I picked up our sidelined cars and followed her to the condo, a spacious penthouse suite with a generous view of Playa Azul. After dumping our stuff in our rooms, Julia opened her laptop to catch up on emails and work, so Marisol and I decided to stroll on the beach before dinner.

The wind was blowing hard, and Marisol kept holding on to her straw hat. We passed only a handful of people at the beach. Some American college kids had a lively touch football game going on. An artist painted the landscape. Several sunburned bodies strewn on blankets, sleeping past the time they should have packed for home. We waved to the beach police patrolling in their dune buggies.

When we reached jagged rocks overlooking an inlet, we sat for a while to take in the view. We sat with our arms and hands behind us, glancing out toward the ocean, Marisol holding her hat between her knees. Menacing clouds hung low; it had been drizzling on and off all the way from Fajardo, although at times bright rays of sun peeked through. We talked about the funeral, the niece with the voice, Rita's family, which neither one of us had ever met.

Marisol lounged back, hat held at her stomach, to catch some sun. I did the same but turned to look at her, my crooked arm supporting my face. I marveled at her full lips, her eyes at times intense while other times sad and exposed, but always expressive. The tiny freckles on her nose which I had grown to like. The wind had blown a strand of curly hair over her face, and I reached to brush it back as she did the same. Our hands bumped and she opened her sleepy eyes, startled.

"I'm here," I said.

She looked up at me, her eyes partly squinting. She stared up at me for a few seconds then sat up.

"Ay, Rennie. Sometimes you're really not."

She was right. Most of the time in Puerto Rico I had felt like I was drifting away. She laughed softly and peered out toward seagulls squawking below.

We didn't speak for a few minutes.

"Everything's changed," I said, breaking the silence. "Except you, you're the same for me, you're my anchor."

The wind had subsided, so she put on her hat, stuffing her hair under it. She looked at me, suspiciously, studying my face, putting her hand over her eyes to protect them from the glare of the setting sun.

"What's that? Like the new ball and chain?"

"No," I cracked up, shaking my head. "Not what I'm saying."

We both laughed. She was busting my chops for sport, a good sign.

"You have a problem with that?"

She grinned, looking at her wiggling feet, then away to the horizon. "Don't know. Never been an anchor before."

She gave me a sly look, and I leaned into her to explain how in the past few weeks she was always on my mind to the point of obsession, to tell her I loved her, but she put a hand on my mouth.

"Rennie, I'm just so tired of being alone. Can you understand that?" I nodded, and she brushed her thumb across my lips.

"Let's go," she said, squeezing my shoulders. "Julia's waiting for us."

We walked back along the water as swirls of orange and purple crowded the darkening sky. At one point, she put her arm around my waist and rested her head against my bicep. And we walked like that for a while.

By the time we returned, Julia had finished her work, showered, dressed and had made reservations at a local restaurant. She chided us for being late, because she was starved, and she hoped we

were in the mood for seafood. "Hurry up and get ready," she said
and scooted us toward our rooms.

El Rincón Sabroso was less than a ten-minute drive. A cozy
place, clean, nestled between the ocean and the highway. Julia
ordered lobsters for us all. We each had a cocktail, and then she
surprised us by ordering champagne.

"What's the occasion?" I asked.

She smiled. "You don't need an occasion to have champagne,
right Marisol?"

Marisol looked at her and shrugged her shoulders. "Of course,
not. Pour, sister."

The conversation drifted into platitudes—weather, food, the
beach—and after a short pause, when it seemed we had exhausted all topics, I said, almost absent-mindedly, "I'm going to miss
Rita."

"She was a good friend and colleague," Marisol said, nodding.

Julia looked at me and rubbed my arm, as she is wont to do
when I look distressed or sad. Where before I might have
clammed up, I grabbed her hand, and she smiled back. Trying to
break the gloomy atmosphere that my previous comment had created, I told Julia about my renewal. At first, she didn't respond,
which surprised me. After a few seconds, she lit a cigarette and
turned to me.

"I'm proud of you, m'ijo, I am. But, down the line you should
transfer out of there." And then she bent past me and spoke to
Marisol, "And that goes for you too." We looked at each other, then
at her.

I kept looking at her face to read for meaning. She whipped out
a brush from her purse and combed her hair while holding the
cigarette between her lips. She put the brush away with a loud
click in her bag and turned to us again, blowing smoke out of her
mouth in that urgent way of hers.

"What are you saying, Julia?"

"Ay, that was the champagne talking. Forget it," she said, tapping my face playfully and ending the conversation. And then, lifting her glass, she added, "It's good to see you both together again."

Marisol and I looked at each other, then away, both blushing. She stared at us, smiling, and her eyes were getting a bit glassy. Rubbing the stem of the flute champagne glass, she told us about how she had met my father, who she reminded us, was a bit older than she.

"We bumped into each other at the Lázaro library," she laughed. "We needed the same book and we had a real debate over who should have the book." She took a sip, looked into the flute glass.

"Juanma used to say that I smiled, or batted my eyelashes or something like that, and he melted and gave in." Julia smiled again, in her tongue in cheek, pursed-lip way that says "Can you believe that?"

Marisol and I both laughed because the thought of Julia doing such a thing was so ridiculous.

"Your father, the revisionist historian."

The food came. Some of the fattest lobster tails I had ever seen, with equally mammoth tostones. We toasted to the lobsters and ate heartily.

Throughout dinner, Julia served bits and pieces of that past. How my father turned over the book with a promise from her for a date. How after that first date, they were inseparable, argued over politics and other issues so often that friends started referring to them as "Crossfire," after the popular pundit show of the time. Laughing out loud, she recounted my father's serenade at her apartment one night.

"He sang so badly for so long my roommates begged me to tell him to stop." He made her laugh, she said as she fondled her silver necklace. In that first year, they roamed every known street of Old San Juan and discovered the secluded ones.

"There wasn't anything immediately attractive about your father, but after I got to know him, I don't know, he had this presence, and I began to appreciate his loveliness, his character, and he became the most handsome man to me."

Marisol stared at my mother with a new sense of appreciation, I could tell, and frankly, so did I. At that moment, Julia was very much a real woman to me.

"Our thing became an obsession, both of us, unable to go a day without thinking about each other, without keeping our hands off each other," she said, shaking her head, closing her eyes. "What did I know about love? I was so young, so näive." She laughed, shaking her head again, and added, "And so stupid."

I kept quiet at this remark, bowing my head. Under the table, Marisol grabbed my hand. Julia saw my face, and horror swept across hers.

"Oh, no," she said, pain transforming her features. "It wasn't like that, René."

I didn't respond.

Crying, she pushed herself from the table and trotted to the ladies' room. Marisol looked at me, agitated and confused, and ran after her. I sat at the table, my hands rubbing my face, running through my hair.

I was grateful it was a short ride. When she parked the car, she turned to me.

"Let me tell you one thing," she said, pointing her finger, slurring her words. "The day I found out I was pregnant with you was the happiest day of my life."

She was shaking, choking on her tears, and I brought her closer to me and embraced her hard. From the back seat, Mari rubbed my mother's shoulder and with the other hand ran her fingers through my hair.

Twenty-One

Jake Foley lived on a highway that locals joked had a curve for every day of the year. It was a two-lane road, with captivating views of what awaited you below if you fell asleep at the wheel or were stupid enough to take it on under the influence. Like a skinny snake, it wound through the cordillera heading toward Guayama and the southern coast. Foley lived no more than seven miles from Baná, but on that road it felt farther. As a truck roared past me, and both my Civic and I shook, I cursed any man crazy enough to live in such a forsaken place. The invitation was for seven, but I had called and told him I was running late. With an exasperated sigh, he said the food was getting cold, so get my ass up there.

By the time I was getting closer, it was getting colder and darker. As my luck would have it, a heavy fog started settling in. I had never seen anything like this in Puerto Rico, or anywhere for that matter, and driving in it was not fun. I had taped Jake's directions to the dashboard—no GPS will get you there, he said—and after circling a few places and turning here and there, I managed to find the long ascending driveway that led to his chalet, now almost covered in mist.

He met me at the door, wearing jeans and a flowery shirt out of some Hawaiian movie. Barefoot, he ordered me to take my shoes off and leave them on a rubber pad near the doorway. It's been my experience that westerners who have this fetish about taking shoes off inside the house have traveled or lived extensively in areas of the world where this is a custom.

A quick pan of the man's crib confirmed he was an aficionado of East Asian culture. I wouldn't have figured Foley for a lover of any type of art, and not someone who collected anything other than paychecks, but in the foyer and throughout the living room, he had pieces of jade sculpture, Japanese lacquer vases, Chinese ceramic vases and Sumi-e paintings. On one wall he had mounted a calligraphic representation of what he told me was the Chinese character for fate, which looked like a man standing and leaning forward at the furthermost point of a sailing boat's bow.

Mounted on a large wall was an impressive collection of masks from the Far East, including a frightening Indonesian one with big teeth and large ears, and several Maori ones. Placidly, and alone, a Nepalese bronze Buddha sat on the middle of a credenza, contemplating the entire scene, which included my big toe sticking out of the hole in my right sock. Foley came back with a bottle of Beaujolais and two glasses. I shoved my foot under the large, square wooden coffee table.

"Well, had to re-heat the food. What the hell took you so long?" He said this as always in that soft tone that would belie any agitation.

"Jeez, Foley, you live out here in the freakin' boonies."

He laughed. "You made it at least. People never visit me; they use the highway as an excuse." He poured two hearty servings of wine. "Hell, I'm kinda glad, to tell you the truth."

"Don't like our colleagues?"

He shrugged his shoulders, dismissed the entire department with a wave of the hand and a roll of the lips. "Don't need to see them day and night."

"You're barely on campus, though," I said, cringing inside after I said it, because I didn't know how he would take it.

He laughed. "Right out of Notre Dame, I came to PR with a doctorate in Anglo-Saxon literature. So, I accepted my obsolescence early, learned to be another brick in the wall."

"And now you teach writing."

"Makes me feel like I'm doing something worthwhile."

"You teach the other stuff too, don't you?"

"A Shakespeare course for the majors, here and there. Early Brit survey." He took a slow sip from his glass. "They couldn't care less about *Beowulf*."

I had barely taken a sip of the Beaujolais when he signaled me to dinner. It was a chatty one, and I found Foley to be as fascinating a conversationalist as he was mysterious. When I mentioned the art, he described his travels in that region of the world, beginning as a child with his military family. His father was a naval officer, stationed in Yokosuka for an extended period, but with stints in Hawaii and San Diego. Young Jake got to see a good portion of the East, and by the time he was off to the University of Virginia for his undergraduate degree, he had an extensive collection of what he called touristy junk. But that initiated his love for the serious art collecting that would come later.

For such a world traveler, he prepared pretty pedestrian food. He started us off with lentils, made from an old family recipe. Not a big fan, but they were tasty along with the homemade bread— he was surely a man of many talents. The main course consisted of steak, potatoes and string beans. The steaks were done to perfection, and the rest of the meal was actually good. I asked where he learned to cook, and he answered that his wife was a horrible cook, so it was either learn or starve.

"The woman has no sense for the subtleties of flavors and taste."

I remarked how he didn't have any pictures of family around the house.

He sat back on the chair, elbow over the top rail. "Don't have kids, unless you count the dogs, and the wife has custody," he said, smiling. "The missus and I are separated these days." Not divorced, he made it clear, because both of them couldn't help being old school Irish Catholics.

"There's just so much love in any human being, Rennie," he said. "Then like a well, it dries up."

After he cleared the table, he poured himself another glass of wine and told me I shouldn't have any more since I had to drive down that highway again, in thicker fog. I wasn't going to argue. But then, he said, "Well, maybe have a wee bit more to toast," and he poured me two fingers worth.

"Toast to what?" I said.

He told me that he had something for me. And, suddenly, I remembered that there was something important he had wanted to tell me. He came back dangling some keys.

"To your house," he said, a bright smile on his face, lifting his glass. With his left hand, he offered me the keys.

"No way," I said.

I stood up and grabbed the keys, mystified.

"Don't leave me hanging, Falto."

I raised my glass and clinked.

"Thanks," I said, not clear what was going on. "But, how?"

He downed the wine and threw himself back on a large armchair. "You sure ask a lot of questions."

"But, it's just so out of the blue. Did Ledesma have anything to do with this?"

Foley snickered. "Martirio is a good lawyer, but he had the legal system to contend with." Then, he widened his blue eyes, which now appeared glossy and reptilian.

"Please sit down, Rennie," he said, and I realized that I was still standing, so I set the keys on the coffee table and sat down quietly.

"The Riveras were trash and they were playing the system. You know it, everyone knows it." He said this as softly as if he were conducting mass, his hands moving gently here and there, almost making the sign of the cross. But I could see in his eyes the malice that accompanies any justification of means. And it worried me, even scared me. Foley was adept at reading people, and he quickly saw this.

"Oh, no harm was done to them," he said, but in a way hinting it could have been arranged. "Mr. Rivera had quite a rap sheet, suffice it to say. He had no problem moving his butt out once we explained the options."

"Who's we?"

Here, his eyes fluttered, closed, and he exhaled loudly, sat back on the armchair and slanted his head toward me.

"What difference is it to you?"

"It involves me, somehow, doesn't it?"

"But, of course."

There was a pause, for whatever he was saying to sink into what he clearly perceived as my thick head. Then, he leaned toward me, his sinewy frame moving closer to me. He sat at the edge of the chair, legs spread, arms dangling off his thighs, hands folded as if in prayer. Lifting his face, he tugged at his ear, then stared at me.

"You've been talking to the Congreso," he said, as a matter of fact, as if he were commenting on the weather. "You've been organizing."

"What does it matter to you?"

He smiled, laughed, shaking his head. "Okay, Rennie. Here it is. You keep this up, you're going to be in a heap of trouble."

"That sounds like a threat."

He shook his head emphatically. "Advice from a senior faculty member."

"What happens if I don't stop?"

"Let's just say the rector is not too happy with you getting politically involved."

His self-assured, smug tone was beginning to irritate me.

"I see."

"Do you, Falto? I don't think you understand half of what's going on. It's a mess, and your mother is partly to blame."

"My mother?"

"Her law firm is initiating a class-action suit against the university and the U.S. Defense Department."

Stunned, I sat silently, as he let that sink in.

"I think you have some thinking to do," he said.

Still shocked, all I could do was nod absent-mindedly.

"The clean-up is getting done, Rennie. No one needs flak at this moment. It will only make matters worse. Talk to your mother, reason with her."

I sneered, then laughed. "You don't know my mother. *I* barely know my mother."

"Well, it would be a shame for you to end your career, and so much damage done all around, based on her misguided zeal."

"Misguided? You think all of these cancer cases are nothing?"

"There's no link whatsoever, Rennie."

"My mother seems to think there's a case."

"Don't be stupid. Tenure-track positions are hard to come by, especially for someone with only an MFA and scanty publications."

He picked up the keys and handed them over to me. I stared at the keys in his palm, then at his stern face and those eyes that had become cold and distant.

"Be smart," he said.

I took the keys and said I was leaving. He escorted me to the door. As I struggled, hurrying to put my shoes on, I looked up and saw a framed copy of *Caedmon's Hymn* hanging on the slender foyer wall. Tying my shoelaces, I looked across the hallway into his opened bedroom. On an end table, I noticed a large, framed picture of him and Rita Gómez, heads together and both smiling.

Foley returned with some leftovers. "Here, I know what it's like to be a young bachelor."

He thanked me for coming, bid me goodbye. "By the way, buy yourself some socks, man," he added, and then told me to drive carefully.

I shuddered to think that people like this guy exist. One minute he's threatening you and the next he's showing concern for your nutrition and safety while standing in front of a religious poem hanging on his wall and cheating on his wife, whom he would never divorce. He had it all philosophically figured out, his worldview all wrapped up like a Christmas package.

The fog had intensified, like cotton gauze running across my windshield. I had to drive slowly and was happy to note that most of the minimal traffic was heading in the opposite direction. Whenever a car was behind me, I would slow down to a crawl and let it pass. The locals were more adept at fog driving than me.

I kept thinking about Foley's words, the fact that Julia was litigating against the university and the U.S. government. I didn't know what to do, and decided that tomorrow I would give it some thought, that was, if I made it through that foggy night. But as I drove closer to Baná, my exhilaration grew as I absorbed that my parents' house was finally mine. I hated to think that in a way I was in collusion with Foley and whomever he represented. As much as I despised them, the Riveras, or anyone for that matter, should not have to be bullied that way. It frightened me to think he could do that, that some authority had empowered him to do it, and that that authority could do something to me or Julia.

But at the moment I hit the intersection heading to Baná, I gripped the keys in my hand and could not wait to enter the house and see it. The streets were deserted, and it was late. In a matter of minutes, I parked in front of the little house. I opened the small gate and, shivering, perhaps feeling something like the presence of my parents, I opened the second gate with one of the keys. My eyes became teary, and I felt silly getting so emotional, but I did.

I unlocked the front door and flung it open, flicked on the lights and saw, spray painted in black across the living room wall, in Spanish, "SHOVE IT UP YOUR ASS MOTHERFUCKER."

Twenty-Two

We were moving to our new home in Jersey, and I was slumped in the back seat, pouting and sighing loudly throughout the trip from the Bronx to Roselle. I was riding with my mother in the Corolla, following my father in the U-Haul truck that contained whatever furnishings they saw fit to bring along. Both had managed to get teaching jobs in the Garden State, in different colleges, so they were ecstatic to find a good deal on a house that was a reasonable driving distance from both of their institutions.

At age ten, I had to leave my friends behind. Despite all the promises adults made about keeping in touch, even then I knew it wasn't going to happen. No, my friends were gone, and I was angry at my parents. And I also liked my school a lot. Adults don't seem to understand, or they forget if it ever happened to them, that it is not easy to start in a new school. What a colossal pain in the butt to have to be introduced to classmates, learn the nooks and crannies of a new school, build immunity to new cafeteria food and deal with that whole new-kid-on-the-block crap. Kids are at the mercy of their parents' whims and dreams. But I was not going to take it lying down. They would know my displeasure. They would suffer like me.

Mami tried to cheer me up with talk about how exciting it was to have a house all to ourselves. No more hearing Mr. Rothman's honking noises as he tried to clear his nose upstairs, or the Screaming Santos downstairs and their French horn playing daughter. But I had found Mr. Rothman's snout cleaning funny, the Santos' arguments entertaining, and after a while I kind of looked forward to Michelle Santos' limited repertoire. I had no problems with our Bronx apartment on the Grand Concourse. It was spacious, and I could retreat to my own room, the benefit among many of being an only child. I had good times there, memories worthy of remembering, and with a few signatures, "poof," it was all gone. Mami tuned in to a radio station that played rock to entertain my budding interest in that genre, but I just looked away into the smoggy sky.

When we arrived, I slithered further down in the seat, immobile, arms crossed. Papi would not have it. After a few minutes, he came out to the car.

"Gee, have some cheese with that whine," he said. "Okay, move your butt out of the car and make yourself useful."

I dragged my body in slo-mo across the green lawn, just to emphasize the grief I was carrying. My entire childhood, at age ten, had been obliterated. I looked at the house and had to admit it was okay, so was the cul-de-sac that my parents kept talking about like it was the greatest thing on earth since sliced bread. I could already see myself riding my bike around the curve without my parents freaking out. Dragging my feet like the Mummy, I entered the house.

Boxes everywhere. Mami had already started unpacking the ones my father had brought into the kitchen. He started on the bigger items, helped by his friend from the old block, Marco. Together they struggled with the sofa.

"Rennie, please, move out of your father's way," Mami yelled.

I shuffled, head down, to the other side of the living room and plopped myself on the carpeted floor.

"Ay, por Dios," Mami said. "Rennie, enough." She came into the living room and ordered me to carry a few small boxes up to my room. "That's all your stuff; you should take care of it."

The thought of unpacking my action figures, books and video games did not get me out of my funk. I carried the boxes upstairs with a frown. I dumped them in what had been decided would be my room, and I started to explore the house. It had more room than our apartment. There were two full bathrooms, a kitchen my mother "loved," a backyard with a big tree to climb that I "should love," and a family room, in which Papi was already installing the television, in between taking sips from his Corona, while Marco brought in the remaining boxes and lighter items from the truck.

"Must take care of the essentials, right, Rennie?"

"Yeah, whatever," I answered.

I went up to the attic, which had been paneled and was an extra room. I thought it would make a great hideout. It had a couple of windows which looked like ship portals. I ran downstairs to ask Mami if I could have that as my room, and she shot the idea down. "That's going to be our office, your father's and mine."

Back went the frown, the Mummy shuffle.

"¡Ay, qué nene más dramático!" My mother laughed. "We gotta sign you up for acting classes."

I went outside, threw my little behind on the grass and started throwing gravel across the backyard I was supposed to love. After a few minutes, my mother came out from the kitchen and told me to stop moping because it was getting on her nerves.

"There are boxes in the family room, go unpack those, okay?"

I mumbled okay and dragged myself to the living room, my mother snapping a dish towel against my sorry ass.

"Stop," I whined.

She came after me playfully and tickled me, forcing me to laugh against my will. She nuzzled my neck, and I kept laughing, and then smothered my face and head with kisses. She wrapped her arms around me hard.

"Everything's gonna be fine, baby, you'll see." She knelt and stared at me. "This is a great moment for us all, Rennie."

She seemed so happy, I didn't want to argue with her.

"Okay. Go work, and dust the ceramics with this." She handed me a rag.

The boxes were already opened, so I started taking out their contents, mostly photo albums and knickknacks my mother had collected. I placed them carefully on the shelves of the wall unit, which already had the television set up. Papi was struggling with the stereo wiring.

I dropped one of the albums and dozens of pictures spilled onto the carpet. I had never glanced at these photos before. Curiosity, boredom and my funky mood led me to inspect them. Photos of Mami and Papi alone, when they were younger, grinning and playful at the beach, or at parties, dancing or posing with me, in one of the many stupid outfits my mother made me wear. Several of our dog, Sasha, who died a year earlier. Then, the others—so many unknown faces. Who were these people and why did my parents keep them around?

One picture slipped from an inside flap. A pretty woman with captivating eyes. She was throwing her head back and laughing while staring at the camera, her long black hair tumbling down her back and one shoulder. I could not stop staring at her. Why was she laughing? Why was she tilting her head like that? And who was taking the picture that she was talking to with her eyes?

Papi snapped the picture from my hands, breaking me out of my trance.

"Where did you get this?"

"It was in here," I said, pointing to the album.

He stared at the photo, and his sparkly eyes turned downcast, his entire body, which had become alive dancing with the music he had succeeded to pump through the stereo, now forlorn and heavy.

"Who is she, Papi?"

"Nobody, son. An old friend."

"She's real pretty."

His lips buttoned up, and he nodded. "Yes, she was."

"Did she die, Papi?"

And with tears in his eyes, he said, "Yes, a long time ago."

He took the picture and stuffed it into his back pocket, and I continued my work.

Twenty-Three

The Riveras had trashed the place. Besides the endearing "goodbye" posted on the wall, Chu Rivera had urinated on the floor. I imagined him drunk and angry spraying the floor and part of the wall.

"What animals," I thought, outraged and hurt to think he was defiling my parents' dream and my legacy.

That night I just shook my head, too tired to investigate the rest of the house. The next morning, I went back and assessed the damage. It was vandalism, nothing major. Whatever Foley had told Rivera had checked his aggression a bit. The house was structurally sound, and everything seemed to be working. They had absconded with the light fixtures, though. Just as well, I thought, they were probably tacky. In fact, the more I thought about it, the more I felt that this presented itself as an opportunity to re-do the entire house. My parents had planned to upgrade this house, a fixer-upper, anyway.

Julia introduced me to an architect friend who did small jobs on the side, and he designed a plan after driving from Guaynabo to visit the place and take measurements. His dedication was a way to please my mother, whom he obviously liked. The Riveras had depleted my patience, but luckily not the money left to me by my parents and from the selling of the Jersey house. Julia offered to pay everything, and I refused. But she insisted.

"A birthday gift," she said.

So, I agreed to let her pay half.

Work on the house had consumed much of my time since the dinner with Foley. I liked to think that taking care of the minor details in redesigning the house, staying on top of the contractor and time schedules, along with teaching four Basic English classes and all the other college stuff, was to blame for my lack of organizing efforts. If I allowed myself some slack, it was difficult, but the truth was Foley had made me reconsider what I was doing. I'm not proud to admit it, but it was what it was. I'm not saying that I had given up, but I just wasn't as motivated as before. Two leaders from the Congreso, Samuel and Felipe, came to my office to talk to me about what was going on. I told them my situation with the house and they understood, having known, like everyone else on campus, about my problem with the squatters. But they gave me dubious glances, like they were checking out my eyes, my face, to see if I had either defected or was a punk who talked the talk but couldn't walk the walk.

These were seasoned labor people who took organizing and political activism seriously, and I felt like a jerk for wasting their time. They told me that without some commitment from faculty the committee would get nowhere, and I was the only one who even expressed awareness of what was going on.

"Besides," said Samuel, "most of those who have gotten sick are faculty, and it's hard to get other people involved when fellow professors don't want to stand up for their own."

I suggested Stieglitz, and they both laughed. "Loco," Samuel, said, rotating his finger close to his ear. No one would rally around him; he was a "yanqui."

"You're an asimilao," Felipe teased, "but at least you're one of us." I thanked him for the backhanded compliment and told them to give me time with the house and I would get back to the work at hand. But I wasn't really convinced of my own words.

I felt nauseous when they left. I thought about Rita and felt even worse. But I didn't know what to do. I didn't want to trouble Julia with my own problems when she was preparing to take on the U.S. Defense Department and the University of Puerto Rico. Her getting involved made me rationalize that she was taking care of it. She had a big firm and all its resources at her disposal. She would fight legally for those afflicted, victimized by the stupidity of the people in charge of the clean-up, of burying explosives near densely populated residential areas. I was being selfish, of course. It would make her case harder if most of us at the university showed indifference and stayed at home.

We were entering Spring Break and the contractor had put the last touches on the house. I was ready to move into my new home, to leave the Guest House, and I had nothing else on my mind but the painting and other chores that awaited me. The place was roomier now, better designed, brighter lit and felt livable. Most of the work went into the former elevated wooden structure, which had been redone in cement, with a higher ceiling and a slanted, terracotta-tiled roof. Designed as a loft area, it had two short stairs at opposite ends leading to a wide space. The level below now contained the dining area, living room and foyer. There were two smaller rooms, an office and guest room. Everything looked new and fresh, including the utility kitchen and expanded bathroom, now holding a Jacuzzi tub.

With a wry smile, Marisol called it a bachelor crib. She had visited to help me out with ideas for furnishing the place, and we enjoyed that time together; it felt like we were doing it as a couple. After our talk at Luquillo, we had taken it slowly, everything from our conversations to our outings were always cautious, like we were building our relationship from scratch. Cautious also was our intimacy. We lingered, kissing and touching like virginal adolescents, but had not made love. The longer we went without committing ourselves, the more awkward it became. We talked about it but thought it was best to let things flow, like we always had, when our passion would sweep us into explosive lovemaking, sometimes in the most unusual times and places.

Julia still believed a younger woman suited me, but didn't push it like before. I guess she had resigned herself to my choice. She even offered us the Luquillo condo whenever we wanted it, or her apartment in San Juan, telling us we needed time together, away from Baná.

So, several things were distracting me from organizing that committee. When Foley came to the house during the break, the last thing on my mind was political activism.

I was painting the dining room area, grooving and singing along to the Red Hot Chili Peppers' "Snow."

The volume on the boom box on the floor dropped, and I turned around and saw Foley standing in my living room. He took off his sunglasses, folded them and hung them on the collar of his opened polo.

"It's looking really good, Rennie," he said, scanning the place, hands in the pockets of his Chinos. "Wouldn't have gone with that color myself, but hey, as the locals say, para gustos hay colores," he said, in a genuine Puerto Rican accent.

"Thanks," I said, and kept painting, reaching the uppermost part of a wall with an extended paint roller.

"Nice to finally move in, huh?" He grinned, arms crossed.

"It sure is," I said, dipping the roller into the pan, more energetically than usual.

He crept over and grabbed the stick. "Well, let's not forget who made it possible." He said this in a low voice, fixing his eyes on mine.

I put down the brush, and wiped my hands with a rag.

"What do you want?"

"It's not all about wanting, Rennie." He pointed to the beer I had in a little cooler. "May I?" he asked.

"I'm sorry, sure, please have one."

He popped the can open and took a hearty gulp, burped.

"The activity pushing the committee is declining," he said.

I didn't comment.

"Don't know what you're doing or not doing, I'm not going to ask. But this is a good thing."

He stared at me in my silence, sipping the beer again.

"You need to work on your mom," he said, pointing to me with the beer can.

"Oh yeah, and what am I supposed to tell her?"

"I don't care what you tell her, but make her reconsider the lawsuit."

I laughed.

"You think this is funny?"

"It's funny that you think my mother is so easily persuaded."

"I think she'll listen to you. She'd do anything for you. Isn't that right?" He snapped open his sunglasses and put them on. "She'd think things over, I don't know . . . " he continued, lips pursed. " . . . if life got a little tougher for her beloved son and he had to return to the States." He took a last sip of beer and put the can on a window ledge.

Slapping the wall, he said "This is solid cement work—don't see it much anymore. A nice little home, Rennie. Just hope you filed all the right papers with the municipality. Could be messy otherwise. By the way, do you know Baná named me an Honorary Son of the City? Helluva an honor."

He smiled that smug smile of his, and was walking out the door when he turned around, raising his finger in the air. "Oh yeah," he said, "Mari is up for tenure in the fall. And, funny thing about language teachers in PR: they're a dime a dozen. Just thought you should know."

Then he placed his hand over his heart, and, in that soft, calm, priest-like voice intoned:

"May you always have walls for the winds,

a roof for the rain, tea beside the fire,

laughter to cheer you, those you love near you,

and all your heart might desire."

He waved and walked away. I wanted to beat him over the head with the roller stick. I grabbed the beer can he had set down and carried it with two fingers as if it were toxic, and threw the remaining liquid down the sink drain, then crushed the can as if it were Foley's head.

"Fuck you, Foley!" I yelled, as I slammed the can into the garbage can.

I paced the apartment, unable to pick up the paint roller again or even stare at the work I had done. I scrambled for my cell phone and thought about calling Julia, but just couldn't. What would I tell her? Lately, things between us were beginning to gel. I had to think and couldn't inside the house. Everything felt claustrophobic, so I locked up and walked down Marcos Bortelli, still wearing my tee and torn jeans stained with paint, my disheveled hair sprouting from under a Yankee cap splattered with flecks of paint. I didn't know where I was going, but the avenue led into town, and after some turns found myself in the plaza. I sat down on the first bench I saw.

For a few minutes, I felt my heart pounding, and I saw everything around me moving but didn't really see anything. My knees fidgeted as I glanced over the plaza. I imagined myself returning to New York City, to what? No job, no apartment. How could I stay in Puerto Rico if I lost this teaching gig? I didn't come down here to live off my newlyfound mother. What about Marisol? I couldn't be the cause of her losing her job. How could we make it together if we both lost our jobs?

I flipped the cell and punched Marisol's number.

"Come get me," I told her.

A slight pause. "What's wrong?"

"I'll tell you later, but please come pick me up. I'm at the town plaza."

She was there in a matter of minutes and found me at the same bench, my knees doing the wave. She bent down and put her hands on my knees, putting her weight on them to stop them.

"You need to calm down."

She knew not to ask me what was going on right away. We had learned when to talk, when to listen, when to keep the silence or simply let the silence speak. She drove us back to her place, one of the tiny former enlisted barracks turned into faculty apartments near the municipal stadium. Marisol got hold of one when we started seeing each other more frequently, so she didn't have to drive from San Juan every day. Her place always calmed me. There was always a cool breeze, shade provided by the many trees around the house, and tranquility, unless there was a game or some religious event in the stadium.

We sat in the backyard, listening to the wind rustle the leaves. She served me a glass of white wine, and I took it gratefully. She sat down with her own glass and stared at me with concerned and expectant eyes, waiting for me to speak. Her peaceful loveliness in the sunset, and the chardonnay, relaxed me. After exhaling, I began to tell her everything.

"That guy's always been creepy," she told me, once I had finished. "No one really knows anything about him. He's like this shadow that comes and goes."

"Micco once joked he was CIA or FBI."

She laughed, but also shrugged. "Who knows? Anything's possible in Puerto Rico. Who knew they had dossiers on people here, right?"

I nodded, remembering what Julia had told me about the one they had on her and how she had worked with the legal team that had consulted and assisted Congressman Serrano to release them. But why would it surprise anyone, when the FBI even had a dossier on Martin Luther King?

Who knew who was behind Foley? One of those two agencies? One of the branches of the military? The company hired to do the clean up? The university and its Byzantine bureaucracy? The defense department?

Foley was a fixer, a go-to guy, someone hired by someone to get a job done, and it didn't matter what or who it was—they wanted results. And he had been doing this for a while. Who comes to Puerto Rico to teach Anglo-Saxon literature? Or maybe he did, but was recruited by someone. Maybe he was like one of those Russian operatives in the United Sates, who had been planted for years to infiltrate circles of influence and obtain any information they could. Who really knew? Who understood people who fabricated paranoid scenarios in the name of national defense or some other rationalization? The bottom line? Foley had some authority behind him pushing him to push me.

I leaned forward, and asked Mari, "What should I do?"

She sucked in her teeth, bit her lip.

"Ay, Rennie, I really don't know."

"I really trust your judgment, Marisol."

She shook her head, stood up and cleared our glasses, went into the kitchen and started soaping them up. I followed her into the kitchen.

"Tell me, please," I said.

She stopped, her hands full of soap. She brushed back a strand of hair, leaving some suds on it, and stared right at me.

"I'm sorry, Rennie, but I can't start all over again, not like that." I nodded, unable to look at her. "I have my condo, loans to pay. And what about your house. After all that hassle and expense, and if that bastard has his way, you can get into all kinds of legal mess. Lawyers here are experts in tying up people in technicalities."

She was pragmatic, realistic, speaking like someone who had witnessed the turmoil wrought by revolution, like an exile trying hard to fit into an adopted land and home, someone content to be left alone to find whatever peace and happiness she could. I sympathized. It made as much sense as anything I could have said. But she must have seen how disappointed, how torn I was over this decision. She came over to me and kissed me on the lips.

"It's hard, I know. But sometimes you have to let the giants battle it out. We little people have to step aside or be stomped on. Your mom's got this, Rennie."

I nodded again, but I couldn't look at her. I had let down Rita and those others who had died too young and without reasonable explanations. The same way I had let down anyone who ever stood up and did what was right. But the conversation ended there.

She asked me to stay for dinner. After I showered and slipped into some clothes I had at her house, we sat down to enjoy one of her best dishes and finish the bottle of wine. My concerns with Foley had consumed the day; it soon turned to evening. She asked me to stay the night, but I wanted to finish painting the house.

"The break will end soon, and I need to finish before the furniture comes and we resume classes," I said.

She nodded and retrieved her car keys to drive me home.

On the way back, I could only think about how to approach Julia, now that it was inevitable. I had not told Marisol about Foley asking me to intervene in the lawsuit. That his real mission was not just to stop me from organizing the college community, but to use me as a wedge to stop my mother. Why put her in a position to come between me and my mother? Especially now that Julia was warming up to her. She didn't need to know that part of it. It was clear that she was frightened. The giants were indeed battling, and I could not avoid getting stomped on, but I would do anything to prevent her from getting hurt. End of story.

She parked in front of my house. We kissed in the car, and I wanted her so badly. She, too, seemed eager to make love for the first time in so long.

"I have so much to do," I said, and she nodded.

"Go, paint," she said, brushing me away with her fingers.

She drove off, and I went back into my refurbished home and turned on the boom box. I painted until sunrise.

Several days passed before I got the nerve to call Julia. She recommended lunch or dinner, but I declined, thinking what I had to lay on her should be done in her office.

Ever since my first meeting with her in that office, I had come to appreciate what she had achieved. From various sources, I had learned the respect other people had for her; they also feared her, because everyone knew her to be a fierce and unwavering litigator. Driving to Hato Rey to meet her, I kept thinking of what I would ask her to do. The hours her firm had put into the lawsuit, the costs involved, the defendants grieving over the early loss of loved ones, the moral imperative of what this case represented—everything, dropped. Because I had no spine, because even though she was my mother, I had not inherited Julia's spirit or will to fight. I was so ashamed, but yet kept driving.

Julia had a broad smile on her face when she saw me. I, too, was happy to see her. With the house and everything else, I had not seen her for a few days. She embraced me, gave me a big kiss on the cheek and then proceeded to wipe off the lipstick, as she usually did, with a little saliva.

She prepared two demitasses of coffee and brought them over to her desk. She didn't have to ask anymore; she knew I liked coffee during the afternoon.

"Well," she asked, stirring her coffee. "What's the big news you needed to come here to tell me?"

I sipped the coffee. Julia raised her eyebrows in anticipation. I sighed and told her. Everything.

It was as if I had thrown a bucket of ice water on her followed by a ton of bricks. She slouched on the lush leather chair, reached for a cigarette, lit it up and stared at me hard before she even took one drag.

"We can get him on this," she said, pointing at me with the cigarette.

"Julia, I don't want to fight this man."

She pushed back from her desk, holding her forehead. She paced like that, holding her hand at her hairline, and then turned to me.

"It's not just about you, Rennie. People's lives have been destroyed. It's about government abusing power. About the senselessness of military proliferation."

"Julia, I know. But it's also affecting my life, and Mari's."

She ran her hands down the sides of her sleek dress, straightening the large belt around her waist. Nervous tics for coping with tension and anger. She poured herself a glass of water, her hands shaking.

"It's not like I can pass this case to another firm. No one will touch this, Rennie, do you understand?"

"Julia . . . " I began.

She banged the glass down on the credenza, spilling the water. "Goddamn it. Call me Mami, mother, mom, anything but Julia," she said, her eyes burning, her face distorted with anger and frustration. "At least do me that favor when you ask me to sell out."

Out of breath, almost hyperventilating, she spun the chair around and threw herself on it, her eyes focused on me.

After a pause, in a low voice, I said, "Mom . . . I'm sorry."

"Hallelujah," she said, staring at me as if I were a toddler pronouncing it for the first time. Then she covered her eyes, broke down and started crying, her shoulders shaking, her mascara running, her hair falling out of place.

I went to hug her and she put her hand out to stop. From her drawer she took out some tissues and blew her nose, and with tissue in hand waved me to sit again.

She stared at me with an odd smile on her face, and I thought she would start crying again. She sighed and fell back on the chair.

Then, she grabbed a picture frame from her desk, one which opens up to hold two pictures. "Read this," she said, handing it to me.

One frame had an old fading Polaroid snapshot of a baby; the other, a quote from Pedro Albizu Campos, the Puerto Rican icon for independence. From what I could make out, the quote was something like, "The law of love and sacrifice does not allow their separation. I have never been absent and have never felt absent."

"I guess the baby's me," I said, giving her back the frame.

She nodded, took it back and passed her hand over it.

"Taken at the hospital. The only picture I had of you until recently."

I recalled the manic way she kept taking photos of me.

"Juanma refused to send me any of you. Your birthdays would pass and not one photograph." Tears again welled up in her eyes. "But that's in the past."

Dabbing her eyes, clutching the tissue by the base of her neck, she said, "I found that quote, and it touched me so deeply that I started to cry. Don Pedro was talking about la patria, but the words made me think of you." The tears trickled down her cheeks, and once again I stood up.

"No, please sit," she told me.

There was a prolonged, lonely silence in that large office. Outside, my mother's secretary clacked away at the keyboard, phones rang, people chatted. Julia glanced toward the large window. She exhaled, then nodding absent-mindedly, said, "I'll drop the case, Rennie."

Twenty-Four

Marisol moved out of faculty housing and into my place. We were living like a couple, doing everything couples do from shopping to cuddling while watching a rented flick. Everything, except sex. We couldn't understand how before we had literally torn each other's clothes off, now we seemed like two asexual beings inhabiting the same space. We loved and desired each other, but that wasn't enough to make things spark when it came to sexual coupling.

The semester was ending, closing a difficult year for me as a rookie prof. I was happy to see it finish, excited to have time to spend with Marisol during the summer. But she was going to teach summer session, as most professors in the college did, just to help ends meet. Summer classes paid time and a half. They were so coveted that a point system, including all kinds of factors, was devised to determine who would receive these summer plums. At the bottom of the list, I had no chance this time around, but I wasn't keen on working the summer anyway. Marisol, on the other hand, at the number two spot, was receiving a regular class.

The others weren't left empty-handed. There were always the remedial summer classes. The majority of students entering the college had to take remedial English classes during the entire month of July. The need was so great to cover these that almost the entire department was involved, and Micco begged me. I agreed and found myself signed up for a month of intensive, week-long, four-hour sessions. After agreeing, I wanted to cry.

But first, I had to teach tedious final review classes, read and evaluate stacks of papers, tabulate and submit grades, with those

pesky borderline cases driving you crazy and attend all the wonderful meetings Micco had lined up for us and the time-consum-
ing committees on which we had to serve.

The calm after the storm did not come. Marisol and I came
home tired, exhausted, mentally drained. Add the everyday routine that absorbs so many precious minutes of your life, and it is
not hard to imagine how sex gets pushed back to the lower part of
your to-do list.

It wasn't all about time, though. Our break-up had shattered an
emotional, sexual connection that had flowed, that had been electric and spontaneous. After many disappointing relationships with
Puerto Rican men who thought cubiches, a negative term for
Cubans, were only good for a good time and ran to marry the first
decent Boricua girl they met, she had found someone promising
in me. But my foot-dragging made her think I was like the rest,
and the break-up deepened her feelings of being unloved and
unwanted. She went through a severe sense of loss. I, too, experienced it, not unlike when someone you love dies, but perhaps
worse because with death you resign yourself to never seeing the
person again and emotionally you make amends. Without
Marisol, my world had sunk into a deep crevice, dark and loveless,
and just now I felt myself creeping out of it and seeing light.

We carried emotional scars that needed healing as we tried to
build our new relationship on trust and a stronger sense of direction. And it wasn't like there weren't sparks, moments that bordered on rekindling the passion. That's what made it more frus-
trating. Marisol and I joked that fate had determined we would
never make love again. One time we had planned to soak in the
Jacuzzi and linger into lovemaking. We set up aromatic candles,
played soft jazz, popped a bottle of wine, and Marisol scattered the
bathroom floor with rose petals. We entered that fragrant bathroom, kissing, undressing each other and then we turned the
water on, and nothing.

We had experienced yet another of the typical unannounced,
unplanned water stoppages. After we both cursed, we had to dress
and gather our water containers and fetch water at a friend's house
for cooking and bathing, but not to soak in leisurely, because we

knew it would be a few days before the water was restored. A few times, the lights went out, and similarly we had to get ice for the items in the refrigerator, get candles and flashlights, and suddenly being in the dark didn't seem all that romantic. Living in a developing country is hazardous to your lovemaking.

Urgent phone calls interrupted our tender moments, or things needed immediate attention, and with every one of these setbacks the awkwardness grew, as did the tension between us. Not having consistent sex is something any bachelor gets used to; you're not happy about it. It gets you depressed, nasty and bitter, but at least you can attribute it to not having anyone special in your life, and that gives you hope. But here I shared the same roof with this wonderful, charming woman, sexy and loving, and *nada*. It's an unusual situation that can lead to anger and other ill feelings. When we had minor spats, initiated by one or the other of us, for the stupidest things, I would think: "Man, we both really need to get laid."

And it's important to get it at home, because outside there are temptations. I'm not saying I condone that. I had been faithful to Marisol during our sexual famine. But that doesn't mean the temptations weren't there, or that I had superhuman emotional control. Marisol didn't fall in love with a stick figure, but a young man made of flesh and bones. And shit happens, or can.

Like what happened at a department function. At the end of the academic year, the department likes to throw the few graduating seniors and honor students a party at one of the professor's homes, usually someone living in Baná or the outskirts. This year Cari Rosas volunteered to have it at her place in Cidra, a spacious, airy house with an expansive backyard ideal for an outside party. Someone had set up a volleyball net and there was a spirited game going on when Marisol and I arrived. One of the students had brought his deejay equipment and was spinning music to the pleasure of the growing numbers grinding and bumping on the grass. The drinking age is eighteen on the island, while it is twenty-one everywhere else in the United States. So, there was liquor at this party, although we restricted it to beer and wine.

We arrived late, and the party was in full swing. Marisol and I made the rounds congratulating the seniors and honor students, saying our hellos to colleagues and attacking the buffet that had been catered. We sat down to eat, sometimes waving to a student or colleague coming in, chatting with Juan Cedeño and his wife and trying to get more than a grunt from Stiegler, all of whom sat on folding chairs near us. I looked up and saw Pedro Roque walk in with Carmela López, who surely had convinced him to come. Roque had been out of mind since his announced leave, staying in the shadows, where he belonged. But he had taught some of these students, shepherded them through their four or five years of studies, so who was I to expect his continued absence. Seeing him, though, upset me, filled me with anger and disgust. Marisol looked at me and whispered if I wanted to leave. He and Carmela made their rounds, skipping our table, and stood to watch the activity. Occasionally, a student approached and greeted him.

"Definitely, in a few minutes," I responded, "but let me go to the little boys' room." I needed to take a leak, throw some water on my face and then leave.

Granted, I didn't knock but the door wasn't locked. I opened the door and bumped into the Green-Eyed Girl brushing up her lip gloss. She was bending toward a little round mirror, her butt sticking out. She stayed in that position and smiled as I walked in. I should have walked out. But that terrific smile of hers and those big sparkling emerald eyes froze me, not to mention the awkwardness of the encounter. She continued applying lip gloss, slowly, running her index finger across her shiny lips. I scoped her curving body, her firm butt snug in tight jeans.

"Hi, professor," she said, again smiling, this time with glittering lips. Her eyes glassy, she had the silly look of someone entertaining a comfortable buzz on a warm tropical day.

"You need to use the bathroom?"

The question was immaterial because her flashing eyes fixed on mine. We stood there just staring at each other for a few seconds.

"Why do you run away from me?" she asked. She took my hands and like an idiot I let her, and she placed them on her breasts.

"Don't you like me?" she asked, as I stood there dumbfounded, flat-footed, looking into those eyes, my hands palming her generous breasts.

I stared in wonder, studying her face in its earnest desire. She tiptoed to kiss me and her newly glossed lips, fruity and waxy, found mine and broke me from the trance. I pushed her and her breasts away.

"No, please, this isn't appropriate," I said, turning my now flushed face away.

The slight shove shook her into embarrassment and reality.

She grinned and whispered, "I'm sorry," and burst out of the bathroom.

I threw myself on the toilet seat, shaking my head, knowing that I was aroused, wondering what had happened.

After throwing cold water on my face, I went out ready to leave. The party was becoming livelier. The entire department, except for Foley, was in attendance. Freddie Rivas was cackling along with Iglesias for some reason. Cedeño and his wife talked. Rosas cleaned up some of the piling garbage. Micco kept asking if there was any rum in the house. The new Department Chair, I noticed, avoided looking in Roque's direction. Roque had taken a seat and sat regally and immovable as ever. The Green-Eyed Girl spotted me and turned to her friend, one of the English majors, who probably had invited her.

"Let's roll," I whispered to Marisol.

We tossed our goodbyes to colleagues and students alike, most of them not acknowledging or noticing our departure.

I wanted to tell Marisol that same day, but couldn't. The sex thing wasn't going well for us. And I couldn't figure out how it got to the point it did. Was I to blame? Did I encourage her? Was I so in dire need of getting laid that my penis took over my better judgment? I felt terrible, and after a few days I sat down with Marisol and confessed.

"What took you so long to take your hands off her tits?"

I looked flustered, because honestly I did not know. Then Mari roughly grabbed my face in her hands.

"Honey, you did the right thing. A little slow," she laughed, rolling her eyes, "but you did. It's obvious she has a crush on you, and she's sexy."

"Nowhere as sexy as you," I said, nuzzling her neck.

She slapped my thigh. "Not now, Romeo, I have papers to grade. And so do you."

And so it went until the end of the semester. Cold turkey. We both knew we had to do something. Having submitted grades and waiting for summer classes to start, we decided it was a good time to take up Julia's offer to borrow the Luquillo condo for a weekend.

We walked the beach during sunset, had a fantastic seafood meal, shared some animated, lighthearted conversation and a bottle of wine nudged us into the mood. We felt giddy, carefree and sexy. We groped and kissed as we bounced around the elevator. I slammed open the door to the condo and carried her to the bedroom in the dark, her legs wrapped around my waist.

Outside the waves slapped the beach, the bright moonlight spread through the window and shrouded our nude bodies. Mari's perfume filled my nostrils with every deep breath I took. The food and wine lingered on our tongues and lips as we kissed.

Naked, exposed to each other, our bodies had not touched like this in months. It was electric, like our skin would pop with sparks at any moment. My hand ran up Mari's curving thighs, her back, as I kissed her navel, lost inside her skin.

The tactile journey ended as my fingertips alighted on her left breast and the lump. She shot up as soon as I stopped, pulling up the bed sheet to cover herself.

"It's nothing," she said.

I sprung from the bed, stumbling, and turned on the table lamp to see her better. "Let me feel it again."

"You just want to cop another feel," she joked.

I looked at her, angry now. "Fuck, Mari. This is no joke."

"What do you know about it?"

I looked at her, my arms crossed now. "Have you had that checked by a doctor?"

"Not yet."

"Holy fuckin' shit," I yelled, looking at her open-mouth and wide-eyed.

"Don't get hysterical on me, okay?"

I slid myself by her side on the bed. "How long have you known this?"

The pause infuriated me.

"Tell me!"

She started crying. "A few weeks. Oh, Rennie, I'm so scared."

I hugged her, kissed her head, her brow.

"I didn't want you to worry," she said in between sobs. "You've had so much on your mind."

We held each other, rocking ourselves for a long time. Her sobs ended, and we continued embracing in silence.

"Tomorrow we'll go see a specialist."

She nodded her wet face into my naked chest.

Twenty-Five

Looking back, the routine comforted me. From Monday to Friday, every week, for seven weeks, I drove Marisol to the Hospital Oncológico in Río Piedras for radiation therapy. Fighting a disease that causes such chaos in the body, following a regiment of procedures that, although necessary, seemed brutal and torture-like. The complete havoc it creates on the lives of patients and those they love; what it does to a person's spirit and psyche—all this was overwhelming for Marisol, of course. But also for me as I tried, as well as I could, to stand with her through that rough period.

I had inspected every inch of that waiting room, so many times. Having absorbed the purposeful sterility of it, having made symbolic acknowledgement of the burning round cell-like ceiling lamps, I felt the loneliness of sitting in interlocking chairs set against white walls, gaining only an occasional sad smile from another person waiting for a loved one to receive the fifteen to thirty minutes of high energy rays to kill rebel cells out to destroy them.

On the last session of her treatment, there were two other visitors in the waiting room. An older woman waiting for her husband who had prostate cancer and someone new, an older gentleman. When these other people got to talking, after seeing them again for a couple of weeks, they wondered why someone as young as I could be there. They were saddened to hear about Marisol, so relatively young, getting breast cancer, about our budding romance being interrupted by the disease. They were short polite conversations—no one wanted to talk much—and anyway, you weren't there for long.

Toward the end of therapy, I had read everything strewn on the coffee and end tables, so I indulged in the comfort of having the routine run its course. I tried to grade exercises I'd brought, but instead concentrated on the photos of beautiful and serene land-scapes carefully placed throughout the room. That last day, I remember focusing on the beach scene, which could have been any-where on the island: eye-popping turquoise water, oatmeal-colored sand, a barefoot, healthy, tanned couple walking arm in arm.

Marisol was worried about wearing a bathing suit after the sur-gery. She loved the beach so much and couldn't stand the idea of not being able to go. She said this although she had only had a lumpectomy, and the cancer had not spread to lymph nodes. But in her mind it was as if the entire breast had been forever dam-aged. Wearing a swimsuit was foreign, impossible now. She refused to let me see the scar. I tried to talk to her, tried to make her see the bigger picture: she was alive and her prognosis was good. But, no, she had seen the statistics, she said, and they told her that there was a 12% chance of not surviving.

In early June, the biopsy had come back positive; the tumor was malignant. Mari was devastated. The doctors told her it was stage II, a treatable cancer. But the reality was that a knife would cut inside her breast in pursuit of something potentially lethal.

At first she would not accept it. We went to another oncologist who could not believe we were seeking a second opinion on what she termed clear evidence of cancer. She told us to act quickly, now that the tumor was relatively small and the cancer highly treatable. I had to shake Mari out of her stupor. She wanted to put it off, and I kept pushing her. We had a big fight.

"I've had enough loss in my life," I told her. "Please don't add to it."

That kind of shook her a bit, and she relented. After surgery, she lost interest in everything. She was so depressed, she gave up her summer class, the money that went with it, along with the vacation she had planned with me to the Dominican Republic.

"You'll be the first on the list next year," I told her.

"If I'm still alive," she snapped back.

Julia's frequent calls during this period kept me balanced, sane. She had the uncanny ability to call when I was approaching a meltdown. At night, after one of Marisol's bad days, or struggling with doctors and appointments, or medical bills, she was there to listen to me vent. Her soothing voice told me how proud she was of me, offered help with bills, gave me advice whenever I asked. My mother gave me the boost to get up the next morning and face another day.

And those days living with Marisol were not fun. She would go off on tangents about her contaminated breasts and wondered how she could breastfeed if we ever had children. Out loud, she asked me if I would be disgusted or repulsed at her breast scar.

"I'm in love with you, not your breast."

"That's what you say now," she huffed. "Men are all alike."

It was July and I was busy teaching the remedial class, which had turned out to be more difficult and challenging than Basic English. Micco had assigned me the late afternoon section, so I could drive Mari to her morning radiation therapy. When I returned from teaching the class, I'd find her with tissues crying in front of a novela. I would turn off the television and suggest running the Jacuzzi, or that I would cook up a favorite dish, without much success. During weekends, she slept late, spent mornings lying around in pajamas. In a way, I was glad that the radiation therapy had begun because it got us out of the house every day. After a therapy session, I planned outings to distract her and make the day pleasurable. She resisted, she just wanted to go home, she would say. The radiation made her tired, and she complained about the skin irritation. She became even more depressed and lost weight.

"Why couldn't the weight come off my thighs and butt?" she asked, as if I'd be stupid enough to answer that.

Even her family could not shake her moods. Marisol's parents—Don Martín and Doña Caridad—and her siblings, Nicki and Carlos, volunteered to drive Mari to the radiation sessions, but it didn't make sense. I lived with her in Baná, and they lived in San Juan. Why should they drive back and forth? They visited her when we stayed weekends in Marisol's condo, or at home in Baná, always bringing food and gifts. That cheered her up a bit, but their leaving then made her sad and despondent. Doña Caridad cried at the end of every visit; to make it worse, Don Martín would reprimand her. Nicki ushered them into the car, rolling her eyes or shaking her head, apologizing for them. You could hear them arguing in the car as they drove away.

Puerto Rican families argued out of love and caring, but it was always loud and animated. Even the most banal discussion required wild hand motions, bodily gesticulations and rising decibels. In my own family it was the norm, and I grew up wanting to retreat somewhere all the time. I grew up avoiding confrontation, avoiding issues, skirting them, not wanting to be bothered. Being an only child helped me create a cocoon, a bubble from which I never needed to answer to other siblings as I isolated myself from my parents.

But I could not run away now. I kept my ground because life without her would be empty. Selfishly, I fought to retain that which made me feel good, and sound, and whole. There was no cocoon to run to, nowhere I could escape without the feeling of abandonment gnawing at my mind and heart. She needed me, and I had to be there for her. I was not going to lose her. But it was tough. Mari was not the best of patients. The door was tempting, such a natural and easy escape. Sometimes she pushed me toward it, when in her worst moments she claimed, always in Spanish, that I was wasting my time with a "vieja ajada, acabada," an old decrepit woman.

"Ay, vete," she would say. "Go find that girl with the green eyes." And she would roll over on her good side and fall asleep.

I had to contain my anger at these outbursts. She was experiencing something difficult, and it wasn't about my feelings. But I loved her, and yet she didn't believe me or feel it. As the radiation came to a close, I suggested counseling for her, and she accepted that she needed help. She attended a support group and saw a therapist regularly. Eventually, I saw positive change. She was smiling more. We began making plans again and talking about the future. The intimacy was not there, though. We slept in the same bed, but didn't even cuddle. She kept her distance, constructed an emotional wall. It was as if the cancer had invaded her, violated her body, and she could not entrust it to anyone because she could not trust it herself. She wasn't ready to share with anyone what she felt was a body out of control, not even with a person she loved. I would bend over to kiss her cheek goodnight and she would stiffen. "I love you," I'd say, and sometimes she would grab my hand on her shoulder and hold it tight, a gift.

I could not stay angry at Mari, because her enemy was lethal and destructive. And it did not escape my mind that perhaps her health, like that of others, had been compromised by authorities making stupid decisions. That someone or something else had to take the blame for her cancer and that of a growing number of others. Marisol made it a point to tell me not to return to any form of activism, just because of her illness. You don't argue with a person fighting cancer, but on this issue I was not going to follow her advice. I kept quiet, focusing on her treatment, on her health and well-being.

But watching her go through everything intensified my outrage, double what I felt when I had learned of Rita's case. It was now personal, and whatever anger I felt at Rita's ill-timed death, this was too close to home to let it ride. Yes, like on so many issues, when it does hit home, it takes on a terrifying significance that only a numb, heartless and vapid person could neglect. Either that, or a coward. As much as I loved her, Marisol was a coward. She was afraid to fight. Her parents had inculcated into her a complete disregard for politics and anything political. All those years living in Puerto Rico and they still cultivated their exile identity. They were Cuban, first and foremost, and beyond fearing independence like the plague—a recipe for communism Don Martín would often say—they were indifferent to issues confronting the island.

No, Marisol's position on this was not the north star. I humored her and, in between driving her to her appointments and attending to her needs at home, I re-initiated talks with the Congreso. To their credit, Felipe and Samuel met with me again; they could have dismissed me with disdain, but didn't. I met them for breakfast at a bakery in town, and they greeted me with stern and doubtful faces and refused my offer to buy them coffee. I explained my desire to continue with the efforts we had previously started. They both looked at each other and then at me.

"You're starting to sound like Peter with the wolf," Felipe said.

Samuel found this amusing and nodded. But he dropped the smile and stared at me as if studying me. "You know what saddens me, compañero?" He didn't wait for any type of answer. "How our people sit around and watch others suffer until the problem affects them personally."

Felipe stuck out his lips and nodded.

"Then it becomes the most important issue on the planet."

I nodded, feeling ashamed. Everything he was saying was true, but it sounded harsher, more truthful in Spanish.

"I'm really sorry about Marisol," he said.

I tensed up. He gestured to the man behind the counter for a coffee. Felipe took out a cigarette and lit up.

"But," he continued, in a deliberate, painfully slow tone, articulating every word, as if this were a lesson, "you have come around, and that's what's important."

"How do we know he's serious this time, Samuel?" asked Felipe, flicking ashes on the floor.

"Look, look in his eyes," he said, stirring his coffee, pointing to me with pursed lips like Puerto Ricans are wont to do. "They have the fire of a man fighting for something that matters to him."

I stared back at him, upset at how casually he was reading me.

He sipped his coffee, shook his head. "René, I'm not the enemy."

I exhaled, sat back on my chair. "You're right," I said, and extended my hand, which he grabbed at the wrist, making me do the same.

That Saturday morning we talked for hours, making plans, considering strategy, writing down an outline of what needed to be done. Felipe wanted to enlist help from the local PIP party. I questioned whether it was wise to bring in partisan politics, and Samuel answered that the PIP was the only party genuinely interested in environmental issues.

"If they want to make it political, that's not important. But they have the machinery useful for getting media attention."

That's what they wanted, to make it a media event to embarrass the university and generally shed some light on the problem.

We planned to disseminate the information we had to the media, organize the various groups and start a series of meetings and rallies to protest the university's inaction and demand answers. Felipe would focus on the community, Samuel on the Congreso and I would work on the students and faculty. This was hard work, the hardest I had ever done in my life, especially because it was here on the island.

"Brother, this is a colony full of colonized minds. It's difficult to move people to action," Samuel advised me so I wouldn't get discouraged.

"Puerto Ricans are obsessed with having fun and spending money," chimed in Felipe.

And they were right. The faculty seemed so stubbornly opposed to doing anything. Everyone was wrapped up in his or her individual world, his or her career, family. What made it even more difficult was that it was summer and, to reach professors, in many cases I had to go to their homes at times when they were not off on vacation somewhere.

There wasn't any proven correlation between the cancer cases and what the Army had deemed HTRW buried under our feet. This was the standard response, and I had to explain that we wanted an independent study done to verify that one way or another. We deserved answers because possibly our health was at stake. Marisol's case gave me some cred with some of the faculty. She was popular, and colleagues by now knew we were an item. Perhaps they felt sorry for us, who knows. But after a few weeks of constant agitation, some began to commit themselves and, at a minimum, sign the petition we were circulating that demanded an independent study to determine the extent of the health hazards, if any.

The student leadership was made up of highly motivated and politicized young people, but we all knew that the students in general were going to be a hard sell. If professors were oblivious or indifferent, how much more would students be? I contacted the student leaders living in Baná, and they managed to get hundreds of signatures on the petition from people in the community. They

J.L. Torres

promised a good turnout from young people in the area for the scheduled rallies.

Foley showed up to the first faculty meeting, a good turnout considering that it was July. I was so tired and at times felt myself nodding out as others spoke. Caring for Marisol at home was exhausting, and the last week of remedial classes was draining. Just trying to make the monotonous exercises engaging and fun every day was in itself tedious and demanding, but in the final week we also had to test the students and assess the progress of the entire group. But I was proud at the turnout for the first meeting. People were becoming alarmed, especially those who had no idea of the clean-up or about the radioactive material buried so close to where they worked. The apparent cover-up was what riled people the most, and their responses addressed that, directly and bitterly. No one wants to feel used and lied to.

Foley sat silently in the last row, his arm slung over the back of the adjacent seat. He was listening, at times leaning forward, his head bowed especially when his colleagues demonstrated hostility toward the college and those involved in the mess. Everyone in that room, except him, was concerned with the health hazards that we could all be experiencing as we went about our daily routine in what appeared to be an idyllic campus.

Foley stood up and spoke in fluid Puerto Rican Spanish with barely a trace of accent. He moved toward the front of the room like a big-time lawyer handling a jury who was in the palm of his hand. This man commanded respect, used words eloquently, even knew when to pause for effect. And most importantly, he knew his audience. All those years in Puerto Rico had taught him that people on this island lived in constant fear. Fear was their mother's milk. They thrived on fear. The Culture of Fear had its origins here way before any social critic labeled it and wrote about it.

Foley outlined the possible fearful scenarios from how radical students would take hold of this issue in their usual irresponsible way and disrupt classes for God knows how long, to the money and time invested in what could be a possibly, and most likely, a false assumption. Money, he said, that in the present budgetary crisis will have to come from some department or program, and that meant jobs. And, he added, who wants to put up with the media circus that will interrupt our quiet community? We will have protests, outsiders coming in to make trouble for sure, people may get hurt. A long pause.

"Who wants all that trouble?" he asked rhetorically. "Colleagues, the authorities are cleaning it up, isn't that what we want? Let them do their work and let's get back to doing ours."

I didn't appreciate the subtle hint at people getting hurt. Did he know something? Or was it a threat?

I had been on this campus long enough to know the rumors circulating about Foley. He cultivated and used that mystery to his advantage. That, and the instinctive fear or ingratiating respect Puerto Ricans had for Americans. After a century, a colonial mindset is not easily shaken. No one stood up to challenge anything he said. There was a silence, unnerving in all of its revelation.

"Mari wants to get back to work, Jake," I responded. My knees felt weak, but I stood up. Then I rattled off names of colleagues who were recuperating from cancer. "They all want to get back to work."

And then I named the twenty-two who had died. "They will not be coming back to work."

I let that sink in. And I looked at Foley square in the eyes. "And neither is Rita."

His faced reddened, his blue eyes ready to pounce. "Now, the high incidence of cancer on this campus may not have any correlation to the ordnance the Army buried so close to the water we drink, the air we breathe, and where we spend so much of our time. Ordnance that the Defense Department itself has deemed hazardous. We know they're cleaning it up, finally." I stopped and raised my voice. "What we want is definitive proof that it has not adversely affected our friends and colleagues, and our loved ones. And if it has, those responsible should be held accountable and make reparations."

I stared at him with equal anger and disgust. "We're fighting for those colleagues and friends, and for loved ones, Jake. Who you fighting for?"

He could have killed me right there, I know it. He marched out, making those in attendance turn back to watch him slam the door as he left. Strange how good that felt. To stand up to him like that. Some colleagues came up and patted me on the back, shook my hand. There was excitement in the room; we were full of that righteous indignation you hear and read about.

I came home late that night. The faculty leadership decided to go out for a few beers to continue our discussion. When I got home I checked on Marisol, who was sound asleep.

I found it funny how she snored but never admitted to it. I vowed one day I'd record her just to prove it to her. I bent down and brushed back a strand of hair covering her face, kissed her on the cheek. She snorted, which made me want to laugh.

I couldn't sleep and went into the living room, threw myself on the sofa, too tired to undress, turned on the television and clicked through the channels. Julia called to tell me she was driving down to visit tomorrow with goodies from my favorite bakery. We talked briefly about Mari, and she hung up.

My cell rang again. It was Foley.

"Great speech, kid."

"Well thank you, Jake. Coming from you that's a real compliment."

A slight chuckle on his end, a rumbling, throaty one that hinted at drinking.

"It's out of my hands, now, Rennie."

"I'll deal with it."

I could hear him breathing, about to click off, then stop and put the phone back to his mouth.

"By the way, the comment about Rita? That was a low blow."

And he hung up. He was right, and I felt my face flush with shame.

But any feelings of regret or guilt for playing the Rita card quickly dissolved, thinking about his chilling words. It's out of my hands, he had said. I had made a decision to get involved. There was no turning back and no room for apologies.

I was fighting giants, after all. I picked up my cell and dialed.

"Mom . . . I need to talk to you."

Twenty-Six

She called me early the next day, a Saturday, and told me to drive to San Juan and meet her for breakfast at one of our favorite hangouts, a bakery which served delicious grilled sandwiches on homemade bread. I followed her instructions and dressed casually, with a pair of sneakers that had good traction. These days, I rarely questioned what my birth mother said. There was always rationale and common sense behind her orders or requests. I laughed to think I had become such an obedient son in my older age.

We sat for a quick breakfast, which was odd. On these outings we would talk for hours, sometimes over several cups of coffee, a few cigarettes for her, and the newspaper, which we shared as I listened to her take on the national political scene.

Where at first I had disliked these sessions, and the "cultural field trips," I began to appreciate them as I accepted my mother's passion and deep-rooted convictions; and the overwhelming idealism I could never hope to emulate. Julia was growing on me. Those feelings were only disrupted by the haunting reason behind her abandonment of me as a baby. I tried to get beyond that, although it gnawed at me. But right now, I was more worried about how I would approach her about my involvement with the committee, how I would ask her to re-start the lawsuit.

Our breakfast at the bakery was shorter than usual, and I didn't ask questions when she ordered ham croquets and sandwiches to go.

She had brought along her Mazda MX5 roadster. I anticipated an adventure. To see her driving that car was an adventure in itself. She worked the gears like a maniac, her booted foot pumping the clutch, her face serious, except on those occasions when a familiar song came on that she felt obligated to sing along with. A horrible voice, squeaky and off pitch, but she put so much feeling into the lyrics. On these trips I never asked where we were going. In the beginning I did and she would tell me, "Be quiet and soak it all in."

And I did. On this trip, I reclined on the leather seat and let the wind hit me as I looked at the untamed greenery, the whitening limestone karst clinging to the hills, enjoying the curious sights that popped up, and joined her in whatever songs we both wanted to mangle. Occasionally, she initiated a conversation in Spanish to make me practice.

We hopped on the 2 going west toward Arecibo, and in less than half an hour we were heading south to the Camuy caves. The first thing she did after easing the car into the parking lot was take off her stiletto boots. I had to peel those off her, and then she slipped into a pair of raggedy sneakers. She looked way shorter without the boots.

"Someone so fashion conscious and those are the kicks you wear?" I asked.

"Because I *am* a fashionista is why I wear these." She shook. "Your generation with this obsession over tenis."

I didn't want to tell her how the use of "tennis shoes" dated her, even her Spanglish version.

"Anyway," she said, "they have good traction and you need that in the caves."

If they made stiletto sneakers with traction, I thought, she'd wear them.

Julia bought tickets and we had to wait for the guide to call our group by number. We sat and talked a bit, about nothing important, as she smoked a few more cigarettes. The tour guide called our group's number and gathered us, about twenty in total, in front of the entrance. He made us wear green hard hats, which made us look ridiculous.

The guide, Ramón, a chubby man with cherubic cheeks and the straggliest of mustaches, herded us into various cars of a neon orange trolley. As the tram maneuvered through thin roads up to the cave, Ramón gave us some geologic history and background. He was professional and knowledgeable, always trying to mix humor in with the educational bits he was offering. Julia seemed distant as he rambled on. Her ears and eyes perked up when we arrived at the entrance to Cueva Clara. She handed me a camera and told me that I would want a photo of this. She was right. Everyone ambled out of the tram and walked carefully on the slippery walkway, holding on to the handrail, to observe a display of light filtering through a hole above us. It looked like a dozen spotlights hitting the cave ground or the beams of a spaceship taking off to faraway galaxies. In between the oohs and aahs, I snapped a few pictures, amazed again at how such a small island contained so many natural wonders.

Ramón pointed to the Río Camuy, the third largest underground river in the world, which rumbled below us undisturbed. In the darkness slept thousands of bats, only their squeaking and guano there to remind us of their presence, as we gawked at the river and surroundings. Back on the trolley, Ramón peppered his formal commentary on the various karst formations with the funny names the guides gave them. "We call that one 10, a skinny man with a fat lady," he explained, smiling. Some of us laughed, but the heavy-set woman next to him stared at him sternly.

One of the final stops was the sinkhole, or sumidero, surrounded by large stalactites. Outside again, we saw the cascade falls, which loomed above us and seeped down to a trickle closer to us. "The Fountain of Youth," Ramón said and urged us to drink from its natural waters.

"I'll take my chances with cosmetic surgery, thank you," Julia whispered to me, while others in the group scooped some of the water up and slurped it or dripped it over their heads.

"I feel younger already," an older American said.

The tram made a final stop in front of the main building, which held the restaurant and souvenir shop.

"Crappy food," Julia whispered and took out the food from the coffee shop we had visited earlier. We sat at a picnic table under a shady jacaranda tree, near a large coquí sculpture that I photographed.

"I love the caves, they're so cool inside," she said, fanning herself.

"Yeah, they're cool that way, too," I said, playing with a croquet.

"Did you know the Taínos believed human beings emerged from caves?"

"That's news to me," I answered.

"To them, we were once spirits dwelling in caves," she said as she waved her sandwich across the air. "One of the myths tells they left their caves only to wander out to eat our native fruit, jobos, at night. One day they stayed too long eating jobos and daylight hit them."

"Must have been some mighty good jobos," I said.

"Sunlight transformed them into humans, and that began the process of humans leaving the caves."

"And you're telling me this because?"

She shrugged. "I like the idea of sunlight making us human." Her eyes widened and she wiped her mouth on a soiled napkin, set her sandwich down. She hadn't eaten much. Holding up a cigarette, she cupped my hand with her one free hand.

"Okay, now tell me why you called me yesterday." She blew smoke away from my face and smiled.

I wanted to tell her but just couldn't. At my silence, she leaned toward me, her eyes expectant, and grabbed both my hands with her delicate, firm hands, the burning cigarette between two fingers.

"René, you know you can tell me anything. There's nothing—nothing—in this world that you can tell me that will change how I feel about you."

I nodded slowly, looking down at my half-eaten sandwich, at her tiny hands gripping mine, her thin veins bulging.

"I've been so tough on you," I said, biting my lower lip, shaking my head. I looked away. "All you did was seek me out. All you've ever done is love me, and I've just been a selfish asshole."

She snuffed out the cigarette on the sole of her torn left "tennis shoe." She looked at me, studying my face, confused. Her eyes flattened, as if my words had deflated the spirit out of them. At seeing my head down, the tears trickling down my cheeks, she rose and hugged me.

She held my chin up. "You listen to me." Her eyes embraced mine. "What happened to tear you apart from me was not your fault. Just know this: I'll never let it happen again. You understand?"

I nodded and she kissed me on the top of my head.

"Okay," she said, sliding back around to the bench. Spreading her manicured fingers on the picnic table, she leaned into me. "Let's talk about the lawsuit."

I looked up at her.

"It's a small island, René." She tossed back her hair, sprung another cigarette from her gold case and waited for me to light it.

I briefed her on my activities with the committee, told her about Foley and his ominous comment, about Marisol's worries.

After I finished, she seemed lost in thought, agitated. She told me she was proud of me and made a few quick phone calls.

"Now, it's personal," she said, snapping her phone shut.

Being surveilled, you can't help feeling trapped in an invisible jail, wondering why someone is watching your every step if you have not done anything illegal. Or, maybe that is the whole point: no reason, they're there just to intimidate you. If the surveillance is professional and competent, you of course have the added mind fuck that you are perhaps imagining that they are watching you. Every possible lingering car becomes suspect, any person lurking too close to you becomes a spy working for someone. You walk down the street, enter or exit a building, and wonder if they've just snapped your picture. Even in freedom, you are not free; you are neither free physically, nor in your mind.

My mother admitted that she assumed wire taps and that she never said anything important or possibly incriminating on the phone or in the house. She told me that she met with clients outside, where there was much noise, near a construction site, for example. All those scenes of wise guys walking and talking outdoors from the mobster flicks flashed in my mind, taking on a different perspective now. She joked about smiling for the cameras.

"I always give them my best side," she added.

"I feel paranoid," I told her.

"That's to be expected, René," she said and quoted Bukowski: "Just because you're paranoid doesn't mean they're not out to get you."

We both laughed into a pause, and then she sighed.

"Welcome to my world," she said.

"I'm sorry you have to live in that world," I said. We were having lunch at Amadeus, one of our favorite places in San Juan.

"Oh, I have something for you," she said, pulling a wrapped gift from her large pocketbook and handing it to me.

"What's the occasion?" I asked.

"Something to help you get through this period."

It was a poem titled "The Lover of a Subversive Is Also a Subversive," by Martín Espada, printed on heavy linen paper, framed in dark teak.

The poem recounts the perspective of a painter whose revolutionary lover was imprisoned for a long time. Yet, she still is being surveilled by "the FBI man."

At the end of the poem, as she paints her lover's portrait by the beach, at a distance the FBI man lurks behind her, waiting for her to sob. But she refuses to cry.

Touched by the poem and my mother's intention in giving it to me, I took it home and hung it by the doorway, to remind me every time I walked out the door to smile for the camera.

Mari was touched by Julia's gesture but not crazy about the idea of having to put up with people spying on us, or that loved ones had to suffer the political actions of their lovers.

"It's just romanticizing a bad situation," she told me.

I kept my renewed organizing efforts a secret from Mari as long as I could. I did not want her to become worried during her convalescence. Since she was pretty much a recluse, I was able to keep it a secret for most of the summer. But Baná is a small town. With her recovery, she started going out more and bumped into someone who told her.

She was furious, first for keeping it from her, and then for threatening her job.

"We talked about this, Rennie. You promised me."

"We'll be fine," I assured her.

"Easy for you to say. You have a high-powered lawyer for a mother, who comes and wipes your ass every time you shit on something. You gonna guarantee my job, Che?"

I exhaled, trying to sift the hurtful things from the valid points she was making.

"We'll fight for your job, if it comes to that."

"Fuck that, Rennie, I'm fighting for *my life*." She banged her chest as she said this. "I can't afford to lose my health care, not now."

I stared at my hands, folded in front of me, anything not to look at her angry face.

"Please," I said, slowly. "Have faith."

"In what? A bunch of revolutionary wannabes? What are you going to get out of this?"

"Stop it!" I said, holding up my hand. "You fighting for your life?" I walked over to her, put my face up to hers. "And why's that? Because some fucks contaminated where we work, that's why. Sometimes you need to get a backbone, Mari."

She grabbed her keys and purse and stormed out of the door.

When she returned, with shopping bags from the mall, she was mellow. Shopping always calmed her down.

I had fallen asleep on the couch. She dropped her bags and slid in next to me, took my arm and wrapped it around her. She told me she was upset and frightened, but had no right to tell me what to believe or how to act.

"Just be careful, please," she said, sleepily.

After that, she tolerated my committee work, sometimes made snide remarks about it, but we had no further fights on the issue. She prepared her file for her upcoming tenure review way in advance, bracing herself for the worst. I didn't think it was the right moment then to tell her about the town building inspector who had come around to ask questions about the recent work I had done on the house. I was also prepping for the struggles to come, thinking about alternatives, possible scenarios, plans of action. All the time, trying to deal with the uneasy feeling of being watched.

Twenty-Seven

My ringtone, Nirvana's "Smells Like Teen Spirit," was blaring from my cell, which lay on the coffee table inside, while my friend Kyle's cousin, Jordan, opened the door to her house. I ran in and grabbed it before Mami was about to hang up.

"Oh my God, where have you been, Rennie?" She sounded desperate, on the brink of crying.

"At Kyle's cousin's, like I told you."

She started crying.

"Mami, you okay?"

"Have you seen the news? Turn it on, *Eyewitness News*."

I asked my friend to turn on the news. On the screen a bunch of guys were spraying water on some women, yelling and acting all rowdy, something about a "wilding" attack in Central Park after the Puerto Rican day parade.

"Damn, Rennie, your people going berserk," joked my friend, Kyle.

"Fuck you," I mouthed at him.

"We were worried to death you might be in the park," my mother said. "How come you didn't return our calls?"

Even before the summer had begun, my parents had pushed me to march in the parade. They had insisted I join Aspira, the Latino youth organization so I could meet other Latino teens—maybe even a nice Boricua girl, my father chimed in—and absorb culture, perhaps even improve my Spanish. I hated the idea. I could care less about Hispanic, Puerto Rican or whatever culture for that matter. I was seventeen, summer was coming, and all I wanted to do was party before entering my senior year of high school, when I knew I had to bear down and get into a good college.

I conceded because Mami said they had scholarships for college. She filled out the application, and then both urged me to march with the Aspira contingent in the Puerto Rican day parade. To me that had to be the lamest waste of a Sunday I could possibly imagine, worse than going to church. People walking down an avenue on a hot, summer day, among crowds who were loud and tacky flaunting Puerto Rican flags on the most discrete parts of their body or flapping them in your face, playing tedious and repetitive music, and wearing big-ass buttons proclaiming, "Kiss me, I'm Puerto Rican." And marching for what? To be seen waving stupid flags all over the place? It was the one time of year I was most embarrassed to be Puerto Rican.

"Show your Puerto Rican pride," my mother said. And I was thinking, pride in what?

"It's a great experience, your mother and I did it a couple of times," my father added. Then they rattled off all the wonderful memories, the friends they made, the little inside jokes, while I stood there embarrassed and shocked, about to puke that they would push this crap on me.

Of course, they couldn't make me, and I was not going to do it, no matter how much they harangued about cultural pride, knowing one's history, and all that nationalistic bullshit. But then my bud Kyle scored KISS tickets for the Farewell Tour. The band was playing at the Jones Beach Amphitheater. I was not a huge KISS fan. My tastes gravitated back then to grunge and alternative rock, and of course, to heavy metal and classic rock. Kyle and his cousin, Jordan, were all KISS Army, plus she had a driver's license and a car. I wanted to party and rock all summer long and KISS, though not a fav, still rocked. Suddenly, the Puerto Rican day parade sounded doable, at least as an alibi.

My parents were overprotective, I thought. Never would they have let me go to a concert like that. Everything was about "wait 'til you're eighteen," the magical age for parents to release responsibility. I think it was just a convenient excuse to pull on the leash. I felt so good that summer. I had done well in school, got honors, had made varsity on the swim team, was beginning to get popular with some of the girls in my class. I was growing into my adult body, losing that awkward geekiness, and I wanted to have fun rockin' and cruisin' with chicks. My parents' main concern was keeping their son from not getting any more gringofied than he was.

I lied to them about the parade. Told them I would go, but they would have to let me stay at my friend's cousin's house that Saturday, the day of the concert, so that I could get into Manhattan Sunday early enough to meet the 11 a.m. start of the parade. They let me go because they knew Kyle and his parents and trusted them. His cousin Jordan lived in a house in Astoria, Queens, a few minutes to Manhattan on the subway. That also saved them a trip driving me into the city. They wanted me to participate, but of course they had other plans for their Sunday. "Been there, done that," my mother said.

It seemed like a perfect plan. Go to the concert, party, and Kyle and I would return on Sunday night, and I'd have all these priceless stories about my experience with my fellow Boricuas. And everybody's happy.

Jordan was twenty-one, so she could buy beer, which was another great thing. Her parents had taken off to somewhere in the Caribbean for vacation and had entrusted her the house, dog and plants. Which was great, too.

She had also captivated my young sexual imagination. She was my ideal rocker babe: sassy, in your face, smart and sexy. She wore tight jeans that looked like she had been poured into, a tee slung over one shoulder, showing off an athletic bra strap, wore platform heels, her hair and face made up as her favorite KISS band member, Gene Simmons. You had to love a girl who could imitate and get away with the Demon's style, including the wagging tongue.

I had to admit, despite my grunge tendencies to criticize anything resembling glam rock, the concert was awesome. Everything seemed magical that night. The bigger than life, iconic band members, dressed in their costumes and outrageous high heel shoes and make-up, playing hard rock the way it should be played: ruthless, unforgiving, relentless. Didn't even mind all the pyrotechnic stuff:

the rotating sparklers and smoke as they plowed through their repertoire of "Black Diamond," "Heaven's on Fire," "Strutter," until they ended with their signature "Rock and Roll All Nite."

At one point, after giving me a shotgun, Jordan grabbed my head and tongue kissed me with such ferocity I almost lost my breath. She slipped both her hands under my jeans and gripped my ass. I think she would have unzipped me right there, and I would have let her if the band hadn't started on a number that had everyone firing up their lighters. Etiquette requires that you, too, light up for the somber occasion of the song. We were all high and happy, young and horny, and it was all good. Then, I was not a Puerto Rican, but just another American teen having fun on a June Saturday night, amid the stirring sounds of bass, drum and Ace's wicked guitar riffs. A regular guy who turned on an "older" hot rocker chick.

After the concert, we went out to eat some burgers, and later we drove to the beach, sat on Jordan's car, listening to tunes on the radio and looking up at the stars. Jordan told Kyle to take a walk and we made out for what seemed like hours. We crashed when we got to Jordan's, and I slept through most of the parade. When we finally got up, half deaf from the blasting speakers, and hungry, we slipped out for some chow. At a diner, Jordan ran her fingertips up my thigh. It was one of the best weekends of my life.

All that good feeling crashed with that call. I was deported back to Puerto Rican Land with my mother's sobbing, worrying lectures about what could have happened to you, a young man of color, among all those "savages."

"'Cause they never arrest the real culprits," she said. "They see a bobo like you, hanging around there gawking, and an hour later we have to go down to the station to bail your ass."

I felt like laughing, but it was actually sad. Years later, when I cared about those issues, I found out that two innocent men were arrested and convicted in what would become known as the "Puerto Rican day parade attacks," although they happened in Central Park after the parade had finished. None of the men shown groping the women on the forty or so videos collected were arrested.

"You have to be constantly watching your step when you're Puerto Rican in America, Rennie," my father informed me. "You need to do twice as much as any gringo to get a crumb of respect, but one little misstep and you're screwed for life."

So many years later, and his words now weigh down on me from his grave.

Twenty-Eight

Perhaps the clowns were a mistake, in hindsight. But how could I, or anybody, know they would have such rabid militancy, especially Miki Tavárez, their leader. Because of his demure stature—and here I risk being political incorrect—I never imagined he possessed such viciousness and hate. At the moment, we were willing to do anything to keep the crowds subdued, and there was the issue of the children. They needed something to keep them entertained. Miki came along, a little odd, for sure, with his long hair pinned up with what looked like a chopstick, his tats and leather pants, and he volunteered to do the clowning with his buddies, also clowns. "All professionals," he said. He was down with the cause, he said, in his accented but excellent English, which had a southern tinge, his having lived in Georgia for some time.

Everyone was down with the cause, at that time. No short supply of commitment and political resolve. Or, so I thought. It started with a simple plan: conduct a series of protests at the college to draw attention to the contamination, with the hope that the media would pick it up and run with it for a while. My mother supported it, because as she put it, "There's nothing better than good publicity for your case." Well, they ran with it, all right, but not for the reasons we had anticipated nor with the results we wanted.

I thought I was doing something tech savvy, bringing in Facebook, Twitter and all the new communication and social networking facilities to political activism in Puerto Rico, right? We set up a Facebook page and announced the first protest. Thousands of people signed up immediately, which surprised me. Then the stream of tweets began. I started to get messages on my cell from all over the island for information. We set up a web page with all the vital links.

The first protest had a better than expected turn out. Felipe and Samuel were impressed at the hundreds who gathered there with signs, musical instruments and loud voices. Impressive when you think that it was early August and students were still on vacation. They could have gone to the beach, slept late, watched TV, played video games, plugged into their iPods. Yet, they came from the four corners of the island. They tweeted each other; it became the island's cyberspace chatting point of the week. Bored with all those things they normally did for fun, this event had become their new political fad.

Still, I can't overlook or underestimate the outrage. The overwhelming majority who gathered at the college to protest was steamed at the arrogance of the authorities, the sneaky methods for covering it up and the lack of concern for those hurt by their stupidity. Puerto Ricans harbored residual anger over Vieques, years after the mobilization to close Roosevelt Roads.

It was the height of arrogance to use Vieques, an island slightly bigger than Manhattan, for target practice, endangering the lives, livelihood and health of human beings. I understood why these protestors had come. Baná college had become another Vieques in their eyes. The hypocrisy of opening a school in the name of "turning swords into plowshares," but secretly burying the ordnance under the feet of those working there was intolerable. The independentistas' outrage that a power like the United States could push Puerto Rico around like that was felt by all Boricuas across the political spectrum. But those of us on the Committee, those who were supposed to lead, including yours truly, should have sensed that singing and dancing, the general festive mood which developed, was not necessarily good political form or discipline.

The bands came much later, because they were down with the cause, but their political chops didn't prevent them from getting free publicity and selling T-shirts and CDs. That first day, and the week that followed, only a few young men and women played congas, drums of all sorts, clapped and set up a drumming circle of resistance against the government and the powers that be. It was all well and good. I was a bit smug, thinking I, rather *we*, had any control over this.

I thought it was out of commitment and duty that the hardcore group remained after the event was officially over. One of the student leaders, with the standard sparse beard and scruffy hair, said, "Compañero, the official time for a movement to end is when the goals are achieved." He had more political acumen than I did. And that made sense, of course, but dedication and resolve don't have to mean chaos and whatever goes.

So, they kept coming, by the hundreds. Contingents from as far as Fajardo, Yabucoa, Rincón and the largest from San Juan, mostly composed of firebrand, youthful independentistas, craving for this type of attention, looking for the next event that would give them an adrenaline high. Within a week, the highways leading to Baná were packed with traffic, vehicles lined up with sleeping bags and other camping paraphernalia tied to the top, slogans sprayed on their windows or doors. Cars parked anywhere space was available; then the buses starting dropping people off. The mayor of the town, a young politician from the minority party, opened the baseball stadium for parking, and soon had to secure other public spaces for the vehicles.

Mom informed me that the mayor lobbied and succeeded in getting the town of Baná to officially join the lawsuit against the present government, the University of Puerto Rico and the Defense Department, and thus the U.S. government. His participation, she said, ensured the basic requirements of a number of people and costs to pursue class-action litigation. Her firm had already started oiling the media machine in anticipation of filing the lawsuit, so she was very pleased with the media attention.

"I'm so proud of you, Rennie," she said at the beginning, when everything was going our way.

Some unions participated at first, when it was still serious, although later the labor leaders removed their support. The leftist parties did the same. But in the beginning, the faithful stayed and grew. They set up camp within the confines of the college, something we had not wanted them to do. They climbed over the fences and overran the main gate, which the poorly outnumbered university guards could not keep closed. Not wanting to create any further bad publicity or a situation which could lead to violence, the university consented to their staying, thinking within a few days they would leave. A week later, there were more tents, ranging from bed sheets to upscale models from Sears, dotting the wide open grounds of the college.

We had to deal with sanitary issues, potential health problems, security and keeping everyone focused on the political reason for gathering there. The last point was the most difficult to sustain. We managed to distribute donated bottles of water to people, a few doctors volunteered their time and set up a medical tent, and from the money the organizing committee had collected, we had to rent portable toilets.

Food kiosks were set up, where townspeople sold food at a reasonable price or distributed it free. The police, in riot gear, kept gathering, lurking outside, while the university guards walked around with their transceivers ready, making sure there was no major destruction to the college or its grounds. They were prepared to communicate any serious legal infraction to the police outside. Committee members also patrolled what the media soon dubbed "Villa Verde," (then later, more cynically, "Villa de Payasos," or Clowns) to make sure nothing got out of hand. I felt as if we were managing an unintended, perverse political Woodstock.

When did the large speakers appear? Did the bands bring them? What possessed us to let them play? We just didn't expect all of these people to come, and then to stay in protest. Now we had this responsibility toward them, and felt we had to keep them centered and focused. Did that mean keeping them entertained? Some of my colleagues thought it could not hurt, since the bands and performers were doing it for free and they were down with the cause. Besides, said Felipe, protest music had always been a part of the movement. I'm thinking what movement? But they all nodded, and what do I know about island politics anyhow.

Each band came with its equipment, roadies and groupies. They stacked enormous, loud speakers up on the stairs of the Administration Building, which had become a makeshift stage with the customary huge Puerto Rican flag in the background, and large signs and banners all around. Once the music started, the mood got livelier, and the groups incited the crowd with patriotic tunes.

The musical highlight was when Roy Brown, the independentista singer-songwriter, appeared out of the Baná fog onto the stage. A wiry young man, who had been serving as emcee, told us he had a surprise, laughed a bit at the buzz and then introduced the bearded, round-faced, gray-haired folk singer. As Brown jumped onto the stage with his guitar, an uproar erupted among the thousands gathered under the stars; they stood up collectively and applauded, whistled, screamed. He spoke about how those who pollute the island have to pay, to the cheers of everyone, and then broke into "Boricua en la Luna," followed by a moving rendition of "Monon," which had everyone up and singing the refrain, "fuego, fuego, los yanquis quieren fuego." The intensity with which the protesters hurled these lyrics into the summer night air gave me chills.

During the week that followed the Brown concert, nevertheless, solidarity began to wear thin. It was hot, even for Baná, which sits at a higher altitude than the coastal cities, and tempers began to flare over the living conditions. For the less committed, the fun was wearing out, the fad quality fading, and they left. Except for the diehards, their outrage was not so easily dampened. They planned to stay as long as needed to make those responsible pay, one way or another. They did not believe in the judicial system, much less the government. They demanded those in charge be held accountable, that they pay for their horrific actions. Ahora.

The government also began to lose patience. The campers officially became squatters; they were informed to "desist and break camp or be in violation of the law." The university became concerned about the ability to offer classes during the approaching Fall semester, to which the protestors responded with a demand to close the college because it presented a hazardous risk to students, faculty and workers.

Micco called me and asked if I could do something to ensure the start of the semester in two weeks. "Think of all those students graduating this year, Rennie."

To which I answered, "This is bigger than me, Micco. I'm just one of many."

He grunted and hung up.

Marisol called daily to tell me she worried for my safety, to question if this was all worth it.

A flurry of accusations flew across the airwaves. I was interviewed, introduced as "the son of the activist lawyer Julia Matos Canales, whose firm is pursuing a class-action suit against the U.S. government." In my accented Spanish, I reiterated our committee's position on the protest, entering its third week. Sitting next to me in the radio studio, Samuel, our official spokesperson, delineated with calm and eloquence. He informed the media that we, under no circumstance, advocated violence and did not want anyone hurt. "But," he said, "we strongly support the right of citizens to assemble and protest peacefully, even if it means civil disobedience." Above all, he claimed, this is "a dignified, united front of indignation" over the continued contamination of the college and the island in general.

Miki Tavárez had other ideas. "Protestin' don't mean you can't have fun, am I right?" That was his mantra for the first few days in the camp. And most of us had to admit he brought humor and needed levity to the situation. Just running around in his wig, clown pants, clown shoes and make-up made us laugh. He had a horn he kept blowing at people's behinds—that always got a laugh. His fellow clowns, twelve in number, patrolled the environs, cheering people up, telling jokes in between the musical acts. He put up a tent for face painting and balloon sculpting for the children and set up a few games in there; soon it was always crowded with children. Why parents brought their kids to a protest-squatters camp was beyond me; they were just kids, and not interested in politics. Restless, they ran around the camp without anything to do, taxing the fragile nerves of everyone, creating tension among parents and tent neighbors. So, we thanked Miki for taking the initiative on that one. Encouraged by our response, he organized kite flying. At first for the kids, but after a few days the adults got into it and scores of kites brightened the cerulean sky, every one of them scribbled with a political slogan.

Maybe we emboldened him too much, who knows. It's strange the way these things happen. Another night had fallen on the camp. Fires burned everywhere; the university had turned off all the electricity. The music continued, as townspeople donated generators that could power mikes and speakers. The music pacified everyone at night; it was the glue which held everything together.

That night I was pleased to see Rita Gómez's niece show up on stage. I had invited her and wasn't sure if she would show up. She came on with a young man who played guitar beautifully. First, she introduced herself, talked about her aunt who worked for the college and had died recently from cancer. To loud cheers she simply asked, "Why can't the university investigate and make sure my aunt and others have not died from this contamination? From those responsible: We want the truth." And the crowd began the chant, "The truth, the truth, we want the truth!" She raised her hands and told us she wanted to sing for us.

Her melodious soprano voice then went through the haunting lyrics of the danza, "Verde Luz," to a silenced, mesmerized audience. I had heard of the song, never heard it sung, and was moved by the beauty of the words and how she cradled every metaphor with love and sincerity. The perfect song for the moment, and everyone there that night knew it.

The last note brought a roar that made me tremble. She left the stage, wiping tears from her eyes. They wanted her to sing another, but this wasn't a concert performance for her. She had come to sing this song and no more, for her aunt and the cause. The audience kept clapping, even after she had left. From the darkness like a mischievous demon, Miki jumped onto the stage. He brought an empty milk carton on which he stood to reach the mike. That brought a laugh from the crowd. In his clown outfit, he started telling rowdy, raunchy jokes about gringos, and then got serious, talking about the serious problem with the environment in Puerto Rico. He pumped everyone up with the previous chant, "we want the truth, we want the truth, now."

Then he silenced the crowd, putting his small hands up in the air. "Gente, I want to inform you that the Puerto Rican colonial government has mobilized the National Guard."

There was a groan, then a wave of murmuring across the multitude.

I turned to Felipe, who looked at Samuel. We scrambled for our cell phones. A few calls confirmed what Miki had said. The Guard was already positioned by the athletic track across from us, not even a quarter of a mile away. The police, in turn, had been ordered to stop any flow of traffic coming into the vicinity of the college. We soon received phone calls and text messages informing us that we had twenty-four hours to evacuate the college or the Guard would dislodge us and arrest any violators.

Foley texted me: "Warned u. Get ur asses out of there now!!!"

Our faces turned grim and anxious, and we stared at each other trying to figure out what to do next. We decided that Samuel should first calmly update the campers on the situation and then try to convince everyone to follow the instructions to avoid harm to anyone. But Miki Tavárez was on a roll.

"We will not be intimidated," the clown Miki shouted.

Samuel struggled through the agitated crowds, now pumping fists, shouting slogans.

"We won't take this anymore." Miki unleashed a harangue of the angriest, most intensely hateful anti-American venom. "Those yanqui sons of bitches are killing our people," he yelled. "They're destroying our island, filling it up with their shit and flushing us down with it!"

He was literally foaming at the mouth, spit flying in all directions. His head's wild movements started to make his wig slide, so he took it off, bringing a strange cheer from those gathered. He had them captivated. And then he started screaming that we should chain ourselves to the bulldozers at the clean-up site, pointing in its direction with his orange wig.

"We won't let them dislodge us, compañeros. ¡Venceremos!" Miki pumped his little fist in the air, his real hair, long and straight, falling all over his face.

"To the bulldozers," he shouted.

By the time Samuel got up to the mike, the other clowns had taken up the people's solidarity chant, "El pueblo unido, jamás será vencido," as they followed Miki to the clean-up area, located about two hundred yards from the center of the camp.

"Amigos, compañeros," Samuel shouted, but his words were lost amid the yelling, chanting and shuffling of feet. The crowd moved like the angry, disgruntled mob it had become, toward the equipment at the clean-up area.

The Guard had received orders that any move toward the equipment justified action. As the mob moved toward it, Miki and his clowns leading the way, the Guard was given the order to move forward.

Faced with the Guard coming toward them, they hesitated. Sane individuals would have stopped as soon as the Guard had circled the equipment area. But Miki gave the command to charge. It was more like a loud screech of frustration.

Felipe tried to calm people down, shouting instructions through a megaphone to stop, and some of the protestors backed off. But dozens charged, following Miki and the clowns, some now running with anchor chains and locks to tie themselves to the equipment. They attempted to break the barricade of soldiers, and as these pushed back, some protesters dropped to the ground but got up again in defiance and anger. They had no weapons, but with their fists they pummeled the soldiers, who continued to force back the horde. Then I saw Miki wrapped around a soldier's leg, biting him. The soldier yelled, and in a flash, he was butting poor Miki with his rifle. The other clowns jumped the soldier, Jaime Cruz, a twenty-four-year-old graduate student from Salinas. Chains started to swing, punches thrown, scuffling, pushing, a litany of obscenities and shouts.

A warning shot was heard and then a high pitch wave of screams. Like a flash flood, there was a massive retreat. I was trying to hold back demonstrators from moving toward the brawl and was knocked down by the retreating mob. I huddled myself into a fetal position on the ground, covering my head. People wailed obscenities, the Guardsmen yelled to move back. I smelled the scent of dirt and grass, and in the distance, heard the steady beat of a lonely drum.

I would have been injured worse if Felipe, who had the body of an offensive lineman, had not blocked people from trampling me, at times pushing others to the ground, while Marco and Mercedes, two student leaders, helped me up. Felipe leading the way, we ran toward the safety of the water fountain in front of the Administration Building.

Luckily, no one was killed. I received cuts and scratches, had to put my left arm in a sling, but nothing was more bruised than my spirit. The weeks that followed the "riot of clowns" were even more painful, though. The media ran with it as a big joke, deviating from the seriousness of our claims and demands. We had to work night and day to bring the issue back to the gravity it deserved. My mother was incensed.

"So much work, René, down the toilet," she said. "How did you let it get to this?" I had no answers. No one could have seen this coming. Felipe and Samuel shook their heads, even laughed, saying you had to take it all in stride and move on.

Marisol visited me in the hospital, hysterical. When she saw my minor injuries, she proceeded to slap my good arm a few times and to tell me she had warned me this political stuff was risky. Then, she sat by me and kissed me on the forehead and face.

"Why do you put me through this, Rennie? What would I do if something happened to you?"

I couldn't respond. It was the best thing to do, not to continue discussion on the topic, and she dropped it.

Marisol was relatively calmer because Mom had recommended her to the Dean at the Bayamón campus, and he had authorized the transfer. She was happy to have her job secured, despite the driving it would involve, and was spending the remaining summer preparing for the move to the new college.

"At least you weren't hurt as bad as that poor little clown," she said, to change the subject.

Miki had sustained serious injuries and had to remain in the hospital for a week. A lawsuit was expected, and he had even approached my mother, who declined the case. But on release from the hospital, Miki became a celebrity. He hit the local talk shows and was invited everywhere to give a speech or talk about his experience in the riot. People celebrated him as a folk hero, or as one of the talk show hosts introduced him, "a man small in stature who stands like a giant in comparison to our politicians." The buzz on the street was that he was a "little guy with big balls." We had to contend with and deflect his status as the face of the movement to end the dangerous pollution of our college.

"Learn from this, René," my mother advised. "Just remember: in Puerto Rican politics, nothing is what it appears to be, and all that it appears to be is nothing."

Twenty-Nine

I was kicking the footbag in our bedroom, when Julia called. After the protest camp debacle, I went to a corner to heal my spiritual and physical wounds. Most likely in that corner I'd be kicking the footbag ragged. There was a difference, though. Once enjoyable and challenging, hacky sack had now become an activity to keep me from the doldrums, a way to forget the events of the past few weeks.

My mother, astute as always, knew my state of mind. "Pack your weekend carry-on," she said in her usual curt way, which I had grown to interpret as "We're off on an adventure somewhere."

I looked forward to these impromptu trips now. Even in an island 100 by 35 miles, there is enough to make you want to jump in the car and explore, and my mother was a great tour guide/historian/road companion.

But it wasn't just that each one of these "cultural field trips" had been educational, as Julia had promised. How dumb for me not to see it at first. Or, maybe, so numbed by my hurt, so simply lost, Julia showed me that when hard times hit, you need to regain a sense of direction. Movement toward something. Rage against the inertia. At first, I thought she was just being pedantic and overbearing, pushing an agenda, when it was her way of just being there for me.

"Where we going now?" I asked, excited.

"The Fiestas in Loíza," she said. "Pick you up in an hour." And she hung up.

We drove up to the house in Guaynabo, and from there we headed toward the condo in Fajardo. We didn't go straight to the condo. Loíza coming first on Route 3, Julia decided to go directly to the festival since it was getting dark and we were hungry. It was Friday, the first day of the three-day festival celebrating Santiago Apóstol, or Saint James' victory over the Moors. Each day of this festival began with a procession in which a group of men carried the saint's statue from the center of town to a barrio approximately three miles away called Las Carreras. The first procession, which we had missed, is dedicated to the men, the second to women and the last one to children. It was essentially the same ritual every time.

"No big whoop," she said. "But the people get dressed in wonderful costumes and it's so much fun, you'll see."

As night fell on the town, the residents of Loíza, and others from all over the island, roamed the streets dressed as the traditional four carnivalesque characters—caballeros, vejigantes, locas and viejos or locos. The caballeros, or knights, wore wide-brim hats, with dangling ornaments or streamers, and they waved wooden swords. Sometimes they rode on horseback, resembling the Spaniards who had conquered the Moors in the medieval Iberian peninsula.

"How bizarre," I observed to my mother. "A town with such an African legacy and the Spaniards are the good guys."

"And what's most African, the vejigantes," she responded, "are demons, the bad guys."

Trickster figures, the vejigantes bounced and pranced in their lavish, vibrant colored jumpsuits that opened wide like wings as they extended their arms and legs. Their ornate, painted masks were spiked with three to eight long, curving horns. They circled the festival grounds in packs, a flock of children following them, chanting, demanding food, drink or money on their behalf. If you refused, they'd strike you with a simulated goat bladder, or vejiga. These days, the "goat bladders" were long plastic sticks with an inflated bag at the end.

I don't know how many times my mother and I were struck with those silly plastic vejigas. Even as we ate our alcapurrias and tacos de chapín, they would walk by us and slap our butts with them. After a while, you just ignored them and their little smacks like gnats floating in the night air.

We passed the various kiosks, surrounded by caballeros and vejigantes. At one point a band of vejigantes rumbled by, and Julia screamed and grabbed my arm. I protected her from the playful vejiga blows, and we both laughed. Closer to the band stand, a group of viejos and locas danced for spectators. The locas had blackened faces, wore wild wigs and exaggerated, padded breasts and butts and hit large tin cans rhythmically to the music. The viejos grinded against the locas, who kept slapping them with brooms and at times emptied their pockets. They harassed dancers and spectators who congregated by the band shell. The locas flirted with the men; the viejos ogled the women.

The crowds were getting rowdier, in the air was a constant stream of animated voices and laughter. The salsa was percolating, and droves of people dancing, but Julia wanted to head back to Fajardo.

"We need to get up early tomorrow to see the procession," she said.

The next day we set out early to have breakfast at a little dive off Route 3 and then we drove to Loíza for the second procession. It was a much more somber event than I had anticipated, quite religious, with praying and chanting. Several men shouldered the platform, carrying the saint's statue. The saint, mounted on a white horse, brandished a sword. He seemed odd displaying that warlike stance festooned with wild flowers and flamboyant streamers.

My mother wanted to walk in the procession. "For your benefit," she said.

I didn't understand what she meant. Not big on religious rituals, I walked to humor her. I never discussed religion with her. To think about it, Mami and Papi didn't push their religious ideology on me. I was baptized, did my First Communion, Confirmation, like every other Catholic kid. My parents continued to practice their faith to their last days. You could say they died because of their faith. As I withdrew, they showed concerned for "my spiritual side," but being intellectuals and scholars, they understood that thinking individuals go through various spiritual periods in their lives.

If I were to meet Julia, not as her reclaimed son but a stranger, I'd say she wasn't a religious person. But I'd be wrong. Perhaps not religious, but as I recalled her at Rita's funeral, and as I walked beside her during this procession, my birth mother's face was lost in spiritual contemplation. I knew that this woman had been through trials from which only faith in something could have delivered her. When I saw her in this light, she always seemed sad and alone.

When they reached the other replica of the saint in Las Carreras, those carrying the statue lowered the platform three times, as if he were bowing. This gesture done, they made a circular pass of the replica and returned to the town. Because this was the women's procession, the women followed immediately after the statue of St. James; they were followed by the various carnivalesque characters, showing more decorum than the previous evening. Behind them was an SUV waving the red and yellow flag of Santiago and the tri-colored flag of the town.

A disorganized mass of people marched behind the official procession, with only one thing in common: the direction toward the town square. Some marchers stood out, like the older man who had strapped around his shoulders a bouncing paper maché horse. The caballeros on beautiful horses, clip-clopping on the asphalt and flamboyant cross-dressed locas with huge umbrellas and bouncing derrieres. Then came a wave of masks, brilliant and bold, in the afternoon sun. Who's behind each mask, I wondered. How must it feel, for one day, to lose yourself in anonymity, to be free to play the trickster?

As the motley congregation approached the town, they grew brasher and livelier. When they arrived, the chanting grew to a high pitch. The religious songs gave way to clapping and strong syncopated rhythms, and the music swelled with the setting of the sun. Around the festival area, everywhere we strolled, clusters of drummers slapped and banged congas, inviting anyone, challenging them, to dance. At one such grouping, seven men lined up behind congas. They had been playing for a while, their tight polos and tees drenched in sweat. Spectators took turns jumping in to battle the drums. Mesmerized, I observed the dancers' moves, the interplay between dancer and drummers. I didn't know much about the music, but you could tell these drummers had experience, their love for the drumming undeniable. They had drawn a substantial crowd of enthusiasts.

An older man, who had been dancing, tipped his baseball cap and bowed to applause and cheers, and, in a flash, I saw Julia, my mother, barefoot in the middle of the circle. My mouth dropped. She gyrated her hips as she approached the drums, bowed her head and then tapped it in reverence and respect to the drums. Easily, she was the whitest person dancing that day. I bent my head down, covered my face with my hand and looked at her through my fingers. She's going to make a fool of herself, I thought. Be booed or insulted away in mockery. But she shook her hips like a natural. With folded wrists on her hips in a sassy gesture, she shuffled her butt backwards, bounced on her feet quickly to the relentless beat of the drums. She bent and shook shoulders toward the lead conguero, shaking her breasts over his drum.

He stood up and took off his shirt, presenting a buffed chest and shoulders, biceps and forearms chiseled by years of drumming. Onlookers cheered and laughed as he fastened a bandana around his head. He cracked his fingers, swiveled his neck. Julia rolled her head back in laughter, while rolling her hips. And as I shook my head in amazement, she signaled the drummer back to work with a finger. They battled for a few minutes. Drummer rocking hard riffs, my mother keeping up. She tossed her head back, the lustrous hair wild and free, and after a frenzied onslaught of the congas, she burst out laughing and fanned herself as to say, "I surrender." And she stopped, to rousing applause and cheers, bowing several times to the conguero, who stood up and slapped her a high five. While she was dancing, an elderly woman wearing a visor had leaned over to me and yelled in Spanish over the music, "Hey, your mom can really dance!"

As Julia returned to my side, fanning herself, perspiring, she wore a wide, almost panting grin on her face.

I looked at her, puzzled.

"What?" she asked, laughing.

"I didn't know you could dance bomba," I said, finally.

She took a napkin the older woman offered her to wipe her sweat. My comment made her grin disappear.

As she patted herself, she turned to me seriously and said, "There's much you don't know about me, m'ijo."

Later that night, back at the condo, we sat out on the balcony, sated from another fine seafood meal, enjoying a bottle of chardonnay and the salty breeze coming in from the sea. She had bought me a vejigante mask. At one point, I put it on to be silly. With the mask on, I played reporter, asked her questions about her "brilliant performance," holding my wine glass like a mike. She giggled, and played along.

"I took dance classes at U Penn while at law school," she said. Her interest in folkloric Puerto Rican dance developed there.

"You said there's much your son doesn't know about you. Can you elaborate?"

She looked down sadly, took a sip of wine. I peeled off the mask, looking into her eyes now watering up.

"Maybe some things are better left unsaid," she said, shrugging.

"Oh," I said, surprised. "I didn't mean for you to get into that." It was true. I hardly thought about that past anymore. Perhaps I wanted to forget it, too. Make it seem like it never happened. What did it matter, anyway? My mother and I were here today, enjoying our lives together.

With two fat tears streaming down her cheeks, she looked back at me, straight on. "No, no. You deserve to know."

With the bottom of her palms she wiped the tears, sat back on the lounge chair and exhaled sharply, so deeply I thought she wouldn't have any air left in her lungs. Resting her head at an angle, she gazed out into the horizon of the night sea for what seemed eternity, as if trying to find in the black distance the thread of her story.

"Your father and I . . . " she began. "We had this passion that at times scared me. I was young and immature." She continued shaking her head. "Juanma, he was twenty-eight, and probably even more immature. And, as liberal as he made himself out to be, he was, al fin, a Puerto Rican man. I became pregnant with you, and we both decided to get married, start a family, despite our career plans.

"I was so scared. I was finishing my first year of law school at UPR, one of a handful of women. My parents had such hopes for me. I had these ambitious dreams. I never hesitated to have you." She looked at me. "But I was frightened that I would fail at being a mother as well as law student. I started having doubts about your father. Were we really in love, or was it a silly romantic notion to cover up the passion at the heart of our relationship?

"I was struggling with classes, with your father who had his own pressures working on his doctoral dissertation, with the attitudes of classmates and professors not accustomed to seeing a pregnant woman in the law school. My days were consumed with anger and resentment toward their stupidity. Your father and I would have monumental fights, dragging into the night. I was always tired, worried if I was eating enough, worried if all this tension could affect you in some way. Worried in the many ways a woman in her first pregnancy fears about what can happen.

"Then, you were born. Both Juanma and I were so happy that day. It seemed that all our troubles had disappeared. You were such a beautiful baby, with those big eyes, such a pleasure to hold. Your father was so tender then. He came with flowers and balloons and all types of things to make me feel comfortable and happy. But after that day, I grew more irritable, lashing at your father for any little thing. I couldn't sleep and was unable to focus. I'd say I felt like I was in a cloud, numb, but deep down I didn't feel anything. I didn't care about anything. I kept thinking, how could I feel this way when I was just blessed with such a beautiful, healthy baby? And I started hating myself for feeling nothing."

She started sobbing.

"You just had the baby blues," I said, holding her hand.

She gave me a sad nod, biting her lip. Her eyes, all around the sockets, wet with tears.

"But we didn't know that. We were so ignorant," she said, her mouth and face twisted with self-hate and anger.

"You kept crying and crying," she said, exploding into heaving sobs. "I couldn't find a way to make you stop. Maybe you were colicky, who knows. I put you down in the crib, still crying, all red. Crying, screaming, and I didn't know what to do. I didn't know. You crying and crying and crying, and me pacing the room, pulling my hair. Yelling at you, 'Be quiet, please!' I just wanted you to stop crying, to stop, I was so tired, I wanted sleep, just a few hours of rest, and your father . . . he . . . he . . . found me with the pillow in my hands, standing over the crib."

She shoved her face into her hands with a howl that I'm sure the neighbors and the people at the beach must have heard. She wouldn't meet my eyes, kept crying into her hands, the tears rolling off her hands. I bent over her on the chair, put my good arm around her, and she wailed into my chest. She slipped to her knees.

"Forgive me, René, por favor, perdóname, hijo." She repeated this in a groaning voice as she embraced my legs with such intensity that I started to cry.

Over coffee, she told me how my father freaked when he saw her gripping that pillow over my crying body. He seized the pillow and pushed her to the floor, yelling at her.

"His eyes said it all," she said. "In a flash, they switched from shock, anger, contempt, disgust, to fear and sadness."

She shook her head, her eyes shut.

"'What kind of mother does that?' he kept screaming. If he had only looked into my eyes, my heart, he would have known I was not well. But, in his mind, he was being the good father, protecting you.

"'You're not fit to be a mother for my son,' he yelled. He grabbed you in his arms, cradling you as you continued crying, and ran downstairs, and drove to his mother's. I ran after him, pleading with him, screaming and beating on the closed door like the mad woman I had become.

"That was the last time I saw you until that day at the cemetery.

"Juanma cancelled the wedding plans. While I was walking in a daze, trying to understand what was happening to me, his fam-

ily's lawyers pushed the papers on me and made me sign over custody of you to Juanma. My parents advised me against it, and to
this day they can't believe I did it, but I did it because I believed I
was an unfit mother, that there was something flawed with my
maternal instincts. What kind of mother tries to suffocate her
baby for crying? Who does that? At the signing, your father told
me to forget you, to never contact you or him ever again. I nodded yes and walked away.

"I withdrew from UPR law school. With the help of some professors, I transferred to U Penn Law, and while there, I learned that
your father had married Magda, and she had become your adopted mother. That night I walked the streets of Philadelphia feeling
such an engulfing emptiness that I thought I'd disappear into
oblivion. I passed a dance studio, which was at street level, and
wandered in just to sit down. It was African dance, and the beat
was inviting.

"The instructor, a black woman with wavy hair, must have seen
my sad face. Instead of throwing me out, she shouted from the
front, 'Come join us.'

"And, I did. I danced, stomping my feet on those mats like I
wanted to smash through the floor and reach a part of me gone
forever. I kept dancing through that semester, that year and afterward. I danced until my muscles ached and knew I was alive. I
danced to forget. I danced and danced. Always remembering, in
my heart, what Beverly, our instructor, would tell us: 'When the
music changes, ladies, so does the dance.'"

Thirty

Lolita Lebrón departed the island she loved and defended so fiercely on an early August morning. My mother was devastated. She kept shaking her head, repeating she could not believe it. Lebrón was ninety, yet my mother and others found it difficult to accept that her days on earth had run out.

"How does one replace an icon, an everyday inspiration?" she asked me.

"You can't," I answered.

The organizers of her funeral asked my mother to deliver one of many eulogies, which she felt honored to do, but not without some trepidation.

"I'll start crying halfway through it, I know it," she said, shaking her head, tears already rolling down her cheeks. "She was my mentor, my strength, like another mother to me."

At the Ateneo Puertorriqueño, my mother gave one of the most stirring eulogies among many. She had to stop a few times, to catch her breath, to fight back the tears, but her words were personal, full of love and respect for a woman who, as my mother said, had received deserved praise for her commitment and courage from Puerto Ricans of all political stripes.

Crowded among the many packed into the building, I could see Lebrón in her polished wooden coffin, her beautiful white hair covered by a lace shawl, her corpse surrounded in pink fabric.

My mother finished her remarks with "Viva Lolita Lebrón" and "Viva Puerto Rico Libre."

Those phrases would echo throughout the day, along with the constant chant of "Se siente, se siente, Lolita está presente," meaning "We feel it, we feel it, Lolita is present." The phrase was intended to mean something deeper, that Lebrón's spirit, her dedication to the movement for independence, was still alive.

I did not share that optimism. I looked around and could not help thinking the movement was literally aging, dying even. My mother, and others like her, represented the type of undying sacrifice and commitment necessary for its success, but they were in short supply. As my mother gave her eulogy, my heart filled with pride for her, a woman who understood love and sacrifice first-hand. Through my mother I had learned to respect and understand Lolita Lebrón, to appreciate the leadership qualities of Puerto Rican women in the vanguard. Exceptional women, extraordinary individuals. But even with this type of leadership, the masses languished under a boulder of inertia and indifference.

So it was that as I walked with my mother and hundreds of others along with Lebrón's casket, toward the cemetery, listening to the militant version of "La Borinqueña," I sensed yet another nail in the coffin of the independence movement, and that along with Lebrón's corpse, the issue was again being buried.

After the funeral, Mom and I found ourselves lunching at Amadeus. Not very hungry, we picked at our food. The conversation naturally turned to the future of Puerto Rico.

"Love for your family or love for your cultural heritage," I told her, referring to the status issue, "for some it always comes down to one choice."

I looked at her, as she shook her head. "Sacrifice and hard work. That's what's needed, and it's missing."

During a pause in our conversation, I blurted out: "I really don't care which side wins."

Before she would have been outraged. But perhaps my mother was tired of fighting, of this polemic, or the sadness in her heart had punctured her combative spirit. Maybe she had mellowed. She looked at me, waiting for the necessary explanation.

I smiled and shrugged. "I can live with statehood or independence. Anything but this mess we have now."

"The worst of two worlds," she joked, laughing softly. "We agree there, m'ijo."

She bounced her cigarette lighter on the table. "The U.S. keeps saying, 'It's up to the Puerto Rican people.' What a cop out," she said, disgusted.

She set her fork down, leaving her dessert half unfinished. After running her tongue over her front teeth, she threw herself back on the chair as she reached for a cigarette. She made a sign for the check.

"The U.S. needs to play parent and give the island some tough love."

We both had decided to attend El Grito this year. This time around, the trip to Lares was filled with grief and sadness, not only because Lolita would not be there in body, although for so many her spirit lived on, but because the future looked so grim. It was much harder for my mother. This time, I was accompanying her because I wanted to go along, but my heart, if not my mind, wasn't really into it.

Marisol was back home fussing over the marriage preparations, and it was supposed to be a small wedding. Teaching at Bayamón required her moving back to her condo for an easier commute. I stayed in the Baná house a good portion of the time but spent weekends with her in San Juan. We planned to live in San Juan when we married, renting out the house in Baná. I worried about her health and if the current stress could affect it. Her last check-up was good, and for that we were thankful.

That move fit my plans to resign from the college after my yearly contract was over. I didn't want to confront Rector Vigo, still upset and feeling betrayed by my "dabbling in politics." I had decided to work as a paralegal in my mother's firm, with an eye toward getting my law degree. The news made her very happy. I loved teaching and the students, but not the university. I told my mother I wanted to focus on environmental law, which she embraced and supported.

"You'll get hands-on experience with the Baná case," she promised.

I was working part-time on the case, which was proceeding well. Rumors circulated about a settlement. Several times during the semester, Micco tried to change my mind about leaving, telling me I was a natural teacher. But changing the island needed finding the surest ways to achieve change. Even Foley agreed with me on that. On one of those rare moments when he was on campus, I met up with him.

"You'll make a helluva litigator," he said, and then with a strange smile told me he was taking an offer for early retirement, heading back home to Chicago. "Back to the dogs and wife, in that order," he said. He didn't get into details, and I didn't ask. He held out his hand to shake. I thought about everything he had done to undermine our efforts. That he was perhaps responsible for something sinister still rifling through my trash can and lurking in the shadows. Who knows what else he had done in all those years living in Puerto Rico. But I shook his hand anyway. He was leaving—that was worth celebrating.

Driving toward Arecibo, "I Hope You Dance," came on the radio. I thought of Rita Gómez and raised the volume. My mother started singing, much to my dismay. I stifled a laugh, looking away, but she saw me and slapped my thigh.

"You can dance, but you can't sing, deal with it," I responded.

"Oh? I was planning to sing at your wedding."

I turned to her, wide-eyed, and she laughed.

I shook my head and we both laughed; and then we listened to the rest of the song, letting the sorrow in our hearts drift into the wind. As the car consumed the curves heading west, my head tilted toward the window. The blistering midday sun melded into the surrounding tropical greenness, and we dissolved into that unbearable green light.

Also by J.L. Torres